Ar

Selections from the Miscellaneous Works of Archbishop Leighton

SALZWASSER VERLAG

Archbishop Leighton

Selections from the Miscellaneous Works of Archbishop Leighton

Reprint of the original, first published in 1863.

1st Edition 2022 | ISBN: 978-3-37500-298-5

Verlag (Publisher): Salzwasser Verlag GmbH, Zeilweg 44, 60439 Frankfurt, Deutschland
Vertretungsberechtigt (Authorized to represent): E. Roepke, Zeilweg 44, 60439 Frankfurt, Deutschland
Druck (Print): Books on Demand GmbH, In de Tarpen 42, 22848 Norderstedt, Deutschland

SELECTIONS

FROM THE

MISCELLANEOUS WORKS

OF

ARCHBISHOP LEIGHTON.

THE WISDOM OF OUR FATHERS.

SELECTIONS

FROM THE

MISCELLANEOUS WORKS

OF

ARCHBISHOP LEIGHTON;

CONSISTING OF

SERMONS, EXPOSITIONS, AND ACADEMICAL ADDRESSES.

WITH A MEMOIR.

LONDON:

PREFACE.

THOUGH Leighton's Commentary upon the First Epistle of Peter has long held a high place amongst our Sacred Classics, his other works are comparatively little known. This may be partly accounted for by the fact that he printed nothing himself. It was only after his death that his writings were collected and published. They were not intended for publication, and are of very unequal merit. The whole would have been held in higher estimation if a selection had been made, and some had been allowed to go down into the oblivion to which the pious author designed them. Besides which, they have never had the benefit of that careful correction and revision which the Commentary has received, and which Dr Doddridge declared to be "the most faulty piece of printing he ever remembered to have seen in any language." Doddridge went on to say, "Considering what an embarrassment it is to common readers to see commas, colons, and periods placed almost in a promiscuous disorder, without any regard to their proper signification, which is the case here at least in every ten lines, I determined to go over the whole, pen in hand, and correct every page as I would have done a proof from the press." The typographical faults of Leighton's Miscellaneous Works require a revision as careful and complete as that bestowed on the Commentary, whilst their great and rare excellence is such as amply to repay it.

In preparing the present volume for the press, the editor has adopted the following method:

1. Those portions of Leighton's Miscellaneous Works which seemed to possess the greatest value have been selected for publication. Many lectures and expositions, scarcely inferior in merit, have indeed been omitted. But it was thought desirable that the size and price of the volume should be such as to bring it within the reach of all.

2. Clauses or sentences which tended to weaken or obscure the sense have occasionally been removed from the text. When it is remembered that Leighton's manuscripts were prepared, not for the press, but for the pulpit, and that they were never revised by him, it is thought that this was not an unwarrantable liberty to take.

3. The punctuation, the arrangement of sentences and paragraphs, and the classification of the heads and divisions of the discourses, have been carefully corrected, so as to remove the confusion caused by want of attention to these important points in former editions.

It is hoped that the publication of this volume will not only extend the reputation of the devout and gifted author, but will promote the great cause to which he devoted his life—the glory of God and the good of man.

MEMOIR.

One of the most remarkable discoveries of modern science is the fact that hurricanes revolve round a centre of perfect calm. Outside the charmed circle, the tempest may rage furiously—within it, all is peace. A similar phenomenon can be found in the moral and spiritual world. In seasons of civil war or theological strife, when "envy, hatred, and all uncharitableness" abound, we may find some tranquil spirits who, undisturbed by the tumult around, seem perpetually to hear their Master whispering to them words of peace. Such a man was Robert Leighton. Though his lot was cast in the stormiest period of our history, though by his family connexions and his ecclesiastical position he was placed in the very centre of the fiercest strifes of contending parties, both in Church and State, yet "the peace of God which passeth all understanding" kept his "heart and mind." He experienced in its fulness and power the truth of the gracious assurance, "Thou wilt keep him in perfect peace, whose mind is stayed on thee." No text was more habitually on his lips than the words of Isaiah, "In returning and rest shall ye be saved; in quietness and confidence shall be your strength." The secret and the source of this "perfect peace" will appear in the following brief sketch of his life.

Dr Alexander Leighton, the father of the future archbishop, was one of the most prominent and violent disputants in that stormy time. Having become obnoxious to the dominant party, he retired to Holland, and there published *Sion's Plea against Prelacie.* On returning to England he was arrested on a warrant issued by Laud, consigned to a loathsome dungeon in Newgate, into which no light was admitted save what came in, together with the rain, through a hole in the roof, and where he was overrun with rats and other vermin. After a protracted imprisonment in this horrible cell, he was sentenced to pay a fine of a thousand pounds, to be twice pilloried, twice publicly whipped, to have his nose slit on both sides, his ears cut off, and to be branded on the cheeks with the letters S. S., denoting Sower of Sedition. Having been thus miserably mutilated, he was again cast into prison, where he remained for nearly ten years, when he was liberated by order of the Long Parliament.

Robert Leighton was the eldest son of this sufferer for conscience' sake. He was born in the year 1611, probably at Edinburgh. Upon most minds the effect of injuries such as these inflicted upon a father would have been passionate indignation against the persecutors. This he doubtless did feel in some measure, but the more lasting result was the deeply-rooted horror of persecution in every form which he carried with him to the grave.

He entered the University of Edinburgh in his sixteenth year; and even at that early age he was remarkable for his piety. Having distinguished himself by proficiency in his studies, he took his degree in 1631, and soon afterwards went abroad, where he remained for some years, residing principally at Douay in France, where a branch of his family had settled. On his return to Scotland in 1641 he received ordination, and, at the unanimous invitation of the congregation, was appointed to the parish of Newbattle near Edinburgh. Here he spent some of the happiest years of his life in the diligent discharge of his duties, in the enjoyment of the beautiful and romantic scenery of the valley of the Esk in which his parish was situated, and in the congenial society of his neighbours, the Earl of Lothian and his pious family.

Leighton was no slothful or hireling shepherd. In addition to the services of the sabbath, he preached or lectured several times through the week, and was assiduous in pastoral work, assembling the families in each household for religious and catechetical instruction. The young engaged his especial care. By precept, by example, and by prayer, he promoted personal, domestic, social, and public piety to the utmost of his power. Partly from his natural aversion to scenes of strife and contention, partly too from his devotion to the work of the ministry, he very seldom attended the meetings of the presbytery, in which much angry controversy prevailed. He was however present on one occasion, as the following anecdote will show. It was customary at these meetings to demand from each minister whether he "preached to the times," that is to say, whether he discussed public affairs in the pulpit. Each one had given a satisfactory answer in the affirmative. Leighton, on being interrogated in his turn, adroitly replied, "If all the brethren have preached to the *times*, may not one poor brother be suffered to preach on *eternity*?"

Whilst at Newbattle, his father died, and he came into possession of a thousand pounds. As it was not very safely invested, his brother wrote urging him to take steps to have security for it. This however involved a journey to London, then a long and difficult undertaking. Leighton replied, admitting the wisdom of the advice, but saying that unless some other business called him away from Newbattle he should not leave his work for such a reason. The result was the loss of the money by the failure of the merchant in whose hands it was placed. The spirit in which he received intelligence of his loss was characteristic. He wrote in reply:

"Your kind advice I cannot but thank you for, but I am not easily taught that lesson. I confess it is the wiser way to trust nobody; but there is so much of the fool in my nature, as carries me rather to the other extreme, to trust everybody. Yet I will venture to take the best means I can in that little business you write of. It is true, there is a lawful, yea, a needful diligence in such things: but, alas! how poor are they to the portion of believers where our treasure is.

"The little that was in Mr E.'s hands hath failed me; but I shall either have no need of it, or be supplied some other way. And this is the relief of my rolling thoughts, that while I am writing this, this moment is passing away, and all the hazards of want and sickness shall soon be at an end. The Lord be with you, and lead you in his ways."

Newbattle, Feb. 4, 1650.

When Leighton visited England, and his recent loss was adverted to by his brother-in-law, Mr Lightmaker, who regretted that he had misplaced his confidence, "Oh, no more of that," cried Leighton, "the *good* man escapes from the care and vexation of that business." "What, is that all you make of the matter?" rejoined his brother-in-law, with surprise. "Truly," answered Leighton, "if the Duke of Newcastle, after losing nineteen times as much of yearly income, can dance and sing, and the solid hopes of Christianity will not avail to support us, we had better be as the world."

It was not merely the loss of money that he could bear with such calmness and tranquillity: he could face death with equal composure. Some time afterwards, being in London, he had taken the water at the Savoy Stairs, in company with his brother, Sir Ellis Leighton, his lady, and some others, and was on his way to Lambeth, when, owing to mismanagement, the boat was in great danger of sinking. While the rest of the party were pale with terror, and most of them crying out, Leighton never for a moment lost his accustomed serenity. To some who afterwards expressed their astonishment at his calmness, he replied, "Why, what harm would it have been if we had all been safe landed on THE OTHER SIDE?" In the habit of dying daily, and of daily conversing with the world of spirits, he could never be surprised or disconcerted by a summons to depart out of the body.

On another occasion he was anxious to visit his brother, who bore arms in the king's service. On his way to the camp he was benighted in the midst of a dense forest, and having deviated from the path he sought in vain for an outlet. Almost spent with fatigue and hunger, he began to think his situation desperate, and dismounting, he spread his cloak upon the ground, and knelt down to pray. He calmly resigned his soul to God, entreating, however, that if it were not the Divine pleasure for him then to conclude his days, some way of deliverance might be opened. Then remounting his horse, he threw the reins upon its neck, and the animal left to itself, or rather to the care of Providence, threaded all the mazes of the wood, and made straight into the high road.

The uncompromising fidelity with which Leighton exposed and denounced the sins and vices of the times, at length made his residence at Newbattle a very uncomfortable one, and he resigned his pastoral charge there in the year 1652. It is probable that the spirit of conciliation and mutual concession which prompted him to secede from the extreme covenanting party, and to advocate the adoption of a modified Episcopacy, had something to do with this step. In the following year he was elected Principal of the University of Edinburgh, a post for which he was admirably qualified. He lectured in Latin once a week, on some theological subject, to the students, and at stated intervals preached to them in the College Chapel. Multitudes who were not members of the University flocked to listen to his prelections, attracted by the singular purity and elevation of his style, the nobleness and grandeur of his thoughts, and his own modest dignity and grace. Some translations from these lectures and discourses will be found in the present volume.

Whilst Leighton was Principal of the University, Cromwell died, Charles the Second was restored to the throne of his ancestors, and the ascendancy of the Puritan party came to an end. Charles, before his accession, had sworn to maintain the Presbyterian form of church government in Scotland. But it soon became evident that no oaths, however sacred, and no engagements, however binding, could control the king, who very speedily took steps to force Episcopacy upon his Scotch subjects. He found a ready tool in Sharpe, who, though one of the Commissioners of the Presbyterians to the king, was persuaded to desert his own party, and received as his reward the archbishopric of St Andrews, and the Primacy of Scotland. Sharpe likewise nominated three of the new bishops. A fourth was wanting. The king's advisers fixed upon Leighton, feeling that his reputation for learning, piety, moderation, and candour, would do much to promote their schemes. This is not the place in which to pronounce an opinion upon Leighton's ultimate acceptance of the office which was thrust upon him. It must suffice to say that he long refused the appointment, and very speedily resigned it. It was only when Charles laid his absolute commands upon him that he reluctantly consented to accept the unwelcome honour. He submitted to the king's peremptory order, in the hope that he might carry forward some measures of conciliation, which, by modifying the extreme pretensions of the opposite parties, should unite both. How soon his amiable illusion vanished we need not say. Whilst the matter was yet pending, he wrote the following letter to a friend, which will illustrate his state of feeling at the time.

"My dear Friend,

"I have received from you the kindest letter that ever you wrote me, and that you may know I take it so, I return you the free and friendly advice never to judge any man before you hear him, nor any business by one side of it. Were you here to see the other, I am confident your thoughts and mine would be the same. You have both too much knowledge of me and too much charity, to think that either such little contemptible scraps of honour or riches sought in that part of the world with so much reproach, or any human complacency in the world, will be admitted to decide so grave a question, or that I should sell (to speak no higher) the very sensual pleasure of my retirement for a rattle, far less deliberately do anything that I judge offends God. For the offence of good people, in cases indifferent in themselves, but not accounted so by them, whatsoever you do or do not, you shall offend some good people on the one side or other. And for those with you, the great fallacy in this business is, that they have misreckoned themselves in taking my silence and their zeal to have been consent and participation; which, how great a mistake it is, few know better or so well as yourself. And the truth is, I did see approaching an inevitable necessity to strain with them in divers practices, in what station soever remaining in Britain; and to have escaped further off (which hath been in my thoughts) would have been the greatest scandal of all. And what will you say, if there be in this thing somewhat of that you mention, and would allow of reconciling the devout on different sides, and of enlarging those good souls you meet with from their little fears, though possibly with little success? Yet the design is commendable, pardonable at least. However, one comfort I have, that in what is pressed on me there is the least of my own choice, yea, on the contrary, the strongest aversion that ever I had to anything in my life: the difficulty, in short, lies in a necessity of either owning a scruple which I have not, or the rudest disobedience to authority that may be. The truth is, I am yet importuning and struggling for a liberation, and look upward for it; but, whatsoever be the issue, I look beyond it and this weary, weary, wretched life, through which the Hand I have resigned it to, I trust, will lead me in the path of his own choosing; and, so that I may please Him, I am satisfied. I hope, if ever we meet, you will find me in the love of solitude and a devout life.

"Your unaltered brother and friend,

"R. L."

On the 15th of December, 1651, the new bishops were publicly consecrated in Westminster Abbey, Leighton being appointed to the See of Dunblane. The religious service was followed by a banquet, at which Leighton was very ill at ease, and openly testified his aversion to the jollity and revelry which succeeded the sacred ceremony. Soon afterwards the new prelates set out for Scotland, all travelling together in one large coach. Leighton, speaking of the journey to Burnet, said that "he believed his companions were weary of him, for he was very weary of them." Finding that they proposed to make a public entrance into Edinburgh, he left them at Morpeth, and proceeded at once in the most private and unostentatious manner to Dunblane.

He retained enough of Presbyterian simplicity and plainness to refuse the title of *Lord*, and almost the only time in which he took his seat in Parliament was when he did so in order to protest against the persecutions to which the Presbyterians were exposed, and to urge moderation and lenity towards them. We need hardly say that so far as his personal influence extended, these tolerant principles prevailed, though he failed in his attempts to impress them upon the Government. Within his own diocese no person suffered for his religious opinions. He constantly met the Presbyterian clergy in conference, and not unfrequently heard them preach.

His labours were incessant. He preached every Lord's day, preferring to do so to small village congregations. When any of the churches of his diocese were vacant he frequently supplied their pulpits himself, and visited them all once a year, instructing the ignorant, consoling the sick and afflicted, and relieving the wants of the poor. He was most assiduous in watching over the clergy under his charge and in aiding them in their responsible work. For himself, he had always desired the smallest cure; partly from his humility, and partly from an apprehension, so lively as to be almost terrible, of the account which must be given in by spiritual overseers at the great tribunal. Often would he commiserate those of the London clergy, the extent of whose cures made it impracticable to pay to each individual of their flock the attention that his soul required. "Were I again," he said in his last retirement, "to be a parish minister, I must follow sinners to their houses, and even to their alehouses." As one of the faults imputed to the Episcopal clergy was unskilfulness in preaching, he was solicitous to remove from his own diocese all colour for this allegation. This he knew could never be effected until the pulpits were filled by holy men. "It is vain," he would say, "for any one to speak of divine things without something of divine affections. An ungodly clergyman must feel weary when preaching godliness, and will hardly preach it persuasively. He has not been able to prevail on himself to be holy, and no marvel if he fail of prevailing upon others. In truth, he is in great danger of becoming hardened against religion by the frequent inculcation of it, if it fail of melting him."

We have seen that Leighton accepted the bishopric in the hope of being able to bring about some scheme of comprehension which should unite all parties in one church, or, if that failed, of introducing such measures of conciliation as to allay the bitterness of the strife between the Presbyterians and Episcopalians. He soon found, however, that all such hopes were vain. The persecutions grew more ruthless, and, by a very natural reaction, the persecuted grew more violent in their hostility to the dominant party. As is not uncommon to peacemakers, Leighton found himself an object of suspicion and aversion to both parties—the Episcopalians regarded him as a traitor, the Presbyterians as an apostate.

At length, wearied with his futile endeavours, disappointed and almost broken-hearted at finding all his efforts to put things in a better train quite ineffectual, Leighton thought that he should be justified in laying down the charge which he had taken up, not as a dignity, but as a cross and a burden. He resolved, however, to go up to London in the first instance, and to lay before the royal eye, which had hitherto been deluded with fallacious representations, a faithful picture of the distempered and convulsed state of Scotland. Having obtained an interview with the king, he declared that the severities practised upon objectors to the new establishment were such as his conscience could not justify, even for the sake of planting Christianity in a heathen land, much less could he agree to them for an end so comparatively insignificant as that of substituting one form of ecclesiastical government for another. He therefore besought permission to resign his bishopric, lest by retaining it he should seem to be a party to violent practices at which his principles and feelings revolted. His Majesty professed disapprobation of the manner in which the affairs of the church were administered by Sharpe, and seemed touched by the pathetic arguments of the advocate of toleration. He pledged himself to stop that application of the secular sword, against which Leighton protested, and he actually annulled the ecclesiastical commission which endeavoured to goad Dissenters into conformity by fines, and gaols, and corporal punishments. But he would not hear of Leighton's vacating his see, and the bishop consented at length to retain it, as he could not be ignorant that, by persisting in his purpose of retirement, he would throw away every chance of holding the king to those engagements into which he had just been impelled. It was, however, with a heavy heart that Leighton returned to his diocese and consented for some time longer to bear his cross. Though longing for repose, he would not seek it by any base desertion of the post of duty. And so he continued to labour for his Master "in word and doctrine," and by the far nobler eloquence of a devout and holy life.

If he had placed any reliance in the king's promises he was again doomed to disappointment, for they were forgotten almost as soon as uttered. Persecution became more rife and bitter than ever. The "oppression which maketh a wise man mad" was goading the Scotch people into open rebellion, and in the year 1666 they took up arms against the Government. Though the insurrection was crushed at the battle of Pentland Hills, the bitter feeling remained undiminished; discontent was only silenced, not allayed. In the west of Scotland sedition was especially active, and numerous partial risings of the people took place. These were suppressed with great and unnecessary violence, which only tended to make the breach yet wider. At this crisis the archbishopric of Glasgow fell vacant. It was at once felt that Leighton was the only man to fill the vacant post and to allay the prevalent discontent. The king ordered him to come up to court for the purpose of overcoming the scruples he was known to entertain, and he was allowed to submit for the royal consideration a scheme of accommodation between the Presbyterians and Episcopalians, which for years had been the object of his desires and the subject of his studies. Charles examined the scheme, or pretended to do so, expressed his approval of it, and promised Leighton his aid and sanction in carrying it into effect. "Hoping against hope," Leighton consented to accept the archbishopric on these terms, resolved to leave no means untried for bringing about a union of the contending parties. But a combination of causes rendered the scheme abortive. Both parties were too much exasperated, and were too jealous of each other, to yield a single point: and there is reason to believe that whilst the king gave Leighton his outward sanction he sent secret instructions to counteract his proceedings. And so the scheme of comprehension came to nothing. Much incidental good was done, however, by the pacific and conciliatory course of the new archbishop and by the conferences which he held with the Presbyterian ministers at Glasgow, Paisley, and Edinburgh. But he failed in his great object. An Episcopacy introduced and maintained by military violence was not likely to be acceptable to the people. Besides which the Presbyterians believed that Leighton was the only bishop, almost the only man in office, who was cordial or even sincere in the proposals which were made. They had been deceived so often that they had become incredulous.

It is most affecting to read the narrative of Leighton's labours at this period. Sometimes we find him contending with Sharpe and the ultra-Episcopalians, who were bitterly opposed to any concessions; then he turned to the ultra-Presbyterians, who were equally obstinate in maintaining the minutest details of their own system; then we find him vainly endeavouring to induce the royal commissioners to adopt a more conciliatory policy, and put a stop to the atrocities and cruelties of military rule. Meanwhile he did not neglect his own specific duties, but was unwearied in his efforts to promote true godliness in his diocese, and especially amongst his clergy. He preached incessantly, urging his hearers to a devout and holy life as the best remedy for the evils of the times. He exhorted the clergy to look up to God for guidance and strength and grace for the due discharge of their duties, besought them to lay aside all thoughts of ambition and revenge, to humble themselves before God, and by fasting and prayer to seek a blessing upon their labours. "This," says Bishop Burnet, "was a new strain to the clergy—they had nothing to say against it, but it was a comfortless doctrine to them. There was no quartering of soldiers and no levying of fines on the malcontents, so they went home as little edified with their new bishop as he was with them." At length even Leighton's hope and faith succumbed to the insuperable difficulties he encountered, and he abandoned his enterprise in despair.

Under these circumstances he again resolved to resign his office and to devote his remaining days to the exercises of private devotion. He announced his determination to his sister, Mrs Lightmaker, in a letter, from which the following is an extract:

"Our joint business is to die daily to this world and self, that what little remains of our life we may live to Him that died for us. For myself, to what purpose is it that I tell you that I grow old and sickly? And though I have here great retirement, yet I am still panting after a retreat from this place, and all public charge, and next, to rest in the grave. It is the most pressing desire I have of anything in the world, and, if it might be, near to you. But our heavenly Father, we quietly resigning all to him, both knows and will do what is best."

About the same time he wrote to the Synod of Glasgow expressing the same intention. The concluding paragraphs of this letter are in the following words:

"As for the confusions and contentions that still abound and increase in the church, and threaten to undo it, I think our wisdom will be to cease from man, and look for no help till we look more upwards, and dispute and discourse less, and fast and pray more, and so draw down our relief from the God of order and peace, who made the heavens and the earth.

"Concerning myself I have nothing to say, but humbly to entreat you to pass by the many failings and weaknesses you may have perceived in me during my abode amongst you; and if in anything I have injured or offended you, or any of you, in the management of my public charge or in private converse, I do sincerely beg your pardon; though I cannot make any requital in that kind, for I do not know of anything towards me from any of you that needs a pardon in the least, you having generally paid me more kindness and respect than a much better or wiser man could either have expected or deserved. Nor am I only a suitor for your pardon, but for the addition of a further charity, and that so great a one, that I have nothing to plead for it but that I need it much—your prayers. And I am hopeful, as to that, to make you some little, though very disproportionate, return; for whatsoever becomes of me (through the help of God) while I live you shall be no one day of my life forgotten by

"Your most unworthy, but most affectionate
"Brother and Servant,
"R. LEIGHTON."

He now proceeded to London to press his resignation upon the king. Charles, who knew Leighton's value, for a time refused to accept it, and used all means in his power to induce him to change his purpose, but in vain. At length the king gave way so far as to consent to his retirement, if at the expiration of the year he still desired it, and gave him a written engagement to that effect. With this Leighton was forced to be content, and returned to Glasgow, to fulfil the period of service required of him, saying that now there was "only one painful stage between him and rest." The year passed slowly and wearily away. At its close he immediately proceeded to London, and, to the joy of his heart, found himself at length free from the trammels which had weighed so heavily upon him.

His sister, Mrs Lightmaker, was now a widow, living with an only son in the mansion of her late husband at Broadhurst in Sussex. Her spirit was congenial with his own; and young Lightmaker was a dutiful son and a respectful nephew. In the bosom of his sister's family Leighton found a retreat provided for him by his heavenly Father, and he entered it with a grateful spirit. He lived in great privacy, spending his time in study, devotion, and works of charity. He preached much in the neighbouring villages, and his labours were eminently blessed. He saw very little company and scarcely visited at all, except amongst the poor and the afflicted. He seldom inquired after public affairs, and seemed dead to the world. One of his chief pleasures was epistolary correspondence with a few chosen friends on practical and experimental religion.

Many anecdotes remain of this period of his life which admirably illustrate his character. We subjoin a few of them. One Sunday the weather was very bad; the archbishop moreover felt very unwell. Most people would have thought these good reasons for staying away from church. Leighton, however, settled in his own mind that he would go. He said that if the day had been fine he would allow his ill health to keep him at home, but since it was bad he must go: "lest I be thought to countenance by my example the irreligious practice of letting trivial hindrances keep us back from public worship." He used to lament that ordinary Christians did not strive to attain to greater heights of holiness, and were so often content to be "low and stunted vines." We have another story of Leighton and the weather. "It is extremely severe," said his sister to him one day, speaking of the season. The good man only said in reply, "But thou, O God, hast made summer and winter." "You have been to hear a sermon," said some one to him. "I have met a sermon," was the answer, "for I met a corpse; and rightly and properly are the funeral rites performed when the living lay it to heart." Thus was his conversation in heaven, and all the passing incidents of the world became transfigured with celestial light.

Let it not be thought, however, that Leighton was a gloomy ascetic. He could sometimes indulge in a vein of quaint quiet humour. He had a ne'er-do-well sort of young fellow for his man-servant, whose thoughtlessness and idleness he bore with the utmost equanimity. We may be very sure, too, that the good Leighton did not fail to give him serious and solemn counsel. One day it so happened that this young fellow took it into his head that he should like to have a day's fishing; he accordingly started off, locked the door, and took the key with him, leaving his master a prisoner. His occupation proved so interesting that he did not think fit to return till evening; and all that the kind bishop said to him for the bad behaviour, that might justly have caused his dismissal, was, "John, when you next go a fishing, remember to leave the key in the door."

His consideration towards the poor was always very great. His liberality was boundless, and he reserved nothing for himself save the bare pittance which his own necessities imperiously demanded. One day at dinner when he was pressed to partake of a delicacy, he refused it. "Shall I eat of this delicacy," he said, "while a poor man wants his dinner?" He compared pleasure to mushrooms, that require so much precaution in eating, that it is best not to eat them at all. One or two more of his sayings are recorded on which we shall do well to ponder. He was told of a person who had changed his persuasion, and his reply was, "Is he more meek, more dead to the world? If so, he has made a happy change." There is a profound though melancholy meaning in this prayer of his: "Deliver me, O Lord, from the errors of wise men, yea, and of good men." He used often to think of death, and often spoke of it, and never in a melancholy tone. His nephew even says that in illness his spirits rose to an unusual gaiety, and he would say that "from the shaking of the prison doors he was led to hope that some of those brisk blasts would throw them open and give him the release he coveted." In a letter supposed to be written shortly before his death he writes thus: "I am grown exceeding uneasy in writing and speaking, yea, almost in thinking, when I reflect how cloudy our clearest thoughts are; but I think again, what other can we do, till the day break and the shadows flee away; as one that lieth awake in the night must be thinking, and one thought that will likely oftenest return, when by all other thoughts he finds little relief, is, *When will it be day?*"

The "day" for Leighton was not far off. In 1684, he came to London to visit an unhappy nobleman who was distressed in mind for his past guilt, and had desired to have the benefit of his counsel. His old friend Burnet, afterwards the celebrated bishop, was pleased to see him looking so well; his hair still black, his movements still lively, his eyes brilliant. Burnet expressed to him the pleasure he felt in seeing him looking "so hearty." Leighton answered that for all that he was very near his end, that work and journey would both soon be over. Burnet says that the words made no great impression upon him at the time, but they proved prophetic. The very next day he was seized with an oppression of the chest, which proved to be pleurisy: speech and sense suddenly went away, and after twelve hours he died without a struggle in Burnet's arms.

In speaking of death, Leighton used to do so with calmness and even with holy joy. He would compare the clod of clay with which the soul was encumbered to the miry boots which the traveller just lays aside when he has completed his journey. It was also a frequent remark of his that if he were to choose a place to die in he would choose an inn; for it looked like a pilgrim going home to whom this world was all as an inn, and who was weary of the noise and confusion in it. He added, according to Bishop Burnet, that the officious tenderness and care of friends were an entanglement to a dying man, and that the unconcerned attendance of those that could be procured in such a place would give less disturbance. It is remarkable that he obtained his wish, for he died at the Bell Inn, in Warwick Lane. Another singular circumstance is mentioned respecting his death. During the time that he was bishop he had shown so much kindness and forbearance in collecting his dues, that at the time of his retirement considerable sums were due to him as arrears. These were gradually paid to him, and were the means on which he subsisted. His last remittance was paid him about six weeks before his death, "so that" (to quote Bishop Burnet) "his provision and journey failed both at once."

His remains were conveyed to Horsted Keynes, the parish in which he had spent the concluding years of his life, and were buried in the chancel. A simple epitaph in Latin marks his tomb. It is in these words. DEPOSITUM ROBERT LEIGHTOUNJ ARCHEPISCOPI GLASGUENSIS APUD SCOTOS QUI OBJT XXV DIE JUNIJ. ANNO DOMIJ 1684. ÆTATIS SUÆ 74.

Burnet, who knew him well, writing some years after his death, says of him: "He had the greatest elevation of soul, the largest compass of knowledge, the most mortified and heavenly disposition I ever yet saw in mortal; he had the greatest parts as well as virtue, with the most perfect humility that I ever saw in man; and had a sublime strain in preaching, with so grave a gesture, and such a majesty both of thought, of language, and of pronunciation, that I never once saw a wandering eye when he preached, and have seen whole assemblies often melt into tears before him; and of whom I can say with truth, that in a full and frequent conversation with him for about two-and-twenty years I never knew him say an idle word that had not a direct tendency to edification, and I never once saw him in any other temper but that which I wished to be in in the last moments of my life." After making allowance for the partial estimate of a friend, this is a remarkable testimony to the life and character of Leighton. That he would most earnestly and emphatically have disclaimed such a eulogium we may be quite sure. Few men have had a deeper and more humbling sense of sin, or cast themselves more entirely upon the pardoning grace of God, than he. Blameless as was his life before men, he felt himself to be guilty before God. He was saved, as the vilest may be saved, through Christ alone, who "is able to save them to the uttermost that come unto God by him, seeing he ever liveth to make intercession for them."

CONTENTS.

CONTENTS.

SERMONS.

SERMON I.

But the wisdom that is from above is first pure, then peaceable, gentle, easy to be entreated, full of mercy and good fruits, without partiality, and without hypocrisy.—James iii. 17.

"God doth know that in the day ye eat thereof, then your eyes shall be opened, and ye shall be as gods, knowing good and evil," Gen. iii. 5, was the first hissing of that old serpent by which he poisoned mankind in the root. Man, not contented with the impression of God's image in which he was created, lost it by catching at a shadow; climbing higher than his station, he fell far below it: seeking to be more than man, to become as God, he made himself less than man. He lodged not a night in honour, but became as the beasts that perish, Psalm xlix. 12. Ever since, nature's best wisdom is full of impurity, turbulency, and distemper; nor can anything rectify it, but a wisdom from above, that both cleanseth and composeth the soul, that is first pure, and then peaceable.

The wisdom that is from above, is first pure; its gentleness can agree with anything except impurity: then, it is peaceable; it offends nobody, except purity offends them: it is not raging and boisterous. It is not only pure, being void of that mire and dirt which the wicked are said to cast out like the sea, Isa. lvii. 20, but peaceable likewise; not swelling and restless like the sea, as is there said of the wicked. Nor is it only peaceable negatively, that is, not offending, but, as the word bears, pacific, disposed to make and seek peace; and as it readily offends none, so is it not easily offended. It is gentle and moderate, and if offended, easily entreated to forgive: and as it easily passeth by men's offences, so it doth not pass by, but looks upon, their distresses and wants, as full of compassion as it is free from unruly and distempered passions. Nor rests it in an affected sympathy; its mercy is helpful, full of mercy and good fruits: and it both forgives and pities and gives. It is, too, without partiality and without hypocrisy. The word "without partiality" may as well bear another sense, no less suiting both with this wisdom and these its other qualities—that is, not taking upon it a censorious discerning and judging of others. They that have most of this wisdom are least rigid to those who have less of it. I know no better evidence of strength in grace, than to bear much with those that are weak in it. And, lastly, as it spares the infirmities of others, so it makes not false and vain shows of its own excellencies; it is without hypocrisy. This denies two things, both dissimulation and ostentation. The art of dissembling, or hypocrite craft, is no part of this wisdom; and as for the other, ostentation, surely the air of applause is too light a purchase for solid wisdom. The works of this wisdom may be seen, yea, they should be seen, and may possibly be now and then recommended; but they should not be done for that low end, either to be seen or to be commended. Surely, no, being of so noble extraction, this having descended from heaven, will be little careful for the estimation of those that are of the earth, and are but too often of the earth, earthy.

The due order of handling these particulars more fully cannot well be missed; doubtless the subject, "wisdom from above," requires our first consideration; next, the excellent qualities that are attributed to it; and lastly, their order is to be considered, the rather because so clearly expressed—first pure, then peaceable, &c.

I. *Wisdom from above.* There be two things in that: there is the general term of wisdom common to divers sorts of wisdom, though most eminently and truly belonging to this best wisdom. Then there is the birth or original of this wisdom, serving to specify and distinguish it from all the rest—wisdom from above. Wisdom in the general is a very plausible word among men. Who is there that would not willingly pass for wise? Yea, often those that are least of all such are most desirous to be accounted such; and where this fails them, they usually make up that want in their own conceit and strong opinion. Nor do men only thus love the reputation of wisdom, but they naturally desire to be wise as they do to be happy; yet through corrupt nature's blindness they do as naturally mistake and fall short both of the one and the other; and being once wrong, the more progress they make, they are further out of the way: and pretending to wisdom in a false way they still befool themselves, as the apostle speaks, Rom. i. 22, "Professing themselves to be wise, they became fools."

Our apostle, ver. 15, speaking of that wicked wisdom that is fruitful of wrongs, strifes, and debates, and that is only abusively to be called wisdom, shows what kind of wisdom it is by three notable characters, earthly, natural, and devilish; which though they be here jointly attributed to one and the same subject, yet we may make use of to signify some differences of false wisdom. (1.) There is an infernal, or devilish wisdom, proper for contriving cruelties and oppressions, or subtle shifts and deceits, that make atheism a main basis and pillar of state policy; such are those that devise mischief upon their beds, Mic. ii. 1. This is serpentine wisdom, not joined with, but most opposite to, the dove-like simplicity. (2.) There is an earthly wisdom that draws not so deep in impiety as that other, yet is sufficient to keep a man out of all acquaintance with God and divine matters, and is drawing his eye perpetually downwards; employing him in the pursuit of such things as cannot fill the soul except it be with anguish and vexation, Ezek. xxviii. 4, 5. The dexterity of gathering riches, when it is not attended with the Christian art of right using them, abases men's souls, and indisposes them wholly for this wisdom that is from above. (3.) There is a natural wisdom far more plausible than the other two, more harmless than that hellish wisdom, and more refined than that earthly wisdom, yet no more able to make man holy and happy than they: natural, it is the word the apostle St Paul useth, 1 Cor. ii. 14, naming the natural man by his better part, his soul; intimating that the soul, even in the highest faculty of it, the understanding, and that in the highest pitch of excellency to which nature can raise it, is blind in spiritual objects: things that are above it cannot be known but by a wisdom from above.

Nature neither affords this wisdom, nor can of itself acquire it. This is to advertise us, that we mistake not morality and common knowledge, even of divine things, for the wisdom that is from above. This may raise a man high above the vulgar, as the tops of the highest mountains leave the valleys below them; yet is it still as far short of true supernatural wisdom as the highest earth is of the highest sphere.

There is one main point of the method of this wisdom that is of most hard digestion to a natural man, and the more natural wise he be the worse he likes it—If any man would be wise, let him become a fool, that he may become wise, 1 Cor. iii. 18. There is nothing gives nature a greater prejudice against religion than this initial point of self-denial. When men of eminent learning hear, that if they will come to Christ they must renounce their own wisdom to be fit for his, many of them go away as sorrowful as the young man, when he heard of selling all his goods and giving them to the poor.

Jesus Christ is that eternal and substantial wisdom that came from above, to deliver men from perishing in their affected folly, as you find it at large, Prov. viii. St Paul in the first chapter of his First Epistle to the Corinthians calls him the wisdom of God, ver. 24; that shows his excellency in himself; and ver. 30, he tells us that he is made, of God, our wisdom; and by him alone is this infused wisdom from above conveyed to us—In him are hid the treasures of wisdom and knowledge, Col. ii. 3. And from his fulness (if at all) we all receive grace for grace; and of all graces, first some measures of his wisdom, without which no man can know himself, much less can he know God.

Now this supernatural wisdom hath in it both speculation and prudence. It is contemplative and practical. These two must not be separated, I wisdom dwell with prudence, Prov. viii. 12. This wisdom in its contemplative part reads Christ much, and discovers in him a new world of hidden excellencies unknown to this old world. There are treasures of wisdom in him, Col. ii. 3, but they are hid, and no eye sees them but that which is enlightened with this wisdom: no, it is impossible to know divine things while God concealeth them. But when the renewed understanding of a Christian is once initiated into this study, it both grows daily more and more apprehensive, and Christ becomes more communicative of himself, and makes the soul acquainted with the amiable countenance of his Father in him reconciled. No man hath seen God at any time; the only begotten Son which is in the bosom of the Father, he hath declared him, St John i. 18. What wonder if the unlettered and despised Christian know more of the mysteries of heaven than the naturalist, though both wise and learned? Christ admits the believer into *his* bosom, and *he* is in the bosom of the Father. But withal know, that all this knowledge, though speculatively high, yet descends to practice; as it learns what God is, so it thence teacheth man what he should be: this wisdom flows from heaven, and a heavenly conversation flows from it, as we find it there charactered by these practical graces of purity, peace, meekness, &c.

Hence I conceive may be fitly learned for our use, that gross ignorance cannot consist with the truth of religion, much less can it be a help and advantage to it. I shall never deny that a false superstitious religion stands in need of it: "Not too much Scripture-wisdom for the people." The pomp of that vain religion, like court masks, shows best by candle-light; fond nature likes it well; the day of spiritual wisdom would discover its imposture too clearly. But to let their foul devotion pass, (for such it must needs be that is born of so black a mother as ignorance,) let this wisdom at least be justified of those that pretend to be her children. It is lamentable that amongst us, where knowledge is not withheld, men should, through sloth and love of darkness, deprive themselves of it. What abundance of almost brutish ignorance is amongst the commons; and thence uncleanness, and all manner of wickedness; a darkness that both hides and increaseth impurity!

And if there be any that think to shroud unpunished amongst the thickets of ignorance, especially amidst the means of knowledge, take notice of this, though it may hide the deformity of sin from your own sight for a time, it cannot palliate it from the piercing eye, nor cover it from the revenging hand, of Divine justice. As you would escape that wrath to come, come to wisdom's school; and how simple soever ye be as to this world, if you would not perish with the world, learn to be wise unto salvation.

And truly it is mainly important for this effect, that the ministers of the gospel be active and dexterous in imparting this wisdom to their people. If they would have their conversation to be holy, and peaceable, and fruitful, the most expedient way is at once to principle them well in the fundamentals of religion, for therein is their great defect. How can they walk evenly and regularly so long as they are in the dark? One main thing is to be often pointing at the way to Christ, the fountain of this wisdom. Without this, you bid them to be clothed, and clothe them not.

How needful then is it that pastors themselves be seers indeed, as the prophets were called of old; not only faithful but wise dispensers, as our Saviour speaks, St Luke xii. 42. That they be able, and apt to teach, 1 Tim. iii. 2. Laudable is the prudence that tries much the churches' storehouses, the seminaries of learning; but withal, it is not to be forgotten, that as a due furniture of learning is very requisite for this employment, so it is not sufficient. When one is duly enriched that way, there is yet one thing wanting that grows not in schools; except this wisdom infused from above season and satisfy all other endowments, they remain common and unholy, and therefore unfit for the sanctuary. Amongst other weak pretences to Christ's favour in the last day, this is one—"We have preached in thy name;" yet says Christ, "I never knew you;" surely then they knew not him, and yet they preached him. Cold and lifeless (though never so fine and well contrived) must those discourses be that are of an unknown Christ. Pastors are called angels, and therefore, though they use the secondary helps of knowledge, they are mainly to bring their message from above, from the fountain, the head of this pure wisdom.

II. *Pure.* If it come from above it must needs be pure originally, being a main trait of God's renewed image in the soul. By this wisdom the understanding is both refined and strengthened to entertain right conceptions of God in his nature and works. And this is primarily necessary, that the mind be not infected with false opinions in religion; if the spring-head be polluted the streams cannot be pure; it is more important than men usually think for a good life. But that which I suppose is here chiefly intended is, that it is effectively and practically pure, it purifies the heart, Acts xv. 9 (said of faith, which in some sense and acceptation differs not much from this wisdom), and consequently the words and actions that flow from the heart.

This purity that true wisdom works is contrary to all pollution. We know then in some measure what it is; it rests to inquire where it is, and there is the difficulty; it is far easier to describe it in itself than to find it among men. Who can say, I have made my heart clean? Prov. xx. 9. Look upon the greatest part of mankind and you may know at first sight that purity is not to be looked for among them; they suffer it not to come near them, much less to dwell with them and within them; they hate the very semblance of it in others, and themselves delight in intemperance and all manner of licentiousness, like foolish children striving who shall go furthest into the mire; these cannot say, they have made clean their hearts, for all their words and actions will belie them. If you come to the mere moralist, the world's honest man, and ask him, it may be he will tell you he hath cleansed his heart; but believe him not. It will appear he is not yet cleansed, because he says he has done it himself, for (you know) there must be some other, besides man, at this work. Again, he, rising no higher than nature, hath none of this heavenly wisdom in him, and therefore is without this purity too. But if you chance to take notice of some well-skilled hypocrite.

everything you meet with makes you almost confident that there is purity; yet if he be strictly put to it, he may make some good account of the pains he hath taken to refine his tongue and his public actions, but he dare not say he hath made clean his heart. It troubles his peace to be asked the question. He never intended to banish sin, but to retire it to his innermost and best room, that so it might dwell unseen within him; and where then should it lodge but in his heart? Yet possibly because what is outward is so fair, and man cannot look deeper to contradict him, he may embolden himself to say he is inwardly suitable to his appearance; but there is a day at hand that shall, to his endless shame, at once discover both his secret impurity and his impudence in denying it.

After these, there follow a few despised and melancholy persons (at least as to outward appearance) who are almost always complaining of abundant sinfulness. And sure, purity cannot be expected in these who are so far from it by their own confession. Yet the truth is, that such purity as is here below will either be found to lodge among these, or nowhere. Be not deceived; think not that they who loathe, and (as they can) fly from the unholiness of the world, are therefore taken with the conceit of their own holiness; but as their perfect purity of justification is by Christ's imputed righteousness, so likewise they well know, and do always acknowledge, that their inherent holiness is from above too, from the same fountain, Jesus Christ. The wisdom from above is pure, this is their engagement to humility, for it excludes vaunting and boasting; and besides that, it is imperfect, troubled and stained with sin, which is enough to keep them humble. Their daily sad experience will not suffer them to be so mistaken; their many faults of infirmity cannot but keep them from this presumptuous fault. There is a generation indeed that are pure in their own eyes (Prov. xxx. 12), and yet are not washed from their filthiness. They that are washed, are still bewailing that they again contract so much defilement. The most purified Christians are they that are most sensible of their impurity. Therefore I called not this an universal freedom from pollution, but an universal detestation of it: they that are thus pure are daily defiled with many sins, but they cannot be in love with any sin at all, nor do they willingly dispense with the smallest sins, which a natural man either sees not to be sin (though his dim moonlight discovers grosser evils), or if he does see them, yet he judges it too much niceness to choose a great inconvenience rather than a little sin. Again, they differ in another particular; a natural man may be so far in love with virtue after his manner, as to dislike his own faults and resolve to amend them, but yet he would think it a great weakness to sit down and mourn for sin, and to afflict his soul, as the Scripture speaks. The Christian's repentance goes not so lightly; there is a great deal more work in it, 2 Cor. vii. 11. There is not only indignation against impurity, but it proceeds to revenge. The saints we read of in Scripture were ashamed of their impurity, but never of their tears for it.

This is the condition of those that are truly, though not yet fully, cleansed from the pollutions of the world by the spirit of wisdom and purity. What mean they, then, that would argue themselves out of this number, because they find yet much dross left, and that they are not so defecated and refined as they would wish to be? On the contrary, this hatred of pollution testifies strongly that the contrary of it, purity, is there; and, though its beginnings be small, doubt not it shall in the end be victorious; the smoking of this flax shows indeed that there is gross matter there, but it witnesseth likewise that there is fire in it too; and though it be little, we have Christ's own word for it, that it shall not be quenched; and if he favour it, no other power shall be able to quench it. You find not indeed absolute holiness in your persons, nor in your best performances; yet if you breathe and follow after it, if the pulse of the heart beats thus, if the main current of your affection be towards purity, if sin be in you as your disease and greatest grief, and not as your delight, then take courage, you are as pure as travellers can be; and notwithstanding that impure spirit, Satan, and the impurity of your own spirits, vex you daily with temptations, and often foil you, yet, in despite of them all, you shall arrive safe at home, where perfection dwells.

Wisdom from above is pure. Be ashamed then of your extreme folly, you that take pleasure in any kind of uncleanness, especially seeing God hath reformed and purged his house amongst us: you that are, or should be, his living temples, remain not unreformed; if you do, church reformation will be so far from profiting you, that, as a clearer light, it will but serve to make your impurity both more visible and more inexcusable. If you mean that the Holy Ghost should dwell with you, entertain him, avoiding both spiritual and fleshly pollutions. Grieve not the good Spirit of God with actions or speeches, yea, or with thoughts, that are impure. The unholy soul, like the mystical Babylon, Apoc. xiii., makes itself a cage of unclean birds and an habitation of filthy spirits: and if it continues to be such, it must, when dislodged, take up its habitation with cursed spirits for ever in utter darkness. But as for those that are sincerely and affectionately pure, that is, pure in heart, our Saviour hath pronounced their begun happiness—Blessed are they that are pure in heart; and assured them of full happiness—for they shall see God. This wisdom is sent from heaven on purpose to guide the elect thither by the way of purity. And mark how well their reward is suited to their labour; their frequent contemplating and beholding of God's purity as they could, while they were on their journey, and their labouring to be like him, shall bring them to sit down in glory, and to be for ever the pure beholders of that purest object: They shall see God. What this is we cannot tell you, nor can you conceive it; but walk heavenwards in purity, and long to be there, where you shall know what it means; for you shall see him as he is.

Now to that blessed Trinity be praise for ever.

SERMON II.

Surely it is meet to be said unto God, I have borne chastisement, I will not offend any more: that which I see not teach thou me: if I have done iniquity, I will do no more.—Job xxxiv. 31, 32.

The great sin and the great misery of man is, the forgetting of God; and the great end and use of his works and of his word is, to teach us the right remembrance and consideration of him. These words do particularly instruct us in the application of our thoughts towards him in the time of affliction. He that speaks here, though the youngest of the company, yet, as a wise and calm-spirited man, closes all with a discourse of excellent temper, and full of grave, useful instructions, amongst which this is one:—

Surely it is meet to be said unto God. This speaking to God, though it may be vocal, yet it is not necessarily nor chiefly so, but is always mainly, and may often be only, mental; without this the words of the mouth, how well chosen and well expressed soever, are to God of no account or signification at all. But if the heart speak, even when there is not a word in the mouth, it is that he hearkens to and regards, though made by a voice that none hears but he, and in a language that none understands but he.

But it is a rare, infrequent thing, this communing of the heart with God, speaking its thoughts to him concerning itself, and concerning him and his dealing with it, which is the speech here recommended; and is that divine exercise of meditation, and soliloquy of the soul with itself, and with God, hearkening to what the Lord God speaks to us, within us, and our hearts echoing and resounding his words, and opening to him our thoughts of them, and of ourselves. Though they stand open, and he sees them all, even when we tell him not of them, yet because he loves us, he loves to hear them of our own speaking; as a father delights in the little stammering, lisping language of his beloved child. And if the reflex affection of children be in us, we love also to speak with our Father, and to tell him all our mind, and to be often with him in the entertainments of our secret thoughts.

But the most of men are little within; either they wear out their hours in vain discourse with others, or possibly vainer discourse with themselves; even those that are not of the worst sort, and possibly that have their times of secret prayer, yet do not so delight to think of God and to speak with him, as they do to be conversant in other affairs and companies, and discourses, in which there is a great deal of froth and emptiness.

Men think, by talking of many things, to be refreshed, and yet when they have done, find that it is nothing; and that they had much better have been alone, or have said nothing. Our thoughts and speeches in most things run to waste, yea, are defiled; as water spilt on the ground is both lost, cannot be gathered up again, and it is polluted, mingled with dust. But no word spoken to God, from the serious sense of a holy heart, is lost; he receives it, and returns it into our bosom with advantage: a soul that delights to speak to him will find that he also delights to speak to it. And this communication certainly is the sweetest and happiest choice, to speak little with men, and much with God. One short word, such as this here, spoken to God, in a darted thought, eases the heart more when it is afflicted, than the largest discourses and complainings to the greatest and most powerful of men, or the kindest and most friendly. It gives not only ease but joy to say to God, I have sinned, yet I am thine; or as here, I have borne chastisement, I will no more offend.

The time of affliction is peculiarly a time of speaking to God, and such speech as this is peculiarly befitting such a time. And this is one great recommendation of affliction, that it is a time of wiser and more sober thoughts; a time of the returning of the mind inwards and upwards. A high place, fulness and pleasure, draw the mind more outwards; great light and white colours disgregate the sight of the eye, and the very thoughts of the mind too. And men find that the night is a fitter season for deep thoughts. It is better, says Solomon, to go to the house of mourning than to the house of feasting: those blacks made the mind more serious. It is a rare thing to find much retirement unto God, much humility and brokenness of spirit, true purity and spiritualness of heart, in the affluences and great prosperities of the world. It is no easy thing to carry a very full cup even, and to digest well the fatness of a great estate and great place. They are not to be envied that have them; even though they be of the better sort of men, it is a thousand to one but that they shall be losers by the gains and advancements of this world; suffering proportionably great abatement of their best advantages by their prosperity. The generality of men, while they are at ease, do securely neglect God, and little mind either to speak to him, or to hear him speak to them. God complains thus of his own people: I spoke to them in their prosperity, and they would not hear. The noises of their coach-wheels, of their pleasures, and of their great affairs, so fill their ears, that the still voice, wherein God is, cannot be heard; I will bring her into the wilderness, and there I will speak to her heart, says God of his church. There the heart is more at quiet to hear God, and to speak to him, and is disposed to speak in the style here prescribed, humbly and repentingly.

I have borne chastisement. The speaking thus unto God under affliction signifies that our affliction is from his hand, and to the acknowledgment of this truth the very natural consciences of men do incline them.

Though trouble be the general lot of mankind, yet it doth not come on him by an improvidential fatality. Though man is born to trouble as the sparks fly upwards, yet it comes not out of the dust (Job v. 7). It is no less true, and in itself no less clear, that all the good we enjoy, and all the evil we suffer, comes from the same hand; but we are naturally more sensible of evil than of good, and therefore do more readily reflect upon the original and causes of it. Our distresses lead us unto the notice of the righteous God inflicting them, and of our unrighteous ways procuring them, and provoking him so to do; and therefore it is meet to speak in this submissive, humble language to him. It is by all means necessary to speak to him; he is the party we have to deal with, or to speak to, even in those afflictions whereof men are the intervenient, visible causes. They are, indeed, but instrumental causes, the rod and staff (Heb. xii. 6) in his hand that smite us; therefore our business is with him, in whose supreme hand alone the mitigations and increases, the continuance and the ending of our troubles lie. Who gave Jacob to the spoil, and Israel to the robbers? Did not the Lord, against whom we have sinned? So Lam. i. 14: The yoke of my transgression is bound on by his hand. Therefore it is altogether necessary in all afflictions to speak to him; it is meet to speak thus to him: I have borne chastisement, I will no more offend.

These words have in them the true composition of real repentance, humble submission, and holy resolution.

I have borne chastisement; that is, "I have justly borne it, and do heartily submit to it: I bear it justly, and take it well: Lord, I acquit thee, and accuse myself." This language becomes the most innocent persons in the world in their suffering. Job knew it well, and did often acknowledge it in his preceding speeches. Though sometimes in the heat of dispute, and opposure to the uncharitable and unjust imputations of his friends, he seems to overstrain the assertion of his own integrity (which Elihu here corrects), you know he cries out, "I have sinned against thee; what shall I do unto thee, O thou preserver of men?" Job vii. 20; and chap. ix. 30, 31: "If I wash myself with snow-water, and make my hands ever so clean, yet shalt thou plunge me in the ditch, and mine own clothes shall abhor me."

Oh that there were such a heart in us! that, instead of empty words that scatter themselves in the wind, our many vain discourses we hold one with another concerning our past and present sufferings, and further fears and disputing of many fruitless and endless questions, we were more abundantly turning our speech this way unto God, and saying, "We desire to give thee glory, and take shame to ourselves, and to bear our chastisement, and to offend no more, to return each from his evil way, and to gain this by the furnace, the purging away of our dross, our many and great iniquities, our oaths, and cursings, and lying, our deceit and oppressions, and pride, and covetousness, our base love of ourselves, and hating one another; that we may be delivered from the tyranny of our own lusts and passions; and in other things, let the Lord do with us as seems good in his eyes." When a stubborn child leaves struggling under the rod, and turns to entreating, the father then leaves striking; nothing overcomes him but that. When a man says unto God, "Father, I have provoked thee to this; but pardon me, and, through thy grace, I will do so no more," then the rod is thrown aside, and the Father of mercies, and his humble child, fall to mutual tenderness and embraces.

What I see not, teach thou me. The great article of conversion is the disengagement of the heart from the love of sin. In that posture, as it actually forsakes whatsoever it perceives to be amiss, so it stands in an absolute readiness to return to every duty that yet lies hidden, upon the first discovery; that is here the genuine voice of a repentant sinner: What I see not, teach thou me.

This is a very necessary suit, even for the most discerning and clearest-sighted penitent, both in reference to the commandment and rule for discovering the general nature and several kinds of sin; and withal, for application of this general light to the examen of a man's own heart and ways, that so he may have a more exact and particular account of his own sins.

The former is the knowledge of the laws of God, and rule by which a man is to try and to judge himself. The most knowing are not above the need of this request, yea, I am persuaded, the most knowing know best how much they need it, and are most humbled in themselves in the conscience of their ignorance and darkness in divine things, and are most earnest and pressing in this daily supplication for increase of light and spiritual knowledge from Him who is the fountain of it; What I see not, teach thou me. On the other side, the least knowing are often the most confident that they know all, and swelled with a conceited sufficiency of their model and determination of all things, both dogmatical and practical; and therefore are the most imperious and magisterial in their conclusions, and the most impatient of contradiction, or even of the most modest dissent.

The wisest and holiest persons speak always in the humblest and most depressing style of their own knowledge, and that not with an affectation of modesty, but in the real sense of the thing as it is, and the sincere account they give of it, and that commonly when they are declaring themselves most solemnly, as in the sight of God, or speaking in supplication to him with whom they dare least of all dissemble. Whosoever he was that spake these words, Prov. xxx. 2, 3, sure he was a man of eminent wisdom and piety, and yet begins thus: "Surely I am more brutish than any man, and have not the understanding of a man. I have neither learned wisdom, nor have I the knowledge of the holy." And though he was so diligent a student, and so great a proficient in the law of God, yet how importunate a petitioner is he for the understanding of it, as if he knew nothing at all! Besides the like expressions in other psalms, in one psalm (Ps. cxix.), that being of such length, hath nothing but the breathing forth of his affection to the word and law of God, how often doth he in it reiterate that, "Teach me thy statutes!" so often, that a carnal mind is tempted to grow weary of it, as a nauseating tautology; but he made it still new, with the freshness and vehemency of his affection. "Make me to understand the way of thy precepts; give me understanding, and I shall keep thy law; and open thou mine eyes, that I may see the wonders of thy law; unseal mine eyes," as if still veiled in dark. These are the earnest and nobly ambitious desires that daily solicit holy hearts, and stir them to solicit the teacher of hearts, to be admitted more into the secrets and recesses of divine knowledge; not those abysses that God intends should be secret still, and from which he hath barred out our curiosity, as the forbidden tree of knowledge—those secrets that belong to himself alone, and concern us not to inquire after; and certainly to be wading in these deeps is the way to be drowned in them. The searcher of majesty shall be oppressed with glory; yet, there is in man a perverse, preposterous desire to pore upon such things as are on purpose hidden that we should not inquire after them, and to seek after useless, empty speculations of them, which is a luxury and intemperance of the understanding, like unto that, and springing from that, which at first undid us in Adam our root.

These are times full of those empty, airy questions, and notions in which there is no clearness nor certainty to be attained, and if it were, yet would serve to little or no purpose, not making the man that thinks he hath found them out, one jot the better or holier man than he was before. What avails it, says a devout author, to dispute and discourse high concerning the Trinity, and want humility, and so displease that Trinity? The light of knowledge, suited according to the intendment of this copy, is of another nature, such as purifies the heart and rectifies the life. "What I see not, teach thou me," that is, of such things as may serve this end, that "if I have done iniquity I may do it no more." This is sound and solid knowledge, such a light as inflames the heart with the love of God, and of the beauties of holiness; and still, as it grows, makes those to grow likewise. Such are still, we see, David's multiplied supplications in that psalm; not to know reserved and unuseful things, but—"Hide not thy commandments from me." "Thy hands have made me and fashioned me." Now, what is that thy creature and workmanship begs of thee? What is that which will complete my being, and make me do honour to my Maker? This is it; "give me understanding, that I may learn thy commandments." You that would be successful supplicants in this request, wean your hearts from this vanity of desire: such knowledge is as the cypress trees, fair and tall, but fruitless and sapless. Apply all you know to the purging out of sin, and intend all the further knowledge you desire to that same end. Seek to be acquainted with higher rules of mortification and self-denial and charity, than yet you have either practised, or, possibly, so much as thought on; that, by these, your affections and actions may be advanced to greater degrees of purity, and conformity with the holiness of God.

And for this end, beg of him to teach you what you see not in the exactness of the law and rule; and withal (which is the other thing in this text), that what you see not in the application of it and search of yourself, he would likewise show you; for in that, we are commonly as undiscerning and dim-sighted as in the other, even where men have some notion of the rule and their duty; yet they perceive not their own, even their gross recessions and declinings from it. Love is a blinding thing, and above all other love, self-love; and every man is naturally his own flatterer, he deals not faithfully and sincerely with himself in the search of his own evils. Now this we are to entreat of God, to be led into ourselves, and be applied to the work of self-searching, by his own hand, not only to have a right apprehension of the law given us, but a true sight of ourselves. Oh! how many hidden, undiscerned, yea, unsuspected impurities and follies are there in the hearts of those that are most diligent in this inquiry, much more in the greater part, even of such as cannot absolutely be denied the name of good men! Some honest intentions and good desires there are in them; but they are slothful, and unwilling to go to this painful business of trying and judging themselves; and when they set to it, many secret corners, and in those many latent inordinancies, do escape their search. "Cleanse me from secret faults," says David; that is, not only those hidden from men, but even from myself, as is clearly his meaning, by the words preceding—"Who can understand his errors?" Therefore it is necessary that we desire light of God. "The spirit of a man is the candle of the Lord," says Solomon, "searching the innermost parts of the belly;" but it is a candle unlighted when He does not illuminate it for that search. Oh! what a deal of vanity and love of this world, envy and secret pride, lurks in many of our hearts, that we do not at all perceive, till God causeth us to see it, leading us in, as he did the prophet in the vision, to see the idolatry of the Jews in his very temple, by which they had provoked him to forsake it, and go far from his sanctuary; and having discovered one parcel, leads him in further, and makes him enter through the wall, and adds often, "Son of man, hast thou seen these? I will cause thee to see yet more abominations." Thus is it within many of us that should be his temples; but we have a multitude of images of jealousy, one lying hid behind another, till he thus discover them to us. Oh, what need have we to entreat him thus: "What I see not, teach thou me!"

Now, in both these, both in the knowledge of our rule and of ourselves, though there may be some useful subserviency of the ministry of men, yet the great teacher of the true knowledge of his law, and of himself, and of ourselves, is God. Men may speak to the ear, but his chair is in heaven that teaches hearts. Matchless teacher! that teacheth more in one hour than men can do in a whole age! that can cure the invincible unteachableness of the dullest heart, give understanding to the simple, and open the eyes of the blind. So, then, would we be made wise, wise for eternity, learned in real living divinity, let us sit down at his feet, and make this our continual request—"What I see not, teach thou me."

And if I have done, &c. That is, "any iniquity that I yet know not of, any hidden sin, let me but once see it, and I hope thou shalt see it no more within me; not willingly lodged and entertained." This speaks an entire, total giving up all sin, and proclaiming utter defiance and enmity against it; casting out what is already found out without delay, and resolving that, still in further search, as it shall be more discovered, it shall be forthwith dislodged, without a thought of sparing or partial indulgence to anything that is sin, or like it, or may befriend it, or be an incentive of it. This is that absolute renouncing of sin, and surrender of the whole soul and our whole selves to God, which, whosoever do not heartily consent to, their religion is in vain, and (which is here the point) their affliction is in vain: whatsoever they have suffered, they have gained nothing by all their sufferings, if their hearts remain still self-willed, stubborn, untamed, and unpliable to God. And this makes their miseries out of measure miserable, and their sins out of measure sinful; whereas, were it thus qualified, and had it any operation this way towards the subjecting of their hearts unto God, affliction were not to be called misery, but would go under the title of a blessedness: "Blessed is the man whom thou correctest, and teachest him out of thy law." That suiting with this, here desired, "I have borne chastisement: what I see not, teach thou me; and if I have done iniquity, I will do it no more." Oh! were it thus with us, my brethren, how might we rejoice, and insert into our praises all that is come upon us, if it had wrought or advanced anything of this kind within us, this blessed compliance with the will of God; finding a pleasure in the denial and destruction of our own most beloved pleasures at his appointment and for his sake, whatsoever is in us, and dearest to us, that would offend us, that would draw us to offend him: were it the right hand, let it be cut off, or the right eye, let it be plucked out: or, to make shorter work, let the whole man die at once, crucified with Jesus, "That we may be henceforth dead to sin, dead to the world, dead to ourselves, and alive only unto God."

SERMON III.

In that day shall the Lord of hosts be for a crown of glory, and for a diadem of beauty, unto the residue of his people, and for a spirit of judgment to him that sitteth in judgment, and for strength to them that turn the battle to the gate.—ISA. xxviii. 5, 6.

ALL the works of Divine Providence are full of wisdom and justice, even every one severally considered; yet we observe them best to be such, when we take notice of their order and mutual aspect one to another, whether in the succession of times, or such passages as are contemporary, and fall in together at one and the same time. As, when the Lord brings notable judgments upon the proud workers of iniquity, and at the same time confers special mercies on his own people; who is there that may not perceive justice and mercy illustrating and beautifying one another? It is true, the full reward and perfect rest of the godly is not here below; they would be sorry if it were: nor is this the place of plenary punishment for the ungodly. Men may look for a judgment too, and the Lord is pleased at some times to give some resemblances and pledges, as it were, of that great and last judgment in remarkable passages of justice and mercy, at one and the same time; and such a time it is that the prophet foretells in this his sermon, which concerns the two sister kingdoms of Israel and Judah. Having denounced a heavy calamity to come upon Israel, under the name of Ephraim, he comforts those of Judah, under the name of the residue of his people. They not being so grossly corrupted as the other were, he stays them with this promise: In that day, saith he, when the other shall be overwhelmed as with a deluge, the Lord of hosts shall be for a crown of glory, and for a diadem of beauty, unto the residue of his people.

The promise is made up of three benefits, yet the three are but one; or rather, one is all the three to them. The Lord of hosts; it is he that shall be their honour, wisdom, and strength. He shall be a crown, a spirit of judgment and strength.

But first, a word of the circumstance of time, *In that day*. That sovereign Lord who at first set up the lights of heaven to distinguish times and seasons by their constant motion, and likewise, by his supreme providence ruling the world, hath fixed the period of states and kingdoms, and decreed their revolutions, their rising, ascending, and their height, with their decline and setting, hath, by a special providence, determined those changes and vicissitudes that befall his church. That which the psalmist speaks, in his own particular, Psa. xxxi. 14, 15, holds of each believer, and of the church, which they make up in all ages and places: "I said, Thou art my God; my times are in thy hand;" a sure and steady hand indeed, and therefore he builds his confidence upon it.

Thus, then, as many as are looking after a day of mercy to the church of God, pray and believe upon this ground, that the time of it is neither in the frail hands of those that favour and seek it, nor of those that oppose it, how strong and subtle soever they be, but in that Almighty hand that doth in heaven and earth what pleaseth him. If he had said, Now, and here, will I give a day of refreshment to my people that have long groaned for it, a day of the purity and power of religion, if, I say, this be his purpose, they must have somewhat more than omnipotence that can hinder it. When his appointed time comes, to make a day of deliverance dawn upon his church, after their long night, either of affliction or of defection, or both; they that contrive against that dayspring, are as vain as if they would sit down to plot how to hinder the sun from rising in the morning. And they that let go their hopes of it, because of great apparent difficulties that interpose betwixt their eye and the accomplishment of that work, they are as weak as if they should imagine, when mists and thick vapours appear about the horizon in the morning, that these could hinder the rising of the sun, which is so far out of their reach, and comes forth as a bridegroom, and rejoices as a mighty man to run his race, says David. Those mists may, indeed, hinder his clear appearance, and keep it from the eye for a time; but reason tells us, even then, that they cannot stop his course. And faith assures us no less in the other, that no difficulties can hold back God's day and work of mercy to his people. But you will say, "All the difficulty is to know whether the appointed time be near or not." It is true we have no particular prophecies to assure us; but certainly when God awakes his children and makes them rise, this is a probable sign that it is near day. I mean, when he stirs them up to more than usual hopes, and prayers, and endeavours, it is very likely that he intends them some special good. But yet more, when he himself is arisen (as it pleaseth him to speak), that is, when he is begun to appear in a more than ordinary manner of working by singular and wonderful footsteps of Providence, this is, no doubt, a sign that he will go on to show remarkable mercy to Zion, and that the time to favour her, yea, the set time is come, Psa. cii. 13.

Howsoever, then, let the wonderful workings of the Lord move those of you that have any power and opportunity, to be now (if ever) active, for the greatest good, both of the present age and of posterity. And you that can be no other way useful, yet you shall be no small helpers if you be much in prayer; let both your hopes and your fears serve to sharpen your prayers. Be not too much dejected with any discouragement, neither be ye carnally lifted up with outward appearances; for the heart of him that is lifted up is not upright in him, Hab. ii. 4; but live, as the just do, by your faith; and if the deferring of your hopes should sicken your hearts, as Solomon speaks, yet stay and comfort them with the cordial of the promises. This you are sure of, you have God's own word engaged for it, that in those latter days Babylon shall be brought to the dust, and the true church of

Christ shall flourish and increase: and this vision is for an appointed time (as Habakkuk says of his); at the end it shall speak, and not lie: though it tarry, wait for it; it will surely come, it will not tarry, Hab. ii. 3.

In that day. In the day of Ephraim's or Israel's calamity, denounced in the former verses, which, as most do conceive, was when the Assyrian oppressed them, and in the end led them captive in the reign of Hosea, as you have the history of it, 2 Kings xvii.; at which time Hezekiah was king of Judah, as you find in the following chapter; and in that notable reformation wrought by him, with those blessings that followed upon it, is found the accomplishment of this promise to Judah, In that day, &c. The parallel of God's different dealing with these two kingdoms, at the time there specified (In that day), does afford divers lessons, which might be here not impertinently taken notice of. Only this:

Though Judah also had its own corruptions when Hezekiah came to the crown, yet it pleased the Lord to spare them, and work a peaceable reformation, making Israel's punishment their warning. Truly that nation, with whom the Lord deals thus graciously, is vilely ingrate if they observe it not with much humility and thankfulness, and with profit too. If the Lord should answer your desires and hopes with a reformation in a peaceable way, and should yet lengthen out your long-continued peace, and should make this shaking of it cause it to take root the faster; if he should, I say, do this, where would ye find fit praises for such a wonder of mercy, especially considering that in the mean while he hath made other reformed churches fields of blood, and made, as it were, the sound of their stripes preach repentance to us? But certainly, if the hearing the voice of the rod prevail not, we shall feel the smart of it, as this people of Judah did afterwards, because they were not so wise as to become wiser and better by Israel's folly and calamity. We are expecting great things at our Lord's hands, and our provocations and sins against him are great; yet there is none of them all puts us in so much danger of disappointment as impenitence. Were there more repentance and personal reformation amongst us, we might take it as a hopeful forerunner of that public reformation which so many seem now to desire.

The Lord of hosts. This style of his, you know, is frequent in the prophets, in their predictions of mercy and judgment; intimating both his greatness and majesty, and his supreme power for accomplishing his word. No created power can resist him; yea, all must serve him. The most excellent creatures can have no greater honour, the greatest are not exempted, nor the meanest excluded from serving him. In Acts xii. 23, you find one of the noblest creatures, and a number of the vilest, made use of at the same time in the same service. Because Herod did accept of the sacrilege of the people, and gave not back to this Lord of hosts his own glory, the angel of the Lord smote him, and the worms devoured him. And in Egypt, you know the employing of the destroying angel, and what variety of hosts this Lord of hosts did employ to plague them. What madness, then, is it to oppose and encounter this great general; even in doubtful cases, to run on blindly, without examining, lest peradventure a man should be found a fighter against God! And on the other side, it is a great weakness to admit any fear under his banner. If a man could say, when he was told of the multitude of the ships the enemy had, Against how many do ye reckon me? How much more justly may we reckon this Lord of hosts, against multitudes of enemies, how great soever! They are to him as the drop of a bucket, and the smallest dust of the balance. It is ignorance and mean thoughts of this mighty Lord that makes his enemies so confident; and it is the same evil, in some degree, or, at the best, forgetfulness of his power, that causeth diffidence in his followers, Isa. li. 12, 13. Now, the same Lord of hosts, you know, is likewise called the God of peace; he is indeed, *et pace et bello insignis,* splendid both in peace and war. The blessing of peace and the success of war are both from him; and to him alone is due the praise of both.

Shall be a crown. He shall dignify and adorn them by his special presence; to wit, in the purity of ordinances and religion amongst them. The profession and flourishing of that shall be their special glory and beauty; for as the other two benefits concern their civil good, justice flourishing within, and wealth and opulency from without, so doubtless this first, this glory and beauty, is religion, as the chiefest of the three, and the other two are its attendants.

If it be thus, that the purity of religion and worship is the crown and glory of a people; and therefore, on the other side, that their deepest stain of dishonour and vileness, is the vitiating of religion with human devices; then, to contend for the preservation or the reformation of it, is noble and worthy of a Christian. It is for a crown of Jesus Christ, which is likewise a crown of glory and diadem of beauty to them, he being their head. It is, indeed, the true glory both of kings and their kingdoms. Labour, then, for constancy in this work; let no man take your crown from you. You know how busy the emissaries of the church of Rome have been to take it from us, or, at least, to pick the diamonds out of it, and put in false, counterfeit ones in their places; I mean, they stole away the power of religion, and filled up the room with shadows and fopperies of their own devising. It is the vanity of that church to think they adorn the worship of God when they dress it up with splendour in her service, which, though some magnify so much, yet may most truly be called a glistering slavery and captivity. Then is she truly free and wears her crown, when the ordinances of God are conformable to his own appointment. It is vanity in men, I say, when they dress it up with a multitude of gaudy ceremonies, and make it the smallest part of itself; whereas, indeed, its true glory consists not in pomp, but in purity and simplicity. We find the church under the name of a woman (Apoc. xii.), richly attired indeed, but her ornaments be all heavenly, the sun her clothing, and her crown of twelve stars: needs she then borrow sublunary glory? No, she treads upon it; the moon is under her feet. There is another woman, indeed, in that same book, arrayed in purple and scarlet, decked with gold and precious stones, and having a golden cup in her hand, but that golden cup is full of abominations and filthiness, and she herself the mother of abominations, Apoc. xvii. 4. The natural man judges according to his reach, but to a spiritual eye there is a most genuine beauty in the service of God and government of his house; and when they are nearest to the rule, the word of God, then is it that the Lord himself is the crown and diadem of his church.

A crown. Again we consider this personally, as belonging in particular to every believer. They are all made kings and priests unto God the Father, Rev. i. 6. They are a chosen generation, a royal priesthood, 1 Pet. ii. 9, how despicable soever to the world. This is their dignity: The Lord is their crown and diadem: he subdues their lust, and makes them kings over their own affections, and more than conquerors over all troubles and persecutions; whereas carnal men are continually hurried like slaves unto base employments, still kept toiling in the ignoble service of their own lusts. They think, indeed, it is their liberty, but that is a baseness of spirit that complies well with so vile and servile a condition; and whereas they judge the godly to be the refuse and dross of the earth, and the proper objects of contempt, this is because their crown, though most glorious, is invisible to the eye of nature. The Lord is a crown: if they knew what this is, they would see enough in it to countervail their outward meanness, and the reproaches the world casts on them, as the apostle St Peter hath it, 1 Ep. iv. 14. "If ye be reproached for the name of Christ, happy are ye, for the spirit of glory and of God resteth upon you:" he is their crown.

And observe, how this crown is opposed to that blasted glory and fading crown of pride, spoken of in the former verses.

Who is there that sees not, in daily experience, the vanity and inconstancy of worldly glory? And yet, how few are there that wean themselves from it, and learn to disdain it! Still men dote upon that which is not, upon a shadow, a nothing. But would you have a glory that fadeth not, a garland that cannot wither, make the Lord your crown and your glory; and if he be so, glory in him and in nothing else. Jer. ix. 23.

You that are noble aspire to this crown, as being so far above your perishing honours and bounded powers; and you that are outwardly meaner and lower, see how little cause you have to complain of your condition, seeing you are not debarred from this best and greatest honour. And that you may discern aright what it is, know that it consists in the renovation of God's image within you, which is in holiness and righteousness: so the Lord becomes your crown in the kingdom of grace; and by this you may discover, whether or no you have attained it. If you can yet delight to wallow in the puddle and pleasures of sin, you are far from this royal condition; but if you find your soul possessed with the love of holiness, and that you are trampling upon profane delights, this may persuade you that God hath enabled you, and crowned you with his grace, and will crown you with glory. Again, try it by this; if the Lord is become your crown, and your glory, you will glory in him, and in nothing else. Though you be wise, you will not glory in your wisdom, nor in strength, nor in riches, nor honours, though you had them all; but if you glory, you will glory in the Lord. And withal, your highest joy will be to see the advancement of his glory, and, if you can, to be any way serviceable to the advancing of it.

And a spirit of judgment. Both to those that sit in judgment, and to the people; for justice is the strongest base and establishment of authority. And withal, the influence of it is most sweet and comfortable to those that are under authority; and where it is wanting, that order and relation of superiors and inferiors, which God hath appointed in the societies of men for their good, tends exceedingly to the damage of both; and, therefore, where God intendeth to continue the peace and welfare of a people, he is liberal in pouring out much of this spirit of judgment on those that sit in judgment. On the contrary, it is for a heavy punishment, when he withdraws his Spirit from rulers, and leaves them wholly to the corruption and vanity of their own spirits.

Now, seeing the spirit of judgment is from the Lord (yea, he is this spirit), it ought to persuade those that sit in judgment, to entreat and pray for this, and to depend upon Him, and beware of self-confidence. Trust in the Lord, saith Solomon, and lean not to thine own understanding; if you do, it will prove but a broken reed. And as they that sit in judgment should entreat his spirit by prayer, so generally, all must share with them in this duty, and make supplication for all that are in authority over them, especially in extraordinary times. And for this end, let all that wish their own good, pray much for abundance of this spirit of judgment to be conferred on them; your eyes and expectations are upon them. If you would enjoy the lamp, you must pour in oil. This spirit, indeed, you cannot pour upon them, but if you pour out many prayers, you may draw it from above; he will give it, who here promises to be a spirit of judgment.

And strength. Observe, the way to be powerful and successful against foreign enemies is, to have religion and justice flourishing at home. And truly, if it please our God to answer the desires of his people at this time, it may so unite the affection and strength of the two kingdoms,* (the Lord of hosts being their strength,) as to make them a terror to their enemies, whereas they were become a scorn and derision to them. For you

* England and Scotland.

particular, labour to make the Lord your glory, to have Christ made unto you, as the apostle speaks, both wisdom, and righteousness, and sanctification, which are the glory and beauty of the soul, and redemption from your spiritual enemies. Draw strength from him to fight and prevail against them, till, after the short combat of this life, you obtain the crown, and dwell in his presence, where you shall fear no more assaults, neither of sin nor affliction, but shall be for ever happy in the blessed vision of his face. To him be glory. Amen.

SERMON IV.

Because the carnal mind is enmity against God: for it is not subject to the law of God, neither indeed can be.—ROM. viii. 7.

THE ordinary workings and actions of creatures are suitable to their nature, as the ascending of light things, and the moving of heavy things downwards; so the vital and sensitive actions of things that have life and sense. The reasonable creature, it is true, hath more liberty in its actions, freely choosing one thing and rejecting another; yet it cannot be denied, that in acting of that liberty, their choice and refusal follow the sway of their nature and condition. As the angels and glorified souls (their nature being perfectly holy, and unalterably such) cannot sin, they can delight in nothing but in obeying and praising that God, in the enjoyment of whom their happiness consisteth. The saints, again, that have not yet reached that home, and are but on their journey, are not fully defecated and refined from sin; there are in them two parts, natural corruption and supernatural grace, and these keep struggling within them; but the younger shall supplant the elder. Grace shall in the end overcome, and in the mean while, though it be not free from mixture, yet it is predominant. The main bent of a renewed man is obedience and holiness, and any action of that kind he rejoices in; but the sin that escapes him he cannot look upon but with regret and discontent. But, alas! they that be so minded are very thin sown in the world, even in God's peculiar fields, where the labourage of the gospel is, and the outward profession of true religion is unanimously received. Yet the number of true converts, spiritual-minded persons, is very small, the greatest part acting sin with delight, and taking pleasure in unrighteousness, living in disobedience to God, as in their proper element; and the reason is, the contrariety of their nature to our holy Lord. The carnal mind is enmity against God.

The carnal mind. Man, in regard of his composition, is, as it were, the tie and band of heaven and earth; they meet and are married in him. A body he has, taken out of the dust, but a soul breathed from heaven, from the Father of spirits; a house of clay, but a guest of most noble extraction. But the pity is, it hath forgot its original, and is so drowned in flesh that it deserves no other but to go under the name of flesh. It is become the slave and drudge of the body, and, as the Israelites in Egypt, made perpetually to moil in clay. What is all your merchandise, your trades and manufactures, your tillage and husbandry, but for the body, in its behalf, for food and raiment? In all these the mind must be careful and thoughtful, and yet itself hath no interest in them. It is true, the necessity of the body requires much of these things, and superfluous custom far more; but it is lamentable that men force their soul to forget itself and its proper business, to attend these things only, and be busy in them. They spend all their time and their choicest pains upon perishing things, and, which is worse, engage their affections to them. They mind earthly things, whose end is destruction, Phil. iii. 19, &c.

Will you consider seriously, that your souls run the hazard of perishing, because you consider not their spiritual nature? When that earthly tabernacle of yours shall fall to the ground (and ere long it must), your souls must then enter eternity; and though you had as large a share of earthly things as your earthly hearts now would wish, they all lose their use in that moment. They are not a proper good for the soul at any time, and least at that time. If you keep it all your life long, busy about the interest and benefit of the flesh, how poor will it be when they part, having provided nothing at all for itself, but the guiltiness of a sinful life, which will sink it into that bottomless pit! Be forewarned then: "for to be carnally minded is death," verse 6.

Now as sin hath abased and degenerated the soul of man, making it carnal, so the Son of God, by taking our nature, hath sublimated it again, and made it spiritual. The souls that receive him are spiritualized; yea, as sin made the soul carnal, grace makes the very body to become spiritual, making it partaker and co-worker in spiritual things, together with the soul, and participant of the hopes too of an everlasting reward. This is the main Christian character our apostle gives here, that they are spiritually minded, and that their actions suit their minds; they walk not after the flesh, but after the spirit. Whereas before, with the rest of the world, they were eager in the pursuit of honours, and profits, and worldly pleasures; the stream of their desires now runs in another channel: they seek after honour, and are very ambitious of it; but it is such honour as the apostle speaks of in this epistle, Rom. ii. 7, By patient continuance in well-doing, they seek for glory, and honour, and immortality: their mind is upon profit and gain, but it is with the same apostle, Phil. iii. 8, that they may win Christ, and they account all other things loss in comparison; and their desires are after pleasure too, but not carnal pleasures, these are both base and of short continuance, but the pleasures they aim at are those that are at God's right hand, and for evermore, Psalm xvi. 11. And that path of life he there speaks of, that way of holiness that leads thither, is their delight. Spiritual exercises they go to, not as their task only, but as their joy and refreshment. And this change the Spirit of God works in the soul, making it (yea, and the body wherein it dwells) of carnal to become spiritual, as the fire, to which the Holy Ghost is compared, refines sand and ashes, and makes of them the purest glass, which is so bright and transparent.

Enmity against God. Sin hath not only made us unlike God, by defacing his beautiful image in us; not only strangers, by making us wander far off from him,—but enemies; nor enemies only, but enmity in the abstract; for that is emphatical—The carnal mind is enmity, nothing else but enmity.

Now this enmity is described in the latter clause of the text, by an antipathy, so to call it, or non-compliance with the law of God; "it is not subject to the law of God, neither can it be," to wit, while it remains such. There is an absolute impossibility in it to suit with the law of God, and consequently with God himself. The reason lies in their opposite qualities: God is spiritual and holy, and so is the law, as our apostle hath it in the preceding chapter; and the opposition he there makes, betwixt his unregenerate part and the law, is wholly true of the unregenerate man. The law is holy, says he, verse 12; and verse 14, it is spiritual; to which he opposes, But I am carnal, sold under sin.

Where are now those that so vilify grace and magnify nature? Or, shall I rather say, nullify grace and deify nature? Here is the best eulogy the apostle will bestow upon the best of natures—enmity against God. Nay, all the sparkles of virtue and moral goodness in civil men and ancient heathens, are no better; besides many other things to be said to the virtues of those philosophers, as ignorance of Christ, by whom alone this enmity is removed.

I should easily confess, nor (I think) can any deny it, that there is in the very ruins of our nature, some character left of a tendency to God, as our chief and only satisfying good, which we may call a kind of love, and when we hear them spoken of, find it flutter and stir; and hence men so abhor the imputation of hating God and being enemies. Yet this is so smothered under sensuality and flesh, that until we be made spiritual, nothing appears but practical, and, as they call it, interpretative enmity.

You would take it hardly, the most profane of you all, if any should come to you, in particular, and tell you you are an enemy to God; but I answer, there is none of you, if you believe the Scriptures, but will confess that all men are naturally such; and therefore, except we find in ourselves a notable alteration from the condition of nature, we must take with it that we are enemies, yea, enmity to God: of strangers to become acquainted with him, yea, which is more, of enemies to become friends, is a greater and more remarkable change than to be incident to a man without any evidence and sign of it. I know there is a very great variety in the way and manner of conversion; and to some, especially if it be in their tender years, grace may be instilled, and dropped in as it were insensibly. But this I may confidently say, that whatsoever be the way of working it, there will be a wide and apparent difference betwixt friendship with God and the condition of nature, which is enmity against him. Do not flatter yourselves; so long as your minds remain carnal, ardent in love to the world and cold in love to God, lovers of pleasures more than lovers of God, (as the apostle speaks,) you are his enemies; for with him there is no neutrality. And this is God's peculiar, that he can judge infallibly of the inside. Those shadows of friendship which men use one with another, will not pass with him. Deceived he cannot be; but men may easily, and, alas! too many do deceive themselves in this matter to their own ruin.

We may learn, hence, how deep sin goes in our nature, and, consequently, that the cure and remedy of it must go as deep; that all the parts of our bodies and powers of our souls are polluted orginally, our very mind and conscience, as the apostle speaks; for it is immersed in flesh, and enslaved to flesh naturally, and therefore goes under its name; we are become all flesh; that is the spring of our mischiefs; we have lost our likeness with our Father, the Father of spirits, the purest and most spiritual Spirit, till renewed by participation of his Spirit on our flesh.

And it is the error, not only of natural men, but somewhat of the godly too, that in self-reformation they set themselves against actual sin, but they lay not the axe to the root of the tree, this root of bitterness, this our inbred and natural enmity against God; and till this be done, the lopping off of some branches will do no good; whilst the root is in vigour these will grow again, and, possibly, faster than before. Bewail every known act of sin as much as you can, for the least of them deserves it: but withal, let the consideration of them lead you into thoughts of this seed of rebellion, the wickedness of our nature, that takes life with us in the womb, and springs and grows up with us; and this will humble us exceedingly, and raise our godly sorrow to a higher tide. We find David taketh this course, Psalm li. 5, where he is lamenting his particular sin of adultery and murder: it leads him to the sinfulness of his nature—I was shapen in iniquity, and in sin did my mother conceive me; which he mentions, not to extenuate and diminish his sin; no, he is there very far from that strain, but adds it as a main aggravation. Indeed, the power of original sin, in the regenerate, is laid very low, yet not altogether extinct, which they find often to their grief, and makes them cry out with our apostle, in the former chapter, O wretched man that I am! who shall deliver me from this body of death? The converted are already delivered (as he adds) from the dominion of it, but not from the molestation and trouble of it. Though it is not a quiet and uncontrolled master, as it was before, yet it is in the house still as an unruly servant or slave, ever vexing and annoying them: and this body of death they shall have still cause to bewail, till death release them. This leprosy hath taken so deep root in the walls of this house, that it cannot perfectly be cleansed till it be taken down; and it is this, more than any other sorrows or afflictions of life, that makes the godly man not only content to die, but desirous; longing, with our apostle, to be dissolved and be with Christ, which is far better.

As this teaches us the misery of man's nature, so it sets off and commends exceedingly the riches of God's grace. Are men naturally his enemies? Why, then, admire his patience and bounty a little, and then we will speak of his saving grace. Could not he very easily ease himself of his adversaries? as he says by the prophet. Wants he power in his right hand to find out and cut off all his enemies? Surely, no; not only he hath power to destroy them all in a moment, but the very withdrawing of his hand that upholds their being, (though they consider it not,) would make them fall to nothing. Yet is he pleased not only to spare transgressors, but to give them many outward blessings—rain and fruitful seasons, as the apostle speaks, Acts xiv. 17; and the earth that is so full of man's rebellion, is yet more full of his goodness: The earth is full of thy goodness. It is remarkable, that that same reason which is given (Gen. vi. 5) of the justice of God in drowning the world, is (viii. 21) rendered as the reason of God's resolved patience ever since. Then,—

His grace, in finding a way of reconcilement, and not sparing his own Son, his only begotten Son, to accomplish it. Nor did he spare himself. Oh, matchless love! to lay down his life, not for friends but for strangers!

Not only so, but enemies, for unrighteous and ungodly persons, such as be at enmity against him, Rom. v. 7, 8. And having done this, he sends his word, the message of reconciliation, to rebels, and sends his Spirit into the hearts of those whom he hath appointed to salvation, to change their spirits, that they perish not in disobedience; he brings them near that were afar off, having slain this enmity by the death of his Son.

As many of you, then, as have hitherto heard this message of reconcilement in vain, be persuaded at last to give ear to it. This is all that God's ambassadors require, according to their instructions from himself,—That men would lay down that enmity against him, and not be so foolish as wilfully to perish in it. 2 Cor. v. 20.

Consider that this enmity is, 1st, unjust; 2nd, unhappy. Unjust it is, being against Him who is the chief object of love, who is altogether goodness, both in himself and towards his creatures. It is too much not to love him with most ardent and superlative affection; but to entertain enmity against him, is madness; as was said to one who asked, Why are the beautiful loved? *It is a blind man's question.* Certainly we are blind, if we see not cause enough not only to desist from enmity, but to be inflamed with his love. One glance of his amiable countenance is sufficient to cause the most rebellious heart to yield, and lay down arms, and for ever devote themselves to his service. No, we know him not, and therefore it is we hold out against him.

Is he not the living spring of all our comforts? Have we not from him life, and breath, and all things? And is he not ready to forgive iniquity, transgression, and sin? Let mercy, those sweet rays of love, melt our hearts to him. Let his loving-kindness overcome these stubborn hearts or spirits of ours. Among enemies, the weaker usually sue first for peace, but here the mighty: Almighty God comes to entreat agreement with sinful clay.

But if this prevail not, then think how unhappy this enmity is. You that are so afraid of men, and these weak men, of men like yourselves, whose breath is in their nostrils, will ye not tremble at his power, and be afraid to continue in terms of hostility against him who is the Lord of hosts, who hath power of the soul and body both, to kill both and cast them into hell? What is the stoutest of men, but as stubble to the flame of his wrath? Our God is a consuming fire. The sinners in Zion are afraid (says the prophet). Who shall dwell, says he, with devouring fire and everlasting burnings? Then if you would not perish, when his wrath is kindled, take that word of Eliphaz, Job xxii. 21: "Acquaint now thyself with him, and be at peace; thereby good shall come unto thee."

And to you, so many as he hath taken into friendship with himself, look backward to the gulf you have escaped, and forward to the happiness you are appointed to, and let the joint consideration of both awaken your hearts and tongues to praises. How can your hearts contain such a wonder of love as he hath manifested to you, and not run over in songs and praise?

And as you owe him praises, so study, being made his friends, to become more like him. To love and hate the same things with him, will be a sure testimony of friendship. And because carnality, or fleshly and earthly mindedness, is here made the character of enmity, mortify these affections, nail them to that cross of Christ, whereby the enmity was taken away. And further, being once admitted into friendship, labour for a further degree of intimacy with him, and forbear everything that may hinder that: use frequent converse with him, for that both entertains and increases friendship. If anything fall on your part (as it too often does) that may occasion any strangeness betwixt you and your God, rest not till it be removed. And if you walk in this way, it shall undoubtedly, at length, bring you where you shall abide in his presence for ever, and shall no more fear any breach or interruption of enjoying him.

SERMON V.

Surely the wrath of man shall praise thee: the remainder of wrath shalt thou restrain.—PSALM lxxvi. 10.

WHAT man is this, (said the passengers in the ship,) that even the winds and the sea obey him? Chris suddenly turns a great tempest into a greater calm, Matt. viii. 27. Surely those are no ordinary words of command, that swelling waves and boisterous winds, in the midst of their rage, are forced to hear, and taught to understand and obey them. Therefore the holding of the seas in the hollow of his hand, the bridling of the wind, and riding upon the wings of it, we find peculiarly attributed to the Almighty. But no less, if not more wonderful, is another of his prerogatives, to wit, his sovereignty over all mankind, over the divers and strange motions of the heart of man. Admirable is it to govern those, both in respect of their multitude and irregularity. Consider we what millions of men dwell at once upon the face of the earth; and again, what troops of several imaginations will pass through the fancy of any one man, within the compass of one day. It is much to keep eye upon them, and to behold them all at once, but far more to command and control them all; yet if they were all loyal and willingly obedient, were they tractable and easily curbed, it were more easy for us to conceive how they might be governed. But to bound and overrule the unruly hearts of men, the most of whom continually are either plotting or acting rebellion against their Lord, to make them all concur and meet at last in one end, cannot be done but by a power and a wisdom that are both infinite. That God whose name we often mention, but seldom think on his excellency, is alone the absolute monarch of men's hearts, and the ruler of all their motions. He hath them limited while they seem most free, and works his own glory out of their attempts while they strive most to dishonour him. Surely the wrath of man shall praise thee: the remainder of wrath thou shalt restrain.

The psalm is made up of these two different sorts of thoughts, the one arising out of particular experience, and the other out of a general doctrine. These drawn from experience are set down in the verses preceding the text and in it. With those that follow is the doctrine, with a duty annexed to it, which two are faith's main supporters. By-past particulars verify the doctrine, and the generality of the doctrine serves to explain the particular experiences to all wise observers. There is not a treasure of the merits of saints in the church (as some dream), but there is a treasure of the precious experiences of the saints, which every believer hath right to make use of; and these we should be versed in, that we may have them in readiness, at hand in time of need, and know how to use them, both to draw comfort from them to ourselves, and arguments to use with God.

The words contain clearly two propositions, both of them concerning the wrath of man. The former hath the event of it, Surely the wrath of man shall praise thee: the latter, the limitation of it, The remainder of wrath thou shalt restrain.

That the virtues and graces of men do praise the Lord, all men easily understand, for they flow from him; his image and superscription is upon them, and therefore no wonder if he has from them a tribute of glory. Who knows not that faith praises him? Abraham believed, and gave glory to God. Good works, the fruits of faith, praise him too. Herein is your heavenly Father glorified (says our Saviour), that ye bring forth much fruit. But that the inordinate wrath of man shall praise him, may seem somewhat strange. Were it God's own wrath (as wrath is attributed to him in Scripture), that might praise him, for it is always most just; or were it a due and moderate anger of man, upon just cause, that were fit for praising him too, in despite of the Stoics. But that wicked and disordered wrath, the wrath of men, that is both uncomely and dishonourable for themselves, that even such a wrath should honour God, and praise him, argues well that he hath good right to praises, when everything, even things that seem contrary to his nature, as well as to his law, do pay them to him; and that he hath great power and wisdom who obtains what is due to him, even from those persons and things that of themselves are most unwilling and unfit to pay it. This is the excellent skill of his wisdom, to draw that which shall go into the making up of the precious composition of his praise out of this poison; for so the word, here used for wrathful heat, doth sometimes signify. And this wrath often proves a deadly poison both to those it is incensed against, and to the very breast that breeds it, and wherein it is kindled.

But for the clearer understanding of this, I conceive it will be requisite to consider more distinctly, (1.) What the wrath of man is. (2.) How it can praise God.

And, lastly, The infallibility of this event: "Surely the wrath of man shall praise thee."

I. In the 148th Psalm, where David summons the creatures to meet in that song of praise, to keep that full concert, he calls not only the heavens, and the inhabitants of it, angels and lights, but those of the lower world, to bear their part in it; and not only men, beasts, cattle, creeping things, and the flying fowl, but those creatures that do most resemble this wrath here spoken of—fire, stormy tempest, and dragons. The tenor of the psalm doth show, that by the wrath of man is to be understood the undue rage of evil and ungodly men against those whom God owns for his people. The word here used signifies a hot or inflaming wrath; and indeed such is the feverish, distempered anger of the church's enemies. And as too much heat is an enemy to solid reason, this hot wrath of theirs makes them incapable of wise deliberation in themselves, and inflexible to the good advice of others. It is true, they take counsel how to execute their wrath, as we shall hear anon, but they take no counsel that may cool it. Now it is a wonder what the powers of the world find in Christ and his harmless flock that can incense them. St James says of the tongue, that it is set on fire of hell. The same is the original of this wrath. Why do the heathen rage? saith the psalmist. That is, not only to what purpose? intimating that it is a fruitless rage: but why? that is, upon what occasion? checking the rage as groundless and without cause, in regard of Christ and his church's innocency. The cause is only within themselves, to wit, that unhappy antipathy of the serpent's seed against the Seed of the woman. Thus this wrath of man is the causeless, malicious enmity of the wicked against the church of God. And under the name of this passion I take to be here comprised likewise all the attendants of it, all their crafty complotments and devices for the acting of their wrath. As there is mention of the nations' rage against Christ, in the 2nd Psalm, so likewise of the consultations of those that are of quality fit for it; The rulers take counsel together. And of all these it is true that God shall gain glory by them: surely the wrath of man shall praise thee.

"The wrath of man (says the apostle) accomplisheth not the righteousness of God," how then can it accomplish his praises? And this is the second thing propounded.

II. Are grapes gathered of thorns, or figs of thistles? Surely no; therefore I called this praise, not the fruit or proper effect of man's wrath, but the event or consequent of it, by the efficacy of Divine providence. "The use which thou wilt make of it shall tend to thy praise. Thou wilt produce such effects from it, both in the church and upon thine enemies, when thou sufferest their wrath to break forth, as shall furnish more matter of thy praises than if thou hadst altogether restrained it." To instance this in some few particulars.

It is the fury of the church's enemies that has made known to the world the invincible courage and patience of the saints. Those ages that have been most monstrous in persecution, have most of all graced Christianity. Had there been no persecuting emperors, who should have heard of those primitive martyrs that triumphed over the cruelty of their torments? Were there no persecution, nor peril, nor sword, against believers, we should not have heard the apostle say immediately after the mention of those, In all these we are more than conquerors. They could not have been so much as conquerors, had there been no conflict.

Again, as the wrath of man praises God in the invincible patience of the saints, so likewise in the immovable stability of the church. Is it not wonderful how so small and weak a company, as the church hath often been reduced to, yea, hath always been, in respect of the world, could escape the mouths of so many lions, so many enraged enemies that were ready to devour it? And, that we may see that this tends solely to the praise of her great Protector, look at the church's song, penned by the royal prophet; it is the 124th Psalm: "If it had not been the Lord that was on our side, when men rose up against us, then they had swallowed us up quick." The great monarchies and kingdoms of the world that have risen with so much splendour, have had their periods, and been buried in the dust. That golden-headed and silver-bodied image degenerated into worse metal as it went lower, and the brittle feet were the cause of the fall and breaking of all the rest. But the kingdom of Jesus Christ, though despicable in the world, and exposed to the wrath of the world in all ages, stands firm, and cannot be removed. There is a common emblem of the winds blowing from all quarters; and upon the globe of the earth, being in the middle of them, is written *Immobilis.* This fitly resembles the church. Why? It seems to be the sport of all the winds, but is indeed so established, that all of them, yea, the very gates of hell, cannot prevail against it. Now the more the church's enemies labour and moil themselves to undo her, the more do their weakness and the power of her Lord appear; so that thus the wrath of man doth praise him.

When was the church free from the world's wrath? To say nothing of the church of the Jews, did not those wicked emperors of Rome think to have made the Christian church short-lived, to have drowned her, newly born, in floods of her own blood? And in later ages, who knows not the cruelties that have been practised by the Turk in the east, and the proud prelate of Rome in the west? By which she hath sometimes been brought to so obscure and low a point, that if you can follow her in history, it is by the track of her blood; and if you would see her, it is by the light of those fires in which her martyrs have been burned. Yet hath she still come through, and survived all that wrath, and still shall, till she be made perfectly triumphant.

Further: Man's wrath tends to God's praise in this, That God, giving way to it, does so manage it by his sublime providence, that it often directly crosses their own ends, and conduces manifestly to his. Pharaoh thought that his dealing more cruelly with the Jews in their tasks and burdens was wisdom: Let us work wisely, says he. But whereas their ordinary servility was become familiar to them, and they were tamed to it, that same accession of new tyranny did prepare and dispose the Israelites for a desire of departure; and their departure made way for Pharaoh's destruction. Undigestible insolency and rage, hastening to be great, makes kingdoms cast them off, which would have been far longer troubled with their wickedness had it been more moderate. Surely, then, the wrath of man commends the wisdom of God, when He makes him by that contrive and afford the means of his own downfall. Job xviii. 7, "The steps of his strength shall be straitened, and his own counsel shall cast him down," says Bildad. And that is a sad fall: as that eagle that was shot with an arrow trimmed with her own feathers.

But to close this point. It is out of all question, that the deserved punishment of man's unjust wrath doth always glorify the justice of God; and the more he gives way to their wrath, the more notable shall be both their punishment and the justice of it. And though God seems neglective of his people and of his praise, while man's wrath prevails, yet the truth is, he never comes too late to vindicate his care of both; and when he defers longest, the enemy pays dear interest for the time of forbearance. In his eternal decree, he resolved to permit the course of man's wrath for his own glory; and when the period which he hath fixed is come, he stops man's wrath, and gives course unto the justice of his own. Nor is there then any possibility of escaping; he will right himself, and be known by executing judgment. Surely the wrath of man shall praise thee. And that is the third thing propounded, the infallibility of the event.

III. The Author of nature governs all his creatures, each in a suitable way to the nature he hath given them. He maintains in some things a natural necessity of working, contingency in others, and in others liberty. But all of them are subject to this necessity of effecting inevitably his eternal purposes; and this necessity is no way repugnant to the due liberty of man's will. Some entertain and maintain the truth; some plot, others act and execute, against it; some please themselves in a wise neutrality, and will appear so indifferent, that it would seem they might be accepted of all sides for judges of controversies. And all these find no less liberty to wind and turn themselves whither they please, than if no higher hand had the winding of them. Shall not only the zeal of the godly, but even the wrath of the enemy, and the cold discretion of the neutral, all tend to his praise whose supreme will hath a secret, but a sure and infallible, sway in all their actions? Whilst some passengers sit, some walk one way, some another, some have their faces towards their journey's end, some their back turned upon it, this wise Pilot does most skilfully guide the ship to arrive with them all at his own glory. Happy they that propound and intend his glory as he himself does; for in them shall the riches of his mercy be glorified. They that oppose him lose this happiness, but he is sure not to lose his glory for all that; to wit, the glory of his justice. His right hand shall find out all his enemies: surely the wrath of man shall praise thee.

The consideration of this truth, thus in some measure unfolded, may serve to justify the truly wise dispensation of God against our imaginary wisdom. Were the matter referred to our modelling, we would assign the church constant peace and prosperity for her portion, and not consent that the least air of trouble should come near her. We would have no enemies to molest her, nor stir against her; or if they did stir, we would have them to be presently repressed; and these, in our judgment, would be the fairest and most glorious tokens of his love and power, whose spouse she is. But this carnal wisdom is enmity against God, and the glory of God, which rises so often out of the wrath of his enemies. Had God caused Pharaoh to yield at the very first to the release of his people, where had been the fame of those miraculous judgments in Egypt, and mercies on the Israelites, the one setting out and illustrating the other? Where had been that name and honour that God says he would gain to himself, and that he did gain out of Pharaoh's final destruction, making that stony-hearted king, and his troops, "sink like a stone in the waters," as Moses sings? Observe his proud boastings immediately foregoing his ruin: "I will pursue," says he; "I will overtake; I will divide the spoil; my lust shall be satisfied on them; I will draw my sword, and my hand shall destroy them:" soon after, the sea quenches all this heat. Commonly, big threatenings are unhappy presages of very ill success. That historian says well of God, "God suffers no other to think highly of himself, but himself alone." And, indeed, as he abhors these boastings, so he delights in the abasing of the lofty heart whence they flow, and it is his prerogative to gain praise to himself out of their wrath. "Hast thou an arm like God? (says the Lord to Job), then look upon the proud and bring them low," Job xl. 9, 12. When Sennacherib came up against Jerusalem, his blasphemies and boastings were no less vast and monstrous than the number of his men and chariots: good Hezekiah turned over the matter unto God, spreading the letter of blasphemies before him: God undertook the war, and assured Hezekiah that the Assyrian should not so much as shoot an arrow against the city, "but return the same way he came," 2 Kings xix. 33. And the deliverance there promised and effected, is conceived to have been the occasion of penning this very psalm. Surely when an angel did in one night slay 185,000 in their camps, that wrath and those threats tended exceedingly to the praise of the God of Israel. The hook that he put in Sennacherib's nostrils (as the history speaks), to pull him back again, was more remarkable than the fetters would have been, if he had tied him at home, or hindered his march with his army.

Who is he, then, that will be impatient because of God's patience, and judge him slack in judgment, while the rage of the wicked prevails awhile? Know that he is more careful of his own glory than we can be; and the greatest height man's wrath arises to, the more honour shall arise to him out of it. Did not his omnipotency shine brighter in the flames of that furnace into which the children were cast, than if the king's wrath had been at first cooled? Certainly, the more both it and the furnace had their heat augmented, the more was God glorified. "Who is that God" (saith he, blasphemously and proudly) "that can deliver you out of my hands?" A question indeed highly dishonouring the Almighty: but stay till the real answer come, and not only shall that wrath praise him, but that very same tongue, though inured to blasphemy, shall be taught to bear a main part in the confession of these praises. Let that apostate emperor* go taunting the head and tormenting the members of that mystical body; his dying with, "Thou hast overcome, O Galilean" (meaning Christ), shall help to verify that. Whether its course be shorter or longer, man's wrath ends always in God's praise. In like manner, the closing of the lions' mouths spake louder to his praise that stopped them, than if he had stopped Daniel's enemies in the beginning of their wicked designs. So hot was their rage, that the king's favourable inclination to Daniel (of which, in other cases, courtiers used to be so devout

* Julian.

observers), yea, his contesting and pleading for him, did profit him nothing; but they hurried their king to the execution of their unjust malice, though themselves were convinced that nothing could be found against him, but only concerning the law of his God. Dan. vi. 14, it is said, he set his heart upon him to deliver him, and laboured to do it till the going down of the sun, and then those counsellors and counsels of darkness overcame him. But upon this black night of their prevailing wrath followed immediately a bright morning of praises to Daniel's God; when the lions that were so quiet company all night to Daniel, made so quick a breakfast of those accursed courtiers that had maliciously accused him. "Even so let thine enemies perish, O Lord: but let those that love thee be as the sun when he goeth forth in his might."

The other proposition concerns the limiting of this wrath: "The remainder of wrath shalt thou restrain."

To take no notice, for the present, of divers other readings of these words, the sense of them, as they are here well rendered, may be briefly this; that whereas the wrath of man to which God gives way shall praise him, the rest shall be curbed and bound up, as the word is; no more of it shall break forth than shall contribute to his glory. Here should be considered divers ways and means, by which God useth to stop the heady course of man's wrath, and hinder its proceeding any further. But only,—

Let us take out of it this lesson: That the most compendious way to be safe from the violence of men is to be on terms of friendship with God. Is it not an incomparable privilege to be in the favour and under the protection of One whose power is so transcendent, that no enemy can so much as stir without his leave? Be persuaded, then, Christians, in these dangers that are now so near us, every one to draw near to him; remove what may provoke him; let no reigning sin be found either in your cities or in your villages: for he is a holy God. Is it a time to multiply provocations now, or is it not rather high time to be humbled for the former? What shameless impiety is it to be now licentious or intemperate! to be proud, to oppress, or extort! to profane God's day and blaspheme his name! All these sins, and many others, abound amongst us, and that avowedly. Without abundance of repentance, for these we shall smart, and the wrath of our enemies, though unjust in them, shall praise God in our just punishment; though, doubtless, he will own his church, and be praised likewise in the final punishment of their wrath that rise against it. There is a remarkable expression in Psalm xcix. 8, of God's dealing with his people: "He was favourable to them, though he took vengeance on their inventions." A good cause and a covenant with God, will not shelter an impenitent people from sharper correction. It is a sad word God speaks by his prophet to his own people— I myself, says he, will fight against you. A dreadful enemy! And none indeed truly dreadful but he. Oh, prevent his anger, and you are safe enough. If perverse sinners will not hear, yet let those that are indeed Christians mourn in secret, not only for their own sin, but let them bestow some tears likewise upon the sins of others. Labour to appease the wrath of God, and he will either appease man's wrath, or will turn it jointly to his benefit and his own glory. Let the fear of the most high God, who hath no less power over the strongest of his enemies than over the meanest of his servants; let his fear, I say, possess all our hearts, and it will certainly expel that ignoble and base fear of the wrath of man. See how the prophet opposes them in Isaiah viii. 12, 13, Fear not their fear, says he, nor be afraid; but sanctify the Lord, and let him be your fear, and let him be your dread: fear not, but fear. This holy fear begets the best courage; the breast that is most filled with it, abounds most in true magnanimity. Fear thus, that you may be confident, not in yourselves, though your policy and strength were great (Cursed is man that trusteth in man, and maketh flesh his arm), but confident in that God who is too wise and vigilant to be surprised, too mighty to be foiled, and too rich to be outspent in provision; who can suffer his enemy to come to the highest point of apparent advantage, without any inconvenience, yea, with more renown in his conquest.

A Christian who is once made sure of this (as easily he may), is little careful about the rest; his love to God prevailing over all his affections, makes him indifferent what becomes of himself or his dearest friends, so God may be glorified. What though many fall in the quarrel, (which God avert!) yet it is sufficient that truth in the end shall be victorious. Have not the saints in all ages been content to convey pure religion to posterity, in streams of their own blood, not of others? Well, hold fast by this conclusion, that God can limit and bind up the most violent wrath of man, that, though it swell, it will not break forth. The stiffest heart, as the current of the most impetuous river, is in his hand, to appoint its channels, and turn it as he pleaseth. Yea, it is he that hath shut up the very sea with bars and doors, and said, "Hitherto shalt thou come, but no further: and here shall thy proud waves be stayed," Job xxxviii. 10, 11. To see the surges of a rough sea come in towards the shore, a man would think that they were hastening to swallow up the land; but they know their limits, and are beaten back into foam. Though the waves thereof toss themselves as angry at their restraint, yet the small sand is a check to the great sea; "yet can they not prevail; though they roar, yet can they not pass over it," says Jeremiah, v. 22.

The sum is this: What God permits his church's enemies to do, is for his own further glory; and reserving this, there is not any wrath of man so great, but he will either sweetly calm it, or strongly retain it.

SERMON VI.

He shall not be afraid of evil tidings: his heart is fixed, trusting in the Lord.—PSALM cxii. 7.

ALL the special designs of men agree in this—they seek satisfaction and quietness of mind, that is, happiness. This, then, is the great question—Who is the happy man? It is here resolved, verse 1, "Blessed is the man that feareth the Lord, that delighteth in his commandments."

The blessedness is unfolded as a rich landscape, through the whole alphabet, in capital letters; and take all and set them together, it is a most full, complete blessedness, not a letter wanting to it.* Amongst the rest that we have in these words, this is of a greater magnitude and brightness than many of the rest—He shall not be afraid of evil tidings.

Well may it begin with a hallelujah, a note of praise to him in whom blessedness lies. Oh what a wretched creature were man, if not provided with such a portion, without which is nothing but disappointment; and thence the racking torment and vexation of a disquieted mind, still pursuing somewhat that he never overtakes.

* This psalm in the *Hebrew* consists of 22 short verses, each of which begins with the letters of the alphabet in their order, till they are all ended. No one letter is here omitted, as is the case in the 25th psalm, where the same order is observed.

The first words are the inscription, The blessedness of that man, &c. So the particulars follow; where outward blessings are so set as that they look and lead higher, pointing at their end, the infinite goodness whence they flow, and whither they return and carry along with them this happy man.

And these promises of outward things are often *evidently* accomplished to the righteous, and their seed after them, and that commonly after they have been brought very low. But when it is otherwise with them they lose nothing. It is good for many, yea, it is good for all the godly that have less of these lower things, to raise their eye to look after higher,—the eye of all, both of those that are held somewhat short, and of those that have abundance in the world.

These temporal promises were more abounding and more frequently fulfilled, in their very kind, in the times of the law; yet still the right is constant, and all ages do give clear examples of the truth of this word. Where it is thus, it is a blessing created by its aspect to this promise, and so differs from the prosperity of ungodly men; and where it is otherwise with the righteous and their seed, it is no shift, but a most solid comfort, to turn their eyes to a higher compensation.

But howsoever it go, this still holds—He shall not be afraid of evil tidings. Notwithstanding the hardest news that can come to his ears, of anything that concerns himself or his children, or the rest of God's chil dren in his charge in the world, his heart is fixed, trusting in the Lord.

I. Let us take a little of the character of this blessed man. Who is it that is thus undaunted? The man that feareth God.

All the passions are but several ebbings and flowings of the soul, and their motions are the signs of its temper. Which way it is carried is mainly to be remarked by the beating of its pulse. If our desires, and hopes, and fears be in the things of this world, and the interest of flesh, this is their temper and disorder, the soul is in a continual fever: but if they move Godwards, then is it composed and calm, fearing and loving him, desiring him, and nothing but him, waiting for him, and trusting in him. And when any one affection is right, and in a due aspect to God, all the rest are so too: for they are radically one, and he is the life of that soul that is united to him; and so in him it moves in a peculiar spiritual manner, as all do naturally in the dependence of their natural life on him that is the fountain of life.

Thus we have here this fear of God, as often elsewhere, set out as the very substance of holiness and evidence of happiness. And that we may know there is nothing either base or grievous in this fear, we have joined with it, delight and trust; "delighteth greatly in his commandments;" which is that badge of love to him, to observe them, and that with delight, and with exceeding great delight. So, then, the fear is not that which love casts out, but that which love brings in. This fear follows and flows from love, a fear to offend, whereof nothing so tender as love; and that, in respect of the greatness of God, hath in it withal a humble reverence. In all love there is a kind of reverence, a cautious and respective wariness towards the party loved; but especially in this, where we not only stand in a lower relation, as children to our Father, but where the goodness that draws our love doth infinitely transcend our reach; therefore there is a "rejoicing with trembling," an awful love, and "the fearing of the Lord and his goodness," Hosea iii. 5. The heart touched by the Spirit of God, as the needle touched with the loadstone, looks straight and speedily to God, yet still with trembling, being filled with this holy fear.

That delighteth. This is not only to do his commandments, but to do them with delight; yea, the very law itself is writ within, not standing as a hard task-master over our head, but impressed within as a sweet principle in our hearts, and working from thence naturally. This makes a soul find pleasure in purging out of sensual pleasures, and ease in doing violence to corrupt self, even undoing it for God, having no will but his; the remainders of sin and self in our flesh will be often rising up, but this predominant love dispels them. So this fear works with delight.

And further, that we may know how serene and sweet a thing it is, it is here likewise joined with confidence, "trusting;" a quickening confidence always accompanying it; and so, undoubtedly, it is a blessed thing. Blessed is he that feareth. Fear sounds rather quite contrary, hath an air of misery; but add, whom? He that feareth the Lord: that touch turns it into gold. He that so fears, fears not: he shall not be afraid; all petty fears are swallowed up in this great fear, as a spirit inured with great things is not stirred nor affected with small matters. And this great fear is as sweet and pleasing as these little fears are anxious and vexing. Secure of other things, he can say, "If my God be pleased, no matter who is displeased; no matter who despise me, if he account me his; though all forsake me, my dearest friends grow estranged, and look another way, if he reject me not, that is my only fear; and for that I am not perplexed, I know he will not." As they answered Alexander, when he sent to inquire what they most feared, thinking possibly they would have said, Lest he should invade us; their answer was, We fear nothing but lest heaven should fall upon us; which they did not fear neither. A believer hath no fear but of the displeasure of Heaven, the anger of God to fall upon him, he fears that; that is, accounts that only terrible; but yet he doth not fear it, doth not apprehend it will fall on him, is better persuaded of the goodness of his God. So this fear is still joined with trust, as here, so often elsewhere, Psalm xxxiii. 18; xl. 3; and cxlvii. 11.

There is no turbulency in this fear; it is calm and sweet; even that most terrible evil, that which this fear properly apprehends and flies, sin; yet the fear of that goes not to a distraction. Though there is little strength, and many and great enemies, mighty Anakim of temptations from without, and corruption within, and so good reason for a holy, humble fear and self-distrust, yet this should not beat us off; yea, is most fit to put us on to trust in Him who is our strength. Courage! the day shall be ours; though we may be often foiled and down, and sometimes almost at a hopeless point, yet our Head is on high, he hath conquered for us, and shall conquer in us; therefore, upon this confidence, to fear is not to fear; "Why should I fear in the days of evil, when the iniquity of my heels shall compass me about?" Ps. xlix. 5, (which I take is some grievous affliction, and that with a visage for punishment of sin; guiltiness is to be read in it, yet not fear). "If I trust in wealth, and boast myself in the multitude of riches," then that being in hazard, I must fear; leaning on that, it failing, I might fall. But this is my confidence, ver. 15—God will redeem my soul from the power of the grave; for he shall receive me; wealth cannot, but he can. It buys not a man out from his hand, but he buys from the hand of the grave. So the word is; for the visible heavens, even their fall, and the dissolution of nature, would not affright a believer, Psalm xlvi.

Alas! most persons have dull or dim apprehensions and shallow impressions of God, therefore they have little either of this fear or this trust. God is not in all their thoughts, but how to compass this or that design; and if they miss one, then to another; they are cast from one wave upon another; and if at any time they attain their purpose, find it but wind, a handful of nothing, far from what they fancied it.

Oh! my brethren, my desire is that the faces of your souls were but once turned about, that they were towards him, looking to him, continually fearing, delighting, trusting in him, making him your all. Can anything so elevate and ennoble the spirit of a man, as to contemplate and converse with the pure, ever-blessed spring, the Father of spirits? Beg that you may know him, that he would reveal himself to you; for otherwise no teaching can make him known. It is to light candles to seek the sun, to think to attain to this knowledge without his own revealing it. "If he hide his face, who then may behold him?" Pray for this quickening knowledge, such a knowledge as will effectually work this happy fear and trust.

You that have attained anything of it, desire and "follow on to know the Lord," particularly so as your hearts may repose on him; so fear, as you may not fear. He would have your spirits calm and quiet, for when they are in a hurry and confusion, they are then fit for nothing; all within makes a jarring, unpleasant noise, as of an instrument quite out of tune.

This fear of God is not, you see, a perplexing doubt, and distrust of his love. Many that have some truth of grace are, through weakness, filled with disquieting fears; so, possibly, though they perceive it not, it may be in some point of wilfulness, a latent, undiscerned affectation of scrupling and doubting, placing much of religion in it. True, where the soul is really solicitous about its interest in God, that argues some grace; but being vexingly anxious about it, argues that grace is low and weak: a sparkle there is even discovered by that smoke; but the great smoke still continuing, and nothing seen but it, argues there is little fire, little faith, little love.

And this, as it is unpleasant to thyself, so to God, as smoke to the eyes. What if one should be always questioning with his friend whether he loved him or no, and upon every little occasion were ready to think he doth not, how would this disrelish their society together, though truly loving each other! The far more excellent way, and more pleasing both to ourselves and to God, were to resolve on humble trust, reverence, and confidence, most afraid to offend, delighting to walk in his ways, loving him and his will in all, and then resting persuaded of his love, though he chastise us; and even though we offend him, and see our offences in our chastisements, yet he is good, plenteous in redemption, ready to forgive. Therefore let Israel trust and hope; let my soul roll itself on him, and adventure there all its weight: he bears greater matters, upholding the frame of heaven and earth, and is not troubled nor burdened with it.

The heart of a man is not sufficient for self-support,

therefore naturally it seeks out some other thing to lean and rest itself on. The unhappiness is, for the most part, that it seeks to things below itself: these being both so mean and so uncertain, cannot be a firm and certain stay to it. These things are not fixed themselves, how can they then fix the heart? Can a man have firm footing on a quagmire, or moving sands? Therefore men are forced in these things still to shift their seat, and seek about from one to another, still rolling and unsettled. The believer only hath this advantage; he hath a rest high enough and sure enough, out of the reach of all hazards. His heart is fixed, trusting in the Lord.

II. The basis of this happiness is, He trusteth in the Lord. So the heart is fixed; and so fixed, it fears no ill-tidings.

The trust is grounded on the word of God, revealing the power and all-sufficiency of God, and withal, his goodness, his offer of himself to be the stay of souls, commanding us to rest on him. People wait on I know not what persuasions and assurances; but I know no other to build faith on but the word of promise, the truth and faithfulness of God opened up, his wisdom, and power, and goodness, as the stay of all these; that, renouncing all other props, will venture on it and lay all upon him. He that believes, sets to his seal that God is true; and so he is sealed for God, his portion and interest secured. "If ye will not believe, surely ye shall not be established," Isa. vii. 9.

This is the way to have peace and assurance, which many look for first: "Thou wilt keep him in perfect peace, whose mind is stayed on thee: because he trusteth in thee," Isa. xxvi. 3. So, here, the heart is fixed by trusting.

Seek then clearer apprehensions of the faithfulness and goodness of God, hearts more enlarged in the notion of free grace, and the absolute trust due to it; thus shall they be more established and fixed in all the rollings and changes of the world.

Heart fixed: or prepared, ready, and in arms for all services; resolved not to give back, able to meet all adventures, and stand its ground. God is unchangeable; and, therefore, faith is invincible that sets the heart on him; fastens it there on the rock of eternity; then let winds blow and storms arise, it cares not.

The firm and close cleaving unto God hath in it of the affection, which is inseparable from this trust—love with faith; and so a hatred of all ways and thoughts that alienate and estrange from God, that remove and unsettle the heart. The holiest, wariest heart is surely the most believing and fixed heart: if a believer will adventure on any one way of sin, he shall find that will unfix him, and shake his confidence, more than ten thousand hazards and assaults from without. These are so far from moving, that they commonly settle and fix the heart more, cause it to cleave closer and nearer unto God; but sinful liberty breeds inquietude, and disturbs all.

Would you be quiet and have peace within in troublous times, keep near to God, beware of anything that may interpose betwixt you and your confidence. It is good for me, says the psalmist, to draw near to God; not only to draw near, but to keep near, to cleave to him, and dwell in him. Oh, the sweet calm of such a soul amidst all storms; thus once trusting and fixed, then no more fear, not afraid of evil tidings, nor of any ill-hearing! Whatsoever sound is terrible in the ears of men, the noise of war, news of death, even the sound of the trumpet in the last judgment, he hears all this undisquieted.

Nothing is unexpected, being once fixed on God; then the heart may put cases to itself, and suppose all things imaginable, the most terrible, and look for them; not troubled before trouble with dark and dismal apprehensions, but satisfied in a quiet, unmoved expectation of the hardest things. Whatsoever it is, yet the heart is not afraid of the news of it, because fixed, trusting on the Lord; nothing can shake that foundation, nor dissolve that union, therefore no fear. Yea, this assurance stays the heart in all things, how strange and unforeseen soever to it—All foreseen to my God, on whom I trust, yea, fore-contrived and ordered by him. This is the impregnable fort of a soul—All is at the disposal and command of my God; my Father rules all, what need I fear?

Every one trusts to somewhat: as for honour, and esteem, and popularity, they are airy, vain things; but riches seem a more solid work and fence, yet they are but a tower in conceit, not really. "The rich man's wealth is his strong city, and as an high wall in his own conceit;" but "the name of the Lord is a strong tower," Prov. xviii. 11, 10. Hence we call you not to vexation and turmoil, but from it; and as St Paul said, Acts xvii. 23, "Whom ye ignorantly worship, him declare I unto you." Ye blindly and fruitlessly seek after the show. The true aiming at this fixedness of mind will make that, though they fall short, yet by the way they will light on very pretty things that have some virtue in them, as they that seek the philosopher's stone: but the believer hath the thing, the secret itself of tranquillity and joy, and this turns all into gold, their iron chains into a crown of gold, 2 Cor. iv. 17, 18.

This is the blessed and safe estate of believers. Who can think they have a sad, heavy life? Oh! it is the only lightsome, sweet, cheerful condition in the world. The rest of men are poor, rolling, unstayed things, every report shaking them, as the leaves of the trees are shaken with the wind, Isa. vii. 2; yea, lighter than so, as the chaff that the wind drives to and fro at its pleasure, Psalm i. 4. Would men but reflect and look in upon their own hearts, it is a wonder what vain, childish things the most would find there. Glad and sorry at things as light as the toys of children, at which they laugh and cry in a breath! How easily puffed up with a thing or word that pleaseth us! Bladder-like, swelled with a little air, and it shrinks in again in discouragements and fear upon the touch of a needle's point, which gives that air some vent.

What is the life of the greatest part but a continual tossing betwixt vain hopes and fears—all their days spent in these? Oh, how vain a thing is a man even in his best estate, while he is nothing but himself! His heart not united and fixed on God, disquieted in vain, how small a thing will do it! He need no other but his own heart, it may prove disquietment enough to itself; his thoughts are his tormentors.

I know some men are, by a stronger understanding and moral principle, somewhat raised above the vulgar, and speak big of a constancy of mind; but these are but flourishes, an acted bravery. Somewhat there may be that will hold out in some trials, but far short of this fixedness of faith. Troubles may so multiply, as to drive them at length from their posture, and come on so thick, with such violent blows, as will smite them out of their artificial guards, disorder all their Seneca and Epictetus, and all their own calm thoughts and high resolves: the approach of death, for instance, though they make a good mien, and set the best face on it; or if not, yet some kind of terror may seize on their spirits, which they are not able to shift off. But the soul trusting in God is prepared for all, not only for the calamities of war, pestilence, famine, poverty, or death, but in the saddest apprehensions of soul; even in the darkest night, it casts anchor in God, and reposes on him when he sees no light, Isa. l. 10. "Yea, though he slay me (says Job), yet will I trust in him;" not only though I die, but though he slay me; when I see his hand lifted up to destroy me, yet from that same hand will I look for salvation.

My brethren, my desire is to stir in your hearts an ambition after this blest estate of the godly that fear the Lord, and trust on him, and so fear no other thing. The common revolutions and changes of the world, and those that in these late times we ourselves have seen, and the likelihood of more and greater coming on, seem dreadful to weak minds. But let these persuade us the more to prize and seek this fixed, unaffrighted station: no fixing but here, where we make a virtue of a necessity.

Oh that you would be persuaded to break off from the vile ways of sin, that embase the soul and fill it full of terrors, and, disengaged from the vanities of this world, to take up with God, to live in him wholly, to cleave to and depend on him, to esteem nothing besides him. Excellent was the answer of that holy man to the emperor, first essaying him with large proffers of honour and riches, to draw him from Christ. Offer these things, says he, to children; I regard them not. Then, after he tried to terrify him with threatening—Threaten, says he, your effeminate courtiers; I fear none of these things.

Well, choose you; but, all reckoned and examined, I had rather be the poorest believer than the greatest king on earth. How small a commotion, small in its beginning, may prove the overturning of the greatest kingdom! But the believer is heir to a kingdom that cannot be shaken. The mightiest and most victorious prince, that hath not only lost nothing, but hath been gaining new conquests all his days, is stopped by a small distemper in the middle of his course: he returns to his dust, then his vast designs fall to nothing; "in that very day his thoughts perish." But the believer, in that very day, is sent to the possession of his crown; that is his coronation-day; all his thoughts are accomplished.

How can you affright him? Bring him word his estate is ruined; Yet my inheritance is safe, says he. Your wife, or child, or dear friend, is dead; Yet my Father lives. You yourself must die; Well, then, I go home to my Father, and to my inheritance.

For the public troubles of the church, doubtless it is both a most pious and generous temper, to be more deeply affected for these than for all our private ones; and to resent common calamities of any people, but especially of God's own people, hath been the character of men near unto him. Observe the pathetical strains of the prophets' bewailing, when they foretell the desolation even of foreign kingdoms, much more for the Lord's chosen people, still mindful of Sion, and mournful for her distresses, Jer. ix. 1, and the whole book of Lamentations. Yet even in this, with much compassion, there is a calm in a believer's mind; he finds amidst all hard news, yet still a fixed heart, trusting, satisfied in this, that deliverance shall come in due time, Psalm cii. 13; and that in those judgments that are inflicted, man shall be humbled and God exalted, Isa. ii. 11, and v. 15, 16;

and that in all tumults and changes, and subversion of states, still his throne is fixed, and with that the believer's heart likewise, Psalm xciii. 2. So Psalm xxix. 10.

In this condition there is so much sweetness, that, if known, a man might suspect himself rather selfishly taken with them than purely loving God. Such joy in believing, or at least, such peace, such a serene calmness, is in no other thing in this world. Nothing without or within a man to be named with this of trusting on his goodness. He commands thee to roll thyself on him. The holy soul still trusts amidst the darkest apprehensions. If it is suggested, Thou art a reprobate, yet will the soul say, "I will see the utmost, and hang by the hold I have, till I feel myself really cast off, and will not willingly fall off. If I must be separated from him, he shall do it himself; he shall shake me off while I would cleave to him. Yea, to the utmost I will look for mercy, and will hope better; though I found him shaking me off, yet will I think he will not do it." It is good to seek after all possible assurance, but not to fret at the want of it; for even without these assurances, which some Christians hang too much upon, there is in simple trust and reliance on God, and in a desire to walk in his ways, such a fort of peace, as all the assaults in the world are not able to make a breach in. To this add the unspeakable delight of walking in his fear, joined with this trust. The noble ambition of pleasing him makes one careless of pleasing or displeasing all the world.

Besides, the delight in his commandments hath a sweetness in it that presently pays itself.

It is the godly man alone, who, by this fixed consideration in God, looks the grim visage of death in the face with an unappalled mind; it damps all the joys, and defeats all the hopes of the most prosperous, proudest, and wisest worldling. Though riches, honours, and all the glories of this world are with a man, yet he fears, yea, he fears the more for these, because here they must end. But the good man looks death out of countenance, in the words of David, Though I walk through the valley and shadow of death, yet will I fear no evil; for thou art with me.

SERMON VII.

Having therefore these promises, dearly beloved, let us cleanse ourselves from all filthiness of the flesh and spirit, perfecting holiness in the fear of God.—2 Cor. vii. 1.

It is a thing both of unspeakable sweetness and usefulness for a Christian, often to consider the excellency of that estate to which he is called. It cannot fail to put him upon very high resolutions, and carry him on in the divine ambition of behaving daily more suitably to his high calling and hopes. Therefore these are often set before Christians in the Scripture, and are pressed here by the apostle upon a particular occasion of the avoidance of near combinements with unbelievers. He mentions some choice promises that God makes to his own people, and of their near relation to, and communion with himself; and upon these he enlarges, and raises the exhortation to the universal endeavour of all holiness, and that as aiming at the very top and highest degree of it.

In the words are, 1. The thing to which he would persuade. 2. The motive.

I. The thing—holiness in its full extension and intension; "purging ourselves from all filthiness of the flesh and spirit, and perfecting holiness in the fear of God."

The purging out of filthiness, and perfecting holiness, express those two parts of renewing grace, mortification and vivification, as usually they are distinguished. But I conceive they are not so truly different parts, as a different notion of the same thing; the decrease of sin and increase of grace being truly one thing, as the dispelling of darkness and augmenting of light. So here the one is rendered, as the necessary result, yea, as the equivalent of the other; purging from filthiness, and in so doing perfecting holiness; perfecting holiness, and in so doing purging from filthiness.

Cleanse ourselves. It is the Lord that is the sanctifier of his people, he purges away their dross and tin, he pours clean water, according to his promises, yet doth he call us to cleanse ourselves; having such promises, let us cleanse ourselves. He puts a new life into us, and causes us to act, and excites us to excite it, and call it up to act in the progress of sanctification. Men are strangely inclined to a perverse construction of things: tell them that we are to act and work, and give diligence, then they would fancy a doing in their own strength, and be their own saviours. Again, tell them that God works all our works in us, and for us, then they would take the ease of doing nothing; if they cannot have the praise of doing all, they will sit still with folded hands, and use no diligence at all. But this is the corrupt logic of the flesh, its base sophistry. The apostle reasons just contrary, Phil. ii. 13. "It is God that worketh in us, both to will and to do." Therefore, would a carnal heart say, we need not work, or at least, may work very carelessly. But he infers, Therefore let us work out our salvation with fear and trembling, i. e. in the more humble obedience to God, and dependence on him, not obstructing the influences of his grace, and, by sloth and negligence, provoking him to withdraw or abate it. Certainly many in whom there is truth of grace, are kept low in the growth of it, by their own slothfulness, sitting still, and not bestirring themselves, and exercising the proper actions of that spiritual life, by which it is entertained and advanced.

From all filthiness. All kind of sinful pollutions. Not as men commonly do reform some things, and take to themselves dispensation in others, at least in some one peculiar sin—their mistress, their Herodias, their

Delilah: no parting with that; yea, they rather forego many other things, as a kind of composition for the retaining of that.

Of flesh and spirit. The whole man must be purified and consecrated to God; not only refined from the gross outward acts of sin, but from the inward affection to it, and motions of it, that so the heart go not after it, (Psalm cxxxi.,) which, under restraints of outward committing sin, it may do, and very often does. As the Israelites lusted after the flesh pots, their hearts remained in Egypt still, though their bodies were brought out. This is then to be done, namely, affection to sins is to be purged out. That is, to cleanse the ground; not only to lop off the branches, but to dig about, and loosen and pluck up the root; though still fibres of it will stick, yet we ought still to be finding them out, and plucking them up.

Further, These not only of the inner part of all sins, but of some sins that are most or wholly inward, that hang not so much on the body, nor are acted by it, those filthinesses of the spirit that are less discerned than those of the flesh; and as more hardly discerned, so when discerned, more hardly purged out—pride, self-love, unbelief, &c., which, though more retired and refined sins, yet are pollutions and defilements, yea, of the worst sort, as being more spiritual, are filthiness of the spirit. Fleshly pollutions are things of which the devils are not capable in themselves, though they excite men to them, and so they are called unclean spirits. But the highest rank of sins, are those that are properly spiritual wickednesses.

These in men are the chief strengths of Satan, the inner works of these forts and strong holds, 2 Cor. x. 4. Many that are not much tempted to the common gross sensualities, have possibly (though an inclination to them, yet) a kind of disdain of them; and, through education, and morality, and strength of reason, with somewhat of natural conscience, are carried above them; who yet have many of these heights, those lofty imaginations that rise against God, and the obedience of Christ, all which must be demolished.

Perfecting holiness. Not content with low measures, so much as keeps from hell, but aspiring towards perfection; aiming high at self-victory, self-denial, and the love of God, purer and hotter, as a fire growing and flaming up, and consuming the earth. Though men fall short of their aim, yet it is good to aim high; they shall shoot so much the higher, though not full so high as they aim. Thus we ought to be setting the state of perfection in our eye, resolving not to rest content below that, and to come as near it as we can, even before we come at it, Phil. iii. 11, 12. This is to act as one that hath such hope, such a state in view, and is still advancing towards it.

In the fear of God. No working but on firm ground, no solid endeavours in holiness where it is not founded in a deep heart, a reverence of God, a desire to please him and to be like him, which springs from love.

This most men are either strangers to wholly, or but slight and shallow in it, and therefore make so little true progress in holiness.

II. Then there is the motive—having these promises; being called to so fair an estate, so excellent a condition, to be the people, yea, the sons and daughters of God. Therefore they are called to come forth from Babel, and separate themselves from sin, and purge it out. Holiness is his image in his children; the more of it, the more suitable to that blessed relation and dignity, and the firmer are the hopes of the inheritance of glory.

Consider sin as a filthiness, hate it. Oh, how ugly and vile is lust, how deformed is swelling pride! And all sin is an aversion from God, a casting the noble soul into the mire, the defacing all its beauty. Turning to present things, it pollutes itself with them, that "he who was clad in scarlet embraces the dunghill," as Jeremiah in another sense laments.

This, then, should be our main study, first to search out our iniquities, the particular defilements of our nature; not only gross filthiness, drunkenness, lasciviousness, &c., but our love of this earth, vanity of mind, self-will, and self-seeeking. Most, even of Christians, are shortsighted in their own secret evils, the filthiness of spirit especially, and use little diligence in this inquiry. They do not seek light from God to go in before him, and to lead them into themselves, as the prophet had in the discovery of idolatries at Jerusalem. Oh that we could once see what heaps of abominations lie hid in us, one behind another!

Then having searched out, we must follow on to purge out; not to pass over, nor spare any, but to delight most in casting out the best beloved sin, the choicest idol, that hath had most of our services and sacrifices, to make room for Jesus Christ.

And never cease in this work, for still there is need of more purging: one day's work in this disposes for and engages to a further, and that to the next; for, as sin is purged out, light comes in, and more clear discoveries are made of remaining pollutions. So, then, still there must be progress, less of the world and more of God in the heart every day. Oh! this is a sweet course of life: what gain, what preferment to be compared to it?

And in this it is good to have our ambition growing: the higher we rise, to aspire still the higher, looking further than before, even towards the perfection of holiness. It is not much we can here attain to, but sure it is commonly far less than we might; we improve not our condition and advantages as we might do. The world is busy driving forward their designs. Men of spirit are animated, both by better and worse success: if any thing miscarry, it sets them on the more eagerly to make it up, in the right management of some other design; and when they prosper in one thing, that enables and encourages them to attempt further. Shall all things seem worth our pains? Are only grace and glory so cheap in our account, that the least diligence of all goes that way? Oh, strange delusion!

Having these promises. Now consider whether it is better to be the slaves of Satan or the sons of God; measure delight in God with the low, base pleasures of sense. Blessed are the pure in heart, for they shall see God; these gradually go on together, and are perfected together.

Why then is there such an invincible love of sin in the hearts of men? At least, why so little love of holiness, and endeavour after it, so mean thoughts of it, as a thing either indecent or unpleasant, when it is the only noble and the only delightful thing in the world? The soul by other things is drawn below itself, but by holiness it is raised above itself, and made divine. Pleasures of sin for a season, the pleasure of a moment, exchanged for those of eternity! But even in the mean time, in this season, the soul is fed with communion with God, one hour of which is more worth than the longest life of the highest of the world's delights.

SERMON VIII.

I will run the way of thy commandments, when thou shalt enlarge my heart.—PSALM cxix. 32.

To desire ease and happiness, under a general representation of it, is a thing of more easy and general persuasion; there is somewhat in nature to help the argument; but to find beauty in, and be taken with the very way of holiness that leads to it, is more rare, and depends on a higher principle. Self-love inclines a man to desire the rest of love; but to love and desire the labour of love, is of a higher and purer strain. To delight and be cheerful in obedience, argues much lóve as the spring of it. That is the thing the holy psalmist doth so plentifully express in this psalm, and he is still desiring more of that sweet and lively affection that might make him yet more abundant in action.

This is the top of his ambition, while others are seeking to enlarge their barns, their lands, or estates, or titles; kings to enlarge their territories or authority, to encroach on neighbouring kingdoms, or be more absolute in their own; instead of all such enlargements, this is David's great desire, an enlarged heart, to run the way of God's commandments.

Let others seek more money or more honour; oh! the blessed choice of that soul that is still seeking more love to God, more affection, and more ability to do him service; that counts all days and hours for lost that are not employed to this improvement; that hears the word in public, and reads it in private for this purpose, to kindle this love, or to blow the sparkle, if any there be in the heart, to raise it to a clear flame, and from a little flame to make it burn yet hotter and purer, and rise higher; but, above all means, is often presenting this in prayer to Him on whose influence all depends, in whose hand our hearts are, much more than in our own. It follows him with this desire, and works on him by his own interest. Though there can be really no accession of gain to him by our services, yet he is pleased so to account with us as if there were. Therefore we may urge this: "Lord, give more, and receive more; I will run the way of thy commandments, when thou shalt enlarge my heart."

We have here in the words a required disposition, and a suitable resolution. The disposition relates to the resolution, as the means of fulfilling it, and the resolution relates to the disposition, both as the end of desiring it, and as the motive of obtaining it. The resolution occurs first in the words

I will run, &c. The way resolved on is that of God's commandments, not the road of the polluted world, not the crooked way of his own heart, but the highway, the royal way, the straight way of the kingdom, and that in the notion of subjection and obedience—the way of thy commandments. This man naturally struggles against and repines at. To be limited and bounded by law is a restraint, and a vain man could possibly find in his heart to do many of the same things that are commanded; but he would not be tied, would have his liberty, and do it of his own choice. This is the enmity of the carnal mind against God, as the apostle expresses it—"It is not subject to the law of God, neither can it be;" it breaks these bonds, and casts away the cords of his authority. This is sin, the transgression of a law, and this made the first sin so great, though in a matter one would think small—the eating of the fruit of a tree: it was rebellion against the majesty of God, casting off his law and authority, and aspiring to an imagined self-deity.

And this is still the treasonable pride, or independency, and wickedness of our nature, rising up against God that formed us of nothing.

And this is the power and substance of religion, the new impress of God upon the heart, and obedience and resignment to him, to be given up to him as entirely his, to be moulded and ordered as he will, to be subject to his laws and appointments in all things, to have every action, and every word, under a rule and law; and the penalty to be so high—eternal death! All this to a carnal or haughty mind is hard; not only every action and word, but even every thought too, must be subject; not so much as thought-free; 2 Cor. x. 5, "Every thought is brought into captivity,"—as the apostle speaks, and so the licentious mind accounts it,—not only the affections and desires, but the very reasoning and imaginations are brought under this law.

Now, to yield this as reasonable and due to God, to own his sovereignty, to approve, yea, to love his law, even where it most contradicts our own corrupt will, this is true spiritual obedience. We should make this our business in the world, and all other things but accessaries, even those lawful things that may be taken in, and used as helps in our way: as the disciples passing through the corn plucked the ears, and did eat in passing, as a by-work; but their business was to follow their Master. And whatsoever would hinder us in this way must be watched and guarded against. Till the heart be brought to this state and purpose, it is either wholly void of, or very low and weak in the truth of religion.

We place religion much in our accustomed performances, in coming to church, hearing and repeating of sermons, and praying at home. But the way of God's commandments is more in doing than in discourse. In many, religion evaporates itself too much out by the tongue, while it appears too little in their ways. Oh, but this is the main; one act of charity, meekness, or humility, speaks more than a day's discourse. All the means we use in religion are intended for a further end, which, if they attain not, they are nothing. This end is to mortify and purify the heart, to mould it to the way of God's commandments in our converse one with another, and our secret converse with ourselves; to have God still before us, and his law our rule in all we do. This, and nothing below this, is the end of religion. Alas! amongst multitudes that are called Christians, some there may be that speak and appear like it, yet how few are there that make this their business and aspire to this—The way of God's commandments!

His intended course in this way he expresses by running. It is good to be in this way even in the slowest motions; love will creep where it cannot go. But if thou art so indeed, then thou wilt long for a swifter motion; if thou do but creep, creep on, yet desire to be enabled to go; if thou goest, but yet halting and lamely, desire to be strengthened to walk straight; and if thou walkest, let not that satisfy thee, desire to run. So here, David did walk in this way; but he earnestly wishes to mend his pace; he would willingly run, and for that end he desires an enlarged heart.

Some dispute and descant too much whether they go or no, and childishly tell their steps, and would know at every pace whether they advance or no, and how much they advance, and thus amuse themselves, and spend the time of doing and going in questioning and doubting. Thus it is with many Christians; but it were a more wise and comfortable way to be endeavouring onwards, and if thou make little progress, at least to be desiring to make more; to be praying and walking, and praying that thou mayest walk faster, and that in the end thou mayest run; not satisfied with anything attained, but yet by that unsatisfiedness not to be so dejected as to sit down, or stand still, but rather excited to go on. So it was with St Paul, Phil. iii. 13: "Forgetting those things which are behind, and reaching forth unto those things which are before, I press forward." If any one thinks that he hath done well and run far, and will take a pause, the great apostle is of another mind—Not as if I had attained. Oh, no! far from that; he still sets forward as if nothing were done, as a runner, not still looking back how much he hath run, but forward to what he is to run, stretching forth to that, inflamed with frequent looks at the mark and end. Some are retarded by looking on what is past; they are not satisfied, they have done nothing, as they think, and so stand still discontented; but even in that way, it is not good to look too much to things behind; we must forget them rather, and press onwards.

Some, if they have gone on well, and possibly run a while, yet if they fall, then they are ready, in a desperate malcontent, to lie still and think all is lost; and in this peevish fretting at their falls, some men please themselves and take it for repentance, whereas, indeed, it is not that, but rather pride and humour; repentance is a more submissive, humble thing. But this is that which troubles some men at their new falls (especially if after a long time of even walking or running), they think their project is now spoiled; their thoughts are broken off, they would have had somewhat to have rejoiced in, if they had still gone on to the end, but being disappointed of that, they think they had as good let alone, and give over. Oh, but the humble Christian is better taught; his falls teach him indeed to abhor himself, they discover his own weakness to him, and empty him of self-trust, but they do not dismay him to get up and go on; not boldly and carelessly forgetting his fall, but in the humble sense of it walking the more warily, but not the less swiftly; yea, the more swiftly too, making the more haste to regain the time lost by the fall. So, then, if you would run in this way, depend on the strength of God, and on his Spirit leading thee, that so thou mayest not fall, and yet if thou dost fall, arise; and if thou art plunged in the mire, go to the fountain opened for sin and uncleanness, and wash there; bemoan thyself before thy Lord; and if hurt, and bleeding by thy fall, yet look on him, desire Jesus to pity thee, and bind up and cure thy wound, washing off thy blood and pouring in of his own.

However it may be with thee, give not over, faint not, run on; and that thou mayest run the more easily and expeditely, make thyself as light as may be; "lay aside every weight," Heb. xii. 1, 2. Clog not thyself with unnecessary burdens of earth, and especially lay aside that, which of all other things weighs the heaviest, and cleaves the closest, the sin that so easily besets us, and is so hardly put off, that folds so connaturally to us, and we therefore think will not hinder so much. And not only the sins that are more outward, but the inner, close-cleaving sins, the sin that most of all sits easily to us; not only our cloak, but our inner coat, away with that too, as our Saviour says in another case, and run the race set before us, our appointed stage, and that with patience, under all opposition and discouragements from the world without and sin within. And to encourage thee in this, look to such a cloud of witnesses that compasseth us about to further us; as troubles, temptations, and sin, do to hinder us. They encountered the like sufferings, and were encountered with the like sins, and yet they ran on and got home. Alexander would have run in the Olympic Games if he had had kings to run with; now, in this race, kings and prophets and righteous persons run; yea, all are indeed a kingly generation, each one heir to a crown as the prize of this race.

And if these encourage thee but little, then look beyond them, above that cloud of witnesses, to the Sun, the Sun of righteousness; looking off from all things here, that would either entangle thee or discourage thee, taking thine eye off from them, and looking to him that will powerfully draw thee and animate thee. Look to Jesus, not only as thy forerunner in this race, but also as thy undertaker in it; the author and finisher of our faith. His attaining the end of the race is the pledge of thy attaining, if thou follow him cheerfully on the same encouragements that he looked to; "who, for the joy that was set before him, endured the cross and despised the shame, and is now set down at the right hand of God."

When thou shalt enlarge my heart. In all beings the heart is the principle of motion, and according as it is more or less perfect in its kind, those motions that flow from it are more or less vigorous. Therefore hath the psalmist good reason, to the end his spiritual course may be the stedfaster, and the faster, to desire that the principle of it, the heart, may be more enabled and disposed, which here he expresses by its being enlarged.

What this enlargement of the heart is, a man's own inward sense should easily explain to him. Sure it would, did men reflect on it, and were they acquainted with their own hearts; but the most are not. They would find the carnal, natural heart, a narrow, contracted, hampered thing, bound with cords and chains of its own twisting and forging, and so incapable of walking, much less of running in this way of God's commandments, till it be freed and enlarged.

The heart is taken generally in Scripture, for the whole soul, the understanding and will, in its several affections and motions; and the speech being here of an enlarged heart, it seems very congruous to take it in the most enlarged sense.

It is said of Solomon, that he had "a large heart, (the same word that is here,) as the sand of the sea shore;" that is, a vast, comprehensive spirit, that could fathom much of nature, both its greater and lesser things. Thus, I conceive, the enlargement of the heart compriseth the enlightening of the understanding. There arises a clearer light there to discern spiritual things in a more spiritual manner; to see the vast difference betwixt the vain things the world goes after, and the true, solid delight that is in the way of God's commandments; to know the false blush of the pleasures of sin, and what deformity is under that painted mask, and not be allured by it; to have enlarged apprehensions of God, his excellency, and greatness, and goodness; how worthy he is to be obeyed and served. This is the great dignity and happiness of the soul; all other pretensions are low and poor in respect of this. Here then is enlargement to see the purity and beauty of his law, how just and reasonable, yea, how pleasant and amiable it is; that his commandments are not grievous, that they are beds of spices; the more we walk in them, still the more of their fragrant smell and sweetness we find.

And then, consequently, upon the larger and clearer knowledge of these things, the heart dilates itself in affection; the more it knows of God, still the more it loves him, and the less it loves this present world; love is the great enlarger of the heart to all obedience. Then nothing is hard, yea, the harder things become, the more delightful.

All love of other things doth pinch and contract the heart, for they are all narrower than itself. It is framed to that wideness at its first creation, capable of enjoying God, though not of a full comprehending him. Therefore all other things gather it in, and straiten it from its natural size, only the love of God stretches and dilates it. He is large enough for it; yea, it, in its fullest enlargement, is infinitely too narrow for him. Do not all find it, if they will ask themsèlves, that in all other loves and pursuits in this world, there is still somewhat that pinches? The soul is not at its full size, but as a foot in a strait shoe, is somewhere bound and pained, and cannot go freely, much less run; though another that looks on cannot tell where, yet each one feels it. But when the soul is set free from these narrow things, and is raised to the love of God, then it is at ease, and at large, and hath room enough; it is both elevated and dilated.

And this word signifies a high-raised soul, and is sometimes taken for proud and lofty; but there is a greatness and height of spirit in the love of God and union with him, that doth not vainly swell and lift it up, but with the deepest humility joins the highest and truest magnanimity. It sets the soul above the snares that lie here below, in which most men creep and are entangled, in that way of life that is on high to the just, as Solomon speaks.

Good reason hath David to join these together, and to desire the one as the spring and cause of the other: an enlarged heart, that he might run the way of God's commandments. Sensible joys and consolations in God do encourage and enlarge the heart; but these are not so general to all, nor so constant to any. Love is the abounding, fixed spring of ready obedience, and will make the heart cheerful in serving God, even without those felt comforts, when he is pleased to deny or withdraw them.

In that course or race is understood Constancy, Activity, and Alacrity; and all these flow from the enlargement of the heart.

1. *Constancy:* A narrow, enthralled heart, fettered with the love of lower things, and cleaving to some particular sins, or but some one, and that secret, may keep foot a while in the way of God's commandments, in some steps of them; but it must give up quickly, is not able to run on to the end, to the goal. But a heart that hath laid aside every weight, and the most close-cleaving and besetting sin (as it is in that place to the Hebrews), hath stripped itself of all that may falter or

entangle it; it runs, and runs on, without fainting or wearying; it is at large, hath nothing that pains it in the race.

2. *Activity:* Not only holding on, but running, which is a swift, nimble race. It stands not bargaining and disputing, but once knowing God's mind, there is no more question or demur. I made haste and delayed not, as in this Psalm the word is; did not stay upon why and wherefore; he stood not to reason the matter, but ran on. And this love, enlarging the heart, makes it abundant in the work of the Lord, quick and active, despatching much in a little time.

3. *Alacrity:* All done with cheerfulness, so no other constraint is needful, where this overpowering, sweet constraint of love is. I will run, not be hauled, and drawn, as by force, but skip and leap, as the evangelic promise is, that the "lame shall leap as an hart, and the tongue of the dumb sing: for in the wilderness shall waters break out, and streams in the desert," Isa. xxxv. 6. The spouse desires her Beloved "to hasten as a roe and hind on the mountains of spices," and she doth so, and each faithful soul runs towards him, to meet him in his way.

It is a sad, heavy thing to do anything in obedience to God, while the heart is not enlarged towards him by his Divine love; but that, once taking possession of and enlarging the heart, that inward principle of obedience makes the outward obedience sweet: it is then a natural motion. Indeed, the soul runs in the ways of God, as the sun in his course, which finds no difficulty, being naturally fitted and carried to that motion; he "goes forth as a bridegroom, and rejoiceth as a strong man to run a race."

This is the great point that our souls should be studious of—to attain more evenness, and nimbleness, and cheerfulness in the ways of God, and for this end we ought to seek above all things this enlarged heart; it is want of this makes us bog, and drive heavily, and run long upon little ground. Oh, my beloved, how shallow and narrow are our thoughts of God! Most, even of those that are truly godly, are led by a kind of instinct, and carried they scarce know how, to give some attendance on God's worship, and to the avoidance of gross sin, and go on in a blameless course. It is better thus, than to run to excess of riot and open wickedness with the ungodly world. But, alas! this is but a dull, heavy, and languid motion, where the heart is not enlarged by the daily growing love of God. Few, few are acquainted with that delightful contemplation of God, that ventilates and raises this flame of love. Petty things bind and contract our spirits, so that they feel little joy in God, little ardent, active desire to do him service, to crucify sin, to break and undo self-love within us, to root up our own wills to make room for his, that his alone may be ours, that we may have no will of our own, that our daily work may be to grow more like him in the beauty of holiness. You think it a hard saying to part with your carnal lusts and delights, and the common ways of the world, and to be tied to a strict, exact conversation all your days. But, oh, the reason of this is, because the heart is yet straitened and enthralled by the base love of these mean things, and that is from the ignorance of things higher and better. One glance of God, a touch of his love, will free and enlarge the heart, so that it can deny all, and make an entire renouncing of all, to follow him. It sees enough in him, and in him alone, and therefore can neither quietly rest on, nor earnestly desire, anything besides him.

Oh that you would apply your hearts to consider the excellency of this way of God's commandments! Our wretched hearts are prejudiced; they think it melancholy and sad. There is no way truly joyous but this: They shall sing in the ways of the Lord, says the prophet. Do not men, when their eyes are opened, see a beauty in meekness, and temperance, and humility, a present delightfulness and quietness in them? Whereas in pride, and passion, and intemperance, there is nothing but vexation and disquiet.

And then consider the end of this way—rest and peace for ever; it is the way of peace, both in its own nature, and in respect of its end. Did you believe that joy and glory that is set before you in this way, you would not any of you defer a day longer, but forthwith you would break from all that holds you back, and enter into this way, and run on in it. The persuasion of these great things above would enlarge and greaten the heart, and make the greatest things here very little in your eyes.

But would you attain to this enlarged heart for this race, and, as you ought, apply your thoughts to these divine things, and stretch them on the promises made in the word, take David's course, seek this enlargement of heart from God's own hand, for it is here propounded and laid before God by way of request: "See what is my desire; I would gladly serve thee better, and advance more in the way of thy commandments. Now this I cannot do till my heart be more enlarged, and that cannot be but by thy hand—When *thou* shalt enlarge my heart." Present this suit often; it is in his power to do it for thee; he can stretch and expand thy straitened heart, can spread and hoist the sails within thee, and then carry thee on swiftly; filling them not with the vain air of man's applause, which readily runs a soul upon rocks and splits it, but with the sweet breathings and soft gales of his own Spirit, that carry it straight to the desired haven.

SERMON IX.

Who shall lay anything to the charge of God's elect? It is God that justifieth. Who is he that condemneth? It is Christ that died, yea rather, that is risen again, who is even at the right hand of God, who also maketh intercession for us.—ROMANS viii. 33, 34.

OTHER men may fancy and boast as they please, but there are none in the world but the godly alone that are furnished with sufficiently strong supports and comforts against all possible hazards, and of these doth the apostle treat most freely, sweetly, and plentifully in this chapter. He secures believers, touching these two great evils, after-condemnation and present affliction, that the one cannot befall them, and the other cannot hurt them.

They are freed from condemnation, and not only so, but entitled and insured to a kingdom. And what hurt then can affliction do? Yea, it doth them good; yea, not only it cannot rob them of their crown, but it carries them on towards it, is their highway to it: "If we suffer with him, we shall also be glorified together." All things to the children of God do prove advantageous: severally taken, in their present sense, they may seem evil; but taken jointly in their after issue, their workings together are all for good. In their simple nature possibly they are poison, yet, contempered and prepared, they shall prove medicinal. "All these things are against me," said old Jacob, and yet he lived to see that even all these were for him. The children of God are indeed so happy, that the harshest things in their way change their nature, and become sweet and profitable. This much is effected by their prayers. They breathe forth the expressions of that love to God, by which they are charactered, "them that love God;" and that is put into their hearts, through the impression of his love to them, to which they are here led by the apostle, as to the spring-head of all. All their comforts and privileges flow thence, yea, all their love, and their faith, appropriating those comforts and privileges. Yea, the very treasury of all together, Jesus Christ himself, is the free gift of this free love; he, as the greatest, assures all things besides as unspeakably less, ver. 32.

These two are such mighty arguments, that no difficulty nor grief can stand before them. "If God be for us, who can be against us?" All the world it may be; but that is as nothing. Once it was nothing; it was that God who is our God, who loves us and is for us, that made it something; and if he will, it may again be nothing. And, as it is at its best, it is nothing being compared with another gift that he hath bestowed on us; and having bestowed that, sure if there be anything in this world can do us any good, we shall not want it. "He that spared not his own Son, but gave him to the death for us, will he not with him give us all things?"

And to close all, he makes these two great immunities good to us in Christ. He fixes there; there we are freed from all fear of condemnation, or of being hurt by affliction. No accusation nor guiltiness can annul the righteousness of Christ, and that is made ours; no distress nor suffering can cut us off from the love of God: and if it cannot do that, we need not fear it; all other hazards are no hazards, that being sure.

And in confidence of this, the apostle gives the defiance, casts a challenge to angels, to men, to all the world, upon these two points, Who shall accuse? Who shall separate? Accuse to God, or separate from him? Whatsoever times may come, the hardest that any can apprehend or foretell, if these two be not sufficient furniture against them, I know not what is.

Men are commonly busied about other events concerning them and theirs, what shall become of this or the other, and what if this or that fall out? but the conscience once raised to this inquiry, the soul being awake to discern the hazard of eternal death, all other fears and questions are drowned and lost in this great question, "Am I condemned or not? Is my sin pardoned or no?"

And then, a satisfying answer received concerning this, all is quiet, the soul reposes sweetly on God, and puts all its other concernments into his hands. "Let him make me poor and despised, let him smite and chastise me—he hath forgiven my sin; all is well." That burden taken off, the soul can go light, yea, can leap and dance under all other burdens. Oh! how it feels itself nimble, as a man eased of a load that he was fainting under. Oh! blessed the man whose sin is taken off, lifted from his shoulders (that is the word, Psalm xxxii. 1), laid over upon Christ, who could bear the whole load, and take it away, take it out of sight, which we could never have done; no, they would have sunk us for ever. That one word "taketh away," John i. 29, signifies both, and answers to the two, Isa. liii. 4, "He hath borne our griefs, and carried our sorrows;" lifted them away. Oh! how sweet a burden, instead of this, is that engagement of obedience and love to him as our Redeemer; and that is all he lays on us. If we follow him, and bear his cross, he is our strength, and bears both it and us. So then this is the great point, the heart's ease, to be delivered from the condemning weight of sin.

And certainly, while men do not think thus, their hearts have very slight impressions of the truth of these things. I fear the most of us scarce believe this condemnation to come, at least very shallowly, and so they cannot much consider the deliverance from it provided to us in Jesus Christ. I cannot see how it is possible for a heart persuaded of these, to be very careful about anything besides. You that eat and drink, and labour and trade, and bestow all your time either in the pains or the pleasures of this earth, what think you of eternity? Is it a light thing for you to perish for ever? After a few days vainly spent, to fall under the wrath of God for ever! Oh that you would be persuaded to think on these things!

And you that have an interest in this free and blessed estate, why are your spirits so cold, so unfrequent in the thoughts of it? Why are you not rejoicing in the Lord; gladdening yourselves in secret when you remember this: "Go the world as it will, my sin is forgiven me; mistake me, accuse me whoso will, my God hath acquitted me in Christ; and he loves me, and lives to intercede for me."

Methinks I hear some say, "Ay, they that could say that might be merry indeed; but, alas! I have no such assurance. Who can lay anything to the charge of God's elect? That is true; but here is the great point of so hard a resolution—am I one of these?"

That the apostle doth thus specify the owners of this consolation, by this high and hidden character of their election, is not to render it doubtful and dark; for his main aim, on the contrary, is both to extend it as far as it can go, and to make it as clear as may be to all that have interest in it. But he designates them by the primitive act of love fixing on them, so as it is now manifested to them in the subsequent effects that flow from the election—called and sanctified, and conformed to Jesus Christ, both by his Spirit within them, and the sufferings that rise against them in the world; such as, being "the sons of God, are led by the Spirit of God, and walk not after the flesh, but after the Spirit."

And these things indeed considered as their characters, the stamp of God on them, the impressions of their election of life, do check the vain confidence of all carnal, ungodly professors of the name of Christ, and tell them that their pretended title to him is a mere delusion. Certainly, whosoever lives in the love of sin, and takes the flesh for his guide, that accursed blind guide is leading him into the pit. What gross folly and impudence is it for any man, walking in the lusts of his own heart, to fancy and aver himself to be a partner of that redemption, whereof so great a part is to deliver us from the power of our iniquities, to renew our hearts and reunite them to God, and possess them with his love!

The great evidence of thy election is love. Thy love to him gives certain testimony of his preceding eternal love to thee; so are they here designated, "they that love God;" thy choosing him is the effect and evidence of his choosing thee. Now this, that needs to be disputed, is not laborious; amidst all thy frailties, feel the pulse of thine affection, which way beats it? ask thy heart whether thou love him or not: in this thou hast the character of thy election.

Know you not, that the redeemed of Christ and Christ himself are one; they live one life, Christ lives in them; and if "any man have not the Spirit of Christ, he is none of his," as the apostle declares in this chapter. So, then, this we are plainly to tell you, and consider it; you that will not let go your sins to lay hold on Christ, have as yet no share in him.

But, on the other side, the truth is, that when souls are once set upon this search, they commonly wind the notion too high, and subtilize too much in the dispute, and so entangle and perplex themselves, and drive themselves further off from that comfort that they are seeking after. Such measures and marks of grace they set to themselves for their rule and standard; and unless they find those without all controversy in themselves, they will not believe that they have an interest in Christ, and this blessed and safe estate in him.

To such I would only say, Are you in a willing league with any known sin? Yea, would you willingly, if you might be saved in that way, give up yourself to voluptuousness and ungodliness, and not at all desire to follow Jesus Christ in the way of holiness? Then, truly, I have not anything as yet to say for your comfort, only there is a salvation provided, and the door is yet open, and your heart may be changed. But, on the other side, are the desires of thy soul after Christ, to be righteousness and sanctification to thee? Wouldst thou willingly give up thyself to be ruled by him, and have him thy King? Hadst thou rather choose to suffer the greatest affliction for his sake, to honour him, than to commit the least sin to displease him? Doth thy heart go out after him, when thou hearest him spoken of? Dost thou account him thy treasure, so that all the world sounds but as an empty shell to thee, when he is named? Says thy soul within thee, Oh that he were mine and that I were his, that I could please him and live to him? Then do not toss thy spirit, and jangle and spin out thy thoughts in fruitless, endless doubtings, but close with this as thy portion, and be of good comfort; thy sins are, or will be, forgiven thee.

I add yet further, if thou sayest, that thou findest none of all this, yet I say, there is warrant for thee to believe and lay hold on this righteousness here held forth, to the end that thou mayest then find those things in thee, and find comfort in them. Thou art convinced of ungodliness, then believe on him that justifies the ungodly; thou art condemned, yet Christ is dead and risen; fly to him as such, as the Lamb slain, he that was dead and is alive, and then say, Who is he that condemneth? It is Christ that died, or rather that is risen. Who shall accuse? It is true, they may clamour and make a noise, both Satan and thy conscience, but how can they fasten any accusation on thee? If they dare accuse, yet they cannot condemn when the Judge hath acquitted thee, and declared thee free, who is greater than all, and hath the absolute power of the sentence; all charges and libels come too late after he hath once pronounced a soul righteous; "and who shall condemn? it is Christ that died." If the sentence of the law be brought forth against thee, yet here is the answer, it ought not to be twice satisfied; now once it is in Christ, he hath died, and that stands for the believer. Whosoever flies to him, and lays hold on him for life, he cannot die again; nor canst thou die for whom he died once,—or rather is risen; that raises the assurance higher, and sets it firmer; for this evidences that in his death all was paid, when he being the surety and seized on for the debt, and once death's prisoner, yet was set free. This clears the matter, that there is no more to be said; and yet further, in sign that all is done, he is raised to the height of honour above all principalities and powers, is set at the right hand of the Father, and there he sits and lives to make intercession, to sue out the fulfilling of all for believers, the bringing of them home—lives to see all made good that he died and covenanted for; so now his righteousness is thine that believest: any challenge must meet with Christ first, and if it seize not on him, it cannot light on thee; for thou art in him, married to him. And the triumph that he speaks, Isa. l. 8 (whence these words are borrowed), is made thine, and thou mayest now speak it in him. I know not what can cast him down that hath this word to rest upon, and to comfort himself in.

SERMON X.

Who shall separate us from the love of Christ? Shall tribulation, or distress, or persecution, or famine, or nakedness, or peril, or sword, &c.?—ROM. viii. 35—39.

Is this he that so lately cried out, O wretched man that I am! who shall deliver me? that now triumphs, O happy man! Who shall separate us from the love of Christ?

Yes, it is the same. Pained then with the thoughts of that miserable conjunction with a body of death, and so crying out, Who will deliver? now he hath found a deliverer to do that for him, to whom he is for ever united; and he glories now in his inseparable union, and unalterable love. So vast a difference is there betwixt a Christian, taken in himself, and in Christ: when he views himself in himself, then he is nothing but a poor, miserable, polluted, perishing wretch; but then he looks again, and sees himself in Christ, and there he is rich, and safe, and happy; he triumphs, and he glories in it above all the painted prosperities, and against all the horrid adversities of the world; he lives in Christ content and happy, and laughs at all enemies.

And he extends his triumph, he makes a common good of it to all believers, speaks it in their name—Who shall separate us? and would have them partake of the same confidence, and speak in the same style with himself. It is vain that men fancy these to be expressions of revelations, or some singularly privileged assurances; then they would not suit their end, which is clearly and undoubtedly the encouragement of all the children of God, upon grounds that are peculiar to them from all the rest of the world, but common to them all, in all ages, and all varieties of condition.

There be indeed some kind of assurances that are more rare and extraordinary, some immediate glances or coruscations of the love of God upon the soul of a believer, a smile of his countenance; and this doth exceedingly refresh, yea, ravish the soul, and enables it mightily for duties and sufferings. These he dispenses arbitrarily and freely where and when he will. Weaker Christians sometimes have them, when stronger are strangers to them; the Lord training them to live more contentedly by faith till the day of vision come.

And that less ecstatical, but the more constant and fixed kind of assurance, is the proper assurance of faith. The soul by believing cleaves unto God in Christ as he offers himself in the gospel, and thence is possessed with a sweet and calm persuasion of his love; that being the proper work, to appropriate him, to make Christ, and in him eternal life, ours. It is the proper result and fruit of that its acting, especially when it acts strongly, to quiet the soul: "Being justified by faith, we have peace with God through our Lord Jesus Christ," and from that peace, joy; yea, even glorying in tribulation, as there follows. And these springing not from an extraordinary sense or view, but from the very innate virtue of faith working according to its own nature.

Therefore many Christians do prejudice their own comfort, and darken their spirits, by not giving freedom to faith to act according to its nature and proper principles; they will not believe till they find some evidence or assurance, which is quite to invert the order of the thing, and to look for fruit without setting a root for it to grow from.

Would you take Christ upon the absolute word of promise tendering him to you, and rest on him, this would engraft you into life itself, for that he is; and so those fruits of the Holy Ghost would bud and flourish in your hearts. From that very believing on him would arise this persuasion, yea, even to a glorying, and an humble boasting in his love—Who shall accuse? who shall condemn? who shall separate?

The undivided companion, and undoubted helper and preserver of this confidence of faith, is an active love to Christ, a constant study of holiness, and strife against sin, which is the grand enemy of faith. As faith grows, holiness will grow, and holiness growing will mutually strengthen and establish faith. The comforts of the Holy Ghost are holy, purifying comforts; and the more the soul is purified and made holy, the more it is cleared and enlarged to receive much of these comforts. Blessed are the pure in heart, for they shall see God; unholiness is as damps and filthy mists in the soul, it darkens all.

Again, it appears that this assurance is no enemy to holy diligence, nor friend of carnal security; on the contrary, it is the only thing that doth eminently ennoble and embolden the soul for all adventures and services. Base fears and doubtings, wherein some place much of religion (and many weak Christians seem to be in that mistake, to think it a kind of holy, spiritual temper to be questioning and doubting), I say these base fears can never produce anything truly generous, nor any height of obedience. They do nothing but entangle and disable the soul for every good work; perfect love casts out this fear, and works a sweet, unperplexing fear, a holy wariness not to offend, which fears nothing else. And this confidence of love is the great secret of comfort, and of ability to do good service. Nothing makes so strong and healthful a constitution of soul as pure love; it dare submit to God and resign itself to him; it dare venture itself in his hand and trust his word, and seek no more but how to please him. A heart thus composed goes readily and cheerfully unto all services, to do, to suffer, to live, to die, at his pleasure; and firmly stands to this, that nothing can separate it from that which is sufficient to it, which is all its happiness—the love of God in Christ Jesus.

That is indeed his love to us; but at the same time it includes inseparably the inseparableness of our love to him. For observe the things specified as most likely, if anything, to separate us—tribulation, distress: now these being endured for his sake, cannot have any likely visage of altering his love to us, but rather confirm us in it; but these shall not separate us neither by altering our love to him, by driving us from him, and carrying us into any way of defection, or denial of his name, and so cut us off from our union with him, and interest in his love; and that is the way wherein the weak Christian will most apprehend the hazard of separation. Now the apostle speaks his own sense, and would raise in his brethren the same confidence, as to that danger.

No fear; not one of these things shall be able to carry us away: these mighty waves shall not unsettle our faith, nor quench the flame of our love; we shall be victors and more, in all; but how? Through him that hath loved us.

This his love makes sure ours; he hath such hold of our hearts as he will not let go, nor suffer us to let go our hold: all is fast by his strength. He will not lose us, nor shall any be able to pluck us out of his hand.

Jesus Christ is the medium of this love, the middle link that keeps all safe together betwixt God and man, so close united in his personal nature, and the persons of men in and by him, to the Father. So here it is first called the love of Christ, and then in the close, the love of God in Christ; the soul first carried to him as nearest, but so carried by him into that primitive love of God that flows in Christ, and that gave even Christ to us as before. And this is the bottom-truth, the firm ground of the saints' perseverance, which men not taking aright, must needs question the matter, yea, may put it out of question upon their suppositions; for if our own purposes and strength were all we had to rely on, alas, how soon were we shaken!

So the love of God in Christ is not only here mentioned as the point of happiness, from which we cannot be removed, but as the principle of firmness that makes itself sure of us, and us of it, and will not part with us.

Now it is no pride in a Christian, but the truest humility, to triumph and glory in this. This is it that makes all sure: this is the great comfort, and the victory of the saints.

He that loved us, and bought us so dear, will not lightly slip from us; yea, upon no terms will he let us go, unless some stronger than he by force bereave him of us—which we know is impossible. He and his Father, who are one in themselves, one in their strength, and one in this love, are greater and stronger than all; and he that once overcame for us, always overcomes in us.

Thus he lets temptations and tribulations assault us, and this neither unargues his love, nor endangers his right to us; yea, it doth but give proof and evidence of the invincible firmness of both. He suffers others to lie soft, and sit warm, and pamper their flesh at leisure; but he hath nobler business for his champions, his worthies, and most of all for the stoutest of them; he calls them forth to honourable services, to the hardest encounters; he sets them on, one to fight with sickness, another with poverty, another with reproaches and persecutions, with prisons and irons, and with death itself: and all this while, loves he them less, or they him? Oh! no; he looks on and rejoices to see them do valiantly; it is the joy of his heart—no sight on earth so sweet to him; and it is all the while by his subduing, and in his strength, that they hold out in the conflict and obtain the conquest.

And thus they are more endeared to him by these services, and these adventures of love for him, and he still likewise is the more endeared to them. Certainly the more any one suffers for Christ, the more he loves Christ, as love doth grow and engage itself by all it does and suffers, and burns hotter by what it encounters and overcomes, as by fuel added to it: as to Jesus Christ, by what he suffered for us, we are the dearer to him, so he is to us by all we suffer for his sake.

Love grows most by opposition from others when it is sure of acceptance, and of mutal love in the party loved. Above all, this heavenly Divine love is strong as death, a vehement flame, and many waters cannot quench it; not all these that here follow one another, tribulation, distress, persecution, famine, nakedness, peril, sword; yea, in the midst of these, I say, it grows; the soul cleaves closer to Christ, the more attempts are made to remove it from him, though killed all the day long. The saints are as in a common butchery in the world, yet not only as sheep for the slaughter, but sometimes as sheep for the altar, men thinking it a sacrifice. They that kill you, says our Saviour, shall think they do God service; yet even this pulls not from him. They part with life: ay, why not? This life is but a death, and he is our life for whom we lose it.

All these do but increase the victories and triumphs of love, and make it more glorious: as they tell of her multiplying labours to that champion, they are not only conquerors, but more than conquerors, by multiplied victories, and they gain in them all both more honour and more strength; they are the fitter for new adventures, and so more than simple conquerors. We overcome, and are sure not to lose former conquests, but to add more, and conquer on to the end; which other conquerors are not sure of: oftentimes they outlive their own successes and renown, and lose on a sudden what they have been gaining a whole lifetime. Not so here: we are secured in the Author of our victories; it is through him that hath loved us; and he cannot grow less, yea, shall still grow greater, till all his enemies be made his footstool.

Having given the challenge, and finding none to answer, and that all, the most apparent, are in a most rhetorical accumulation silenced—tribulation, distress, persecution, famine, nakedness, peril, sword—he goes on confidently in the triumph, and avers his assurance of full and final victory against all imaginable power of all the creatures; neither death nor life, not the fear of the most terrible death, nor the hope or love of the most desirable life; and in the height of this courage and confidence, he supposes impossible enemies, angels, principalities, &c., unless you take it of the angels of darkness only; but if it could be possible that the other should offer at such a thing, they would be too weak for it. No sense of any present things, or apprehensions of things to come, not anything within the vast circle of the world above or below, nor any creature, can do it. Here sin is not specified, because he is speaking of outward oppositions and difficulties expressly, and because that is removed by the former challenge, Who shall accuse? That asserting a free and final acquittance of all sin, a pardon of the curse, which yet will never encourage any of these to sin that live in the assurance of this love. Oh! no; and these general words do include it too, nothing present nor to come. So it is carried clear, and is the satisfying comfort of all that Jesus Christ hath drawn after him, and united in his love.

It is enough: whatsoever they may be separated from, the things or persons dearest in this world, it is no matter, the jewel is safe, none can take my Christ from me; and I safe in him, as his purchase, none can take me from him. And being still in his love, and through him in the Father's love, that is sufficient. What can I fear? What can I want? All other hazards signify nothing. How little value are they of! And for how little a while am I in danger of them! Methinks all should look on a believer with an emulous eye, and wish his estate more than a king's.

Alas! poor creatures, rich men, great men, princes and kings, what vain things are they that you embrace and cleave to! Whatsoever they be, soon must you part; can you say of any of them, Who shall separate us? Storms may arise, and scatter ships that sail fairly together in fair weather: thou mayest be removed, by public commotions and calamities, from thy sweet dwellings, and societies, and estates. At last you must part, for you must die: then farewell parks and palaces, gardens and honours, and even crowns themselves; then dearest friends, children and wife, must be parted with. And what hast thou left, poor soul, that hast not Christ, but that which thou wouldest gladly part with, and canst not—the condemning guilt of all thy sins?

But the soul that is in Christ, when other things are pulled away, he feels little or nothing; he cleaves to Christ, and these separations pain him not. Yea, when that great separatist, death, comes, that breaks all other unions, even that of the soul and body; yet so far is it from separating the believer's soul from its beloved Lord Jesus, that, on the contrary, it carries it into the nearest union with him, and fullest enjoyment of him for ever.

SERMON XI.

Behold, the Lord's hand is not shortened, that it cannot save; neither his ear heavy, that it cannot hear: but your iniquities have separated between you and your God, and your sins have hid his face from you, that he will not hear.—ISA. lix. 1, 2.

OUR vain minds are naturally fruitful in nothing more than in mistakes of God; for the most part we think not of him, and when we do it, we fancy him according to our own affections, which are wholly perverse and crooked.

Men commonly judge it a vain thing to spend much pains and time in worshipping him; and if they are convinced in this, and tied to it by the profession of his name, then they think all religion is a shell of external diligences and observances, and count it strange if this be not accepted. In the former chapter we find this, in the prophet's contest with the people about their fasting, and their opinion of it; he cuts up their sacrifices, and lets them see what was within: the skin was sound and looked well, but being opened, the entrails were found rotten. And here he enters into another contest, against the latent atheism of their hearts; who, after their manner of seeking God, not finding him, and not being delivered, are ready to think that he either cannot or will not help, and rather rest on that gross mistake, than inquire into themselves for the true cause of their continuing calamities; they incline rather to think it is some indisposition in God to help, than what it truly is, a want of reformation in themselves that hinders it. It is not likely that they would say thus, nor speak it out in plain terms, no, nor possibly not speak it formally and distinctly within, not so much as in their thoughts; and yet they might have a confused, dark conceit of this.

Impenitency of men, in any condition, and particularly under distress, is from the want of clear apprehensions and deep persuasions of God, of his just anger provoked by their sin, and of his sweetness and readiness to forgive and embrace a returning sinner; his sovereign power, able to rid them out of the greatest trouble; his ear quick enough to hear the cries, yea, the least whispering of a humbled heart in the lowest deep of his sorrow; and his arm long enough to reach them, and strong enough to draw them forth. He that comes unto God must believe that he is, says the apostle. So certainly he that believes that, must come; it will sweetly constrain him: he cannot but come that is so persuaded.

In the words of these two verses, these two things appear; I. A sad condition, and, II. The true cause of it.

I. The *condition*, I think I have reason to call sad; it is God hiding his face that he will not hear. This may be the personal estate of his children, or the public estate of his church. From a soul he hides his face, not so much in the withdrawing of sensible comforts and sweet tastes of joy, but in a suspension of that lively influence of his Divine power, for raising the mind to the contemplation of him, and communion with him; and the returns of it appear in beating down the power of sin, making the heart more pure and heavenly, more to live by faith in Christ, to be often at the throne of grace, and to receive gracious answers. Now, when there is a cessation and obstruction of these and such like workings, the face of God is hid, the soul is at a loss, it seeks still, and cannot find him whom it loves. And in this condition it cannot take comfort in other things; they are too low. It is higher and nobler than to be satisfied or diverted with the childish things that men delight in that know not God. Set thee in a palace, and all delights about thee, and a crown on thy head; yet if his love has ceased on thy heart, these are all nothing without him. It was after David was advanced to his kingdom, and is in the Psalm of the dedication of his royal house, that he said, "Thou didst hide thy face, and I was troubled," Ps. xxx. 7. "All is dark, all the shining marble, and the gold and azure, lose their lustre, when thou art not here dwelling with me."

And thus too for the church, God is the light, the beauty, the life of it. Deck it with all this world's splendour, with all the dresses of pompous worship; these are not its genuine beauty. And they provoke him, who is its ornament (Jer. ii. 32), to depart. But give it the native purity and beauty of holy ministers, and ordinances well regulated, yet even that is but a dead comeliness, proportion and feature without life, when God is absent.

And for matter of deliverances and working for it, which is here the thing in hand, none can do anything in that, not the wisest nor the best of men, with all their combined wit and strength, when he retires and comes not forth, doth not show himself on the behalf of his people, and work for them.

We ought to inquire if this be not our condition at this time; hath he not hid his face from us? Are we not left in the dark, that we know not which way to turn us? Either we must sit still and do nothing, or if we stir we do but rush one upon another, as in darkness, contesting each to have the way, and yet when we have it given us, we know not well which way to go; as in this chapter, ver. 9, "We wait for light, but behold obscurity; for brightness, but we walk in darkness: we grope for the wall as blind, and stumble at noonday as in the night." By all debates little or no clearing of things is attained, but our passions are more inflamed, and parties are further off, the light of sound judgment gone, and with it the heat of love; instead of which that miserable, infernal heat, heat without light, mutual hatreds and revellings, both sides (verbally at least) agreeing in general terms, and yet falling out about modes and fashions of them. Desires and prayers we have presented, and see as yet no appearance of an issue, but further confusions, even "fasting for strife and debate."

And where are there any that look like persons to stand in the gap, lifting up holy hands, without wrath or doubting? Hearts are still unhumbled, and lives as unreformed as ever; new intestine troubles are most likely to arise, few or none laying it to heart, and with calm, lowly spirits mourning before God for it; Ephraim against Manasseh, and Manasseh against Ephraim, "and they both against Judah; and for all this his anger is not turned away, but his hand is stretched out still."

But generally men ought to be less in descanting one on another, and more in searching and inquiring each into himself: even where it may seem zeal, yet nature and passion may more easily let in the other; but this self-search and self-censure is an uneasy task, the most unpleasant of all things to our carnal self-loving hearts; but the heavy hand of God shall never turn from us, nor his gracious face turn towards us, till there is more of this amongst us.

Most say their prayers, and as they are little worth, they look little after them, and inquire not what becomes of them. But, my brethren, would we continue to call, and find favourable answers, we must be more within; the heart made a temple to God, wherein sacrifices do ascend: but that they may be accepted, it must be purged of idols, nothing left in any corner, though never so secret, to stir the jealousy of our God, who sees through all. Oh, happy that heart that is, as Jacob's house, purged, in which no more idols are to be found, but the holy God dwelling there alone as in his holy temple.

II. Much of all knowledge lies in the knowledge of causes, and in practical things much of the right ordering them depends on it; the true cause of a disease found out is half the cure. Here we have the miseries of an afflicted people reduced to their real cause; that which is not the cause is first removed. "Behold, the Lord's hand is not shortened," &c.

We are not only to be untaught this error, but to be taught the truth, that God is still the same in power and goodness, to keep up the notion of it in our hearts, so we may call in past experiences, and relations of God's former workings for his people, and that with much use and comfort. He that brought forth his people out of Egypt with an outstretched arm, can again deliver his people when at the lowest, Isa. l. 2, where the like words to these.

And in this belief we shall not faint in the time of deep distress, our own or the church's; knowing the unalterable, invincible, infinite power of our God, that all the strength of all enemies is nothing and less than nothing to his, their devices knots of straw. What is it that is to be done for his church, if her and his glory be interested in it? There remains no question in point of difficulty; that hath no place with him. The more difficulty, yea, impossibility for us or any human strength, the more fit for him: "Because it is hard for you, shall it also be hard for me?" saith the Lord in the prophet. And where Jeremiah uses that argument in prayer, he hath his answer returned in the same words, as the echo to the prayer, resounding from heaven, Jer. xxxii. 17, 27.

Men think it an easy, common belief, and that none doubt of the omnipotency of God. But oh! the undaunted confidence it would give to the heart, being indeed firmly believed, and wisely used and applied to particular exigencies. Men either doubt, or which, for the use of it, is all one, they forget, who the Lord is, when their hearts misgive them, because of the church's weakness and the enemies' power. Remember whose is the church—God's, and what his power is; and then see if thou canst find any cause of fear. Isa. xli. 14: "Fear not, thou worm Jacob, and ye men (few or weak, so the word is) of Israel, I will help thee, saith the Lord, and thy Redeemer, the Holy One of Israel." So Isa. li. 12, 13: "I, even I, am he that comforteth you: who art thou, that thou shouldest be afraid of a man that shall die, and of the son of man which shall be made as grass? And forgettest the Lord thy Maker, that stretched forth the heavens, and laid the foundations of the earth." Do but think aright on him, and then see if it be possible for thee to fear. All thy little doubts and despondencies of mind will fly and vanish away before one clear thought of thy God. Though the world were turning upside down, it shall go well with them that fear him.

And as this apprehension of God strengthens faith,

so it quickens prayer, it stirs thee up to seek to him for help, when thou knowest and rememberest that there it is. There is help in him, power enough, and no want of readiness. If we apply ourselves to seek him aright, his hand is as strong to save, and his ear as quick to hear as ever. And in this, that his ear is not heavy, is both signified his speedy and certain knowledge of all requests sent up to him, and his gracious inclination to receive them. Now these persuasions do undoubtedly draw up the heart towards him.

Again, as they strengthen faith and quicken prayer, they teach us repentance, direct us inward to self-examination, to the searching, and finding out and purging out of sin when deliverance is delayed; for we are sure it stops not on God's part, either shortness of his hand or dulness of his ear. Whence is it then? Certainly it must be somewhat on our side that works against us. So here you see the clear aim of it, "Behold, the Lord's hand is not shortened, that it cannot save; nor his ear heavy, that it cannot hear." What is it then that hinders? Oh! it is this, out of all doubt, "Your iniquities separate."

Old sins unrepented of, and new sins still added; this separates between you and God, for he is a holy God, a just God, hates iniquity; he will be sanctified in those that are near him, in them especially; their sin is greatened much by that relation. *Your* God, to sin against him so grossly, so continuedly, with so high a hand, and so impenitent hearts, not reclaimed by all his mercies, by the remembrance of his covenant made with you, and mercies bestowed on you, nor by the fear of his judgments threatened, nor by the feeling of them inflicted; no returning nor relenting, not even of his own people to their God. Sure, you must be yet more punished. "You only have I known of all the families of the earth; therefore will I punish you for all your iniquities." "I let others escape with many things that I cannot pass in you; you fast and pray, it may be, you howl and make a noise, but you amend nothing; you would be delivered, but do not part with one of your lusts, or wicked customs. It is that that is a huge wall betwixt us, betwixt me and your prayers, and betwixt you and my helping hand; and though I do hear and could help, yet I will not, till this wall be down; you shall not see me, nor find by any gracious sign that I hear you." This hides his face, that he will not hear.

This way God hath established in his ordinary methods with his people; though sometimes he uses his own privilege, yet usually he links sin and calamity together, and repentance and deliverance together.

Sin separates and hides his face, not only from a people that professes his name, but even from a soul that really bears his name stamped upon it. Though it cannot fully and for ever cut off such a soul, yet in part, and for a time, it may, yea, to be sure, it will separate, and hide the face of God from them. Their daily inevitable frailties do not this, but either a course of careless walking, and many little unlawful liberties taken to themselves, that will rise and gather as a cloud, and hide the face of God; or some one gross sin, especially if often reiterated, will prove as a firm stone wall, or rather as a brazen wall, built up by their own hands betwixt them and heaven, and will not be so easily dissolved or broke down; and yet, till that be, the light of his countenance, who is the life of the soul, will be eclipsed and withheld from it.

And this considered, will make us wary to sin; though we were sure not to be altogether separated from the love of God by it. Thou that hast any persuasion of that love, darest thou venture upon any known sin? Thou art not hazardless and free from all damage by it (if thou hast need of that argument to restrain thee); then, before thou run upon it, sit down and reckon the expenses, see what it will cost thee if thou do commit it. Thou knowest that once it cost the heart-blood of thy Redeemer to expiate it; and is it a light matter to thee? And though that paid all that score—nothing thou canst suffer being able to do anything that way—yet as unavoidable present fruit of it, it will draw on this damage; thou shalt be sure for a time, it may be for a long time, possibly most of thy time, near all thy days, it may darken much of that love of God to thee. It changes not in him, but a sad change will sin bring on thee, as to thy sight and apprehension of it; many a sweet hour of blest communion with thy God shalt thou miss, and mourn after him, and yet find thyself, and sighs, and tears shut out. Now this distance from God, and all this turmoiling, and breaking, and crying ere he appear again, consider, if any pleasure of sin can countervail this damage. Sure, when thou art not out of thy wits, thou wilt never make such a bargain for all the pleasure thou must make out of any sin, to breed thyself all this pains, and all this grief; at once to displease thy God, and displease thyself, and make a partition between him and thee. Oh! sweet and safe ways of holiness, walking with God in his company and favour: he that orders his conversation aright, he sees the loving-kindness of the Lord; it is shown to him; he lives in the sight of it.

But if any such separation is made, yet is it thy great desire to have it removed? Why, then, there is hope. See to it, labour to break down, and pray to him to help thee, and he will put to his hand, and then it must fall; and in all thy sense of separation, look to him that brake down the middle wall, Eph. ii. 14. There it is spoken of as betwixt men, Jews and Gentiles, but so as it was also between the Gentiles and God, separated from his people, and from himself; ver. 16, "To reconcile both to God in one body;" and ver. 18, "Through him we have access by one Spirit to the Father;" and then he adds, that they were no more strangers and foreigners, as the word is, but fellow-citizens.

Oh that we knew more what it were to live in this sweet society, in undivided fellowship with God. Alas! how little is this living in him understood, separated from sin and this world, which otherwise do separate from him; solacing our hearts in his love, and despising the base, muddy delights that the world admires; hoping for that new Jerusalem, where none of these walls of sin, nor any one stone of them, are, and for that bright day wherein there is no cloud nor mist to hide our sun from us!

Now for the condition of the church—know sin to be the great obstructor of its peace, making him to withdraw his hand, and hide his face, Isa. i. 15; Jer. xiv. 12. The quarrel stands; sin not repented and removed, oaths, and sabbath-breaking, and pride, and oppression, and heart-burning, still remaining. Oh, what a noise of religion and reformation; all sides are for the name of it, and how little of the thing! The gospel itself is despised, grown stale, as trivial doctrine. Oh, my beloved, if I could speak many hours without intermission, all my cry would be, "Repent and pray! Let us search and try our ways, and turn unto the Lord our God." Oh, what walls of every one's sin are set to it! Dig diligently to bring down thine own; and for these huge walls of public, national guiltiness, if thou canst do nothing to them more, compass them about as Jericho, and look up to Heaven for their downfall. Cry, "Lord, these we ourselves have reared, but without thee who can bring them down? Lord, throw them down for us: a touch of thy hand, a word of thy mouth, will make them fall." Were we less busied in impertinences, and more in this most needful work, it might do some good: who knows but the Lord might make his own way clear, and return and visit us, and make his face to shine that we might be saved?

MEDITATIONS,

CRITICAL AND PRACTICAL,

ON PSALMS XXXII. AND CXXX.

Translated from the Latin.

PSALM XXXII.

VER. I. *Blessed is he whose transgression is forgiven, whose sin is covered.*

IT would be a vain and ridiculous labour to light up a great number of lanterns and torches, and go out and look for the sun in the night; but when the appointed hour of morning comes, he rises, as of his own accord, and freely manifests himself by his own lustre to every beholder. The wisest of the heathens undertook to find out the Supreme Being, and the Supreme Good; but wandering through the devious ways of multiplied errors, they could attain to neither. Nor was it the least of their errors, that they sought them as two different things, when it is most certain that both are united in One. For it is the only and ultimate happiness of man to be united to that first and supreme Being and Good, from which he drew his original. But since there has so sad a distance and disagreement arisen between God and man, by our deplorable apostasy from him, there could not be the least hope of attaining that union, did not infinite goodness and mercy propose the full and free pardon of our offences. So that the true determination of this grand question about happiness, is evidently this—Blessed and happy is that man whose transgression is forgiven, and whose sin is covered. Innocence was the first means of obtaining happiness; which being once violated, the only plank that can save us after our shipwreck, is repentance and remission; which two things the whole Scripture assures us that the Divine wisdom has connected, as with an adamantine band. And this Psalm which is now before us, is a signal declaration of it, which since it inculcates so grand a topic of religion, may well be styled as it is, *Maschil*, a lesson of instruction: for, as St Augustine well observes, "That is instruction indeed, which teaches us that man is not saved by the merit of his works, but by the grace of God."

Blessed. Or, Oh! blessed man! or, Oh! the felicity of that man! and to denote the most entire, supreme, and perfect blessedness. He only has attained to complete felicity, whose numerous debts are remitted: though, far from being able to pay them, he could not so much as reckon them up; and blessed is he that knows it, as the proverb is, "No man is happy but he who thinks himself so."

The man whose iniquity is forgiven. As the word is *nesevi,* it might be rendered, Blessed is the man who is eased of the heavy burden of his sin. A burden indeed too heavy for the strongest man upon earth; a burden so dreadfully great, that God's angels are not able to stand under it: for many of the chief of them were pressed down to hell by it, and can rise no more. But though no giant on earth or in heaven could bear it, a lamb subjected himself to it: but it was a lamb without blemish and without spot, burdened with no load of his own sin, nor stained with the least spot of pollution. The Lamb of God, the Son of God, who is himself God, is he who takes away all the sins of the world, as one sin: taking the burden upon himself, he bears it and carries it away.

Covered. That sinners may more clearly apprehend, and more easily and firmly believe a thing which seems so difficult to admit as the free and full remission of sin, it is pointed out by various beautiful expressions and figures in the sacred Scriptures—washing, cleansing, blotting out, scattering like a cloud, entirely forgetting, casting into the bottom of the sea, and here by that of taking away and covering, and by that phrase which explains both, of not imputing them; and this expression of covering them, is with great propriety added to the former phrase of lightening the sinner of the burden of them: and that there may be no fear of their returning again, or coming into sight, when God has not only taken the heavy load from our shoulders, but for ever hidden it from his eyes, and the veil of mercy has taken it away; that great covering of Divine love which is large enough to overspread so many and so great offences. Thus it does, as it were, turn away the penetrating eye of his justice, which the most secret iniquity could not elude, did not he himself in pity voluntarily avert it.

But you will know what is our propitiatory, what the covering of the mercy-seat; even Jesus who was typified by that Caporeth in the temple, which the Septuagint renders a propitiatory covering; by which title our great Redeemer is marked out, Rom. iii. 25, as the same Hebrew word Caphar signifies both to cover and to expiate. But that the thing may be more evident and certain, the thought is repeated again in the second verse.

VER. 2. *Blessed is the man unto whom the Lord imputeth not iniquity, and in whose spirit there is no guile.*

Aben-ezra paraphrases it, of whose sins God does not think, does not regard them so as to bring them into judgment, reckoning them as if they were not; does not count or calculate them, or charge them to account; does not require for them the debt of punishment. To us the remission is entirely free, our Sponsor having taken upon him the whole business of paying the ransom. His suffering is our impunity, his bond our freedom, and his chastisement our peace; and therefore the prophet says, The chastisement of our peace was upon him, and by his stripes we are healed. Distracted creatures that we are, to indulge those sins which brought death upon our dear Redeemer, and to be so cold in our affections to that Redeemer who died for these sins!

This weighty sentence, of itself so admirable, Paul renders yet more illustrious, by inserting it into his reasonings on the topic of justification, as a celebrated testimony of that great article of our faith. "David," says he, "thus describeth the blessedness of that man, saying, Blessed is he whose iniquities are forgiven." So that this is David's opinion concerning true happiness: he says not, Blessed are those that reign over kingdoms; blessed those generals who are renowned for their martial bravery and success, though he himself had both these titles to boast of. It is not the encomiums of the greatest multitudes, nor the breath of popular applause, nor any other degree of human honour, which entitles a man to this character. It is not said, Blessed is he who ploughs many thousand acres of land, or who has heaped together mountains of gold and silver; not he who has married a beautiful and rich woman; nor blessed is he who understands the secrets of nature, or even the mysteries of religion: but, Oh happy man whose sins are pardoned, and to whom the Lord does not impute iniquity, and in whose spirit there is no guile; whose breast is full, not of feigned repentance, but of a fervent love of holiness, and hatred of sin! This makes life happy, nay, absolutely blessed: but alas! when we inculcate these things, we sing to the deaf. The ignorance and folly of mankind will not cease to pronounce the proud and the covetous happy, and those who triumph in successful wickedness, and who, in chase of these lying shadows of happiness, destroy their days and their years, and their souls.

"Alas," says the wise Roman, "how little do some who thirst most impatiently after glory, know what it is, or where to be sought!" which is equally applicable to that true calm and serenity of mind which all pursue, but few are able to attain. But as for us who enjoy the celestial instruction of this sacred volume, if we are ignorant of it, our ignorance is quite inexcusable, obstinate and affected, since we are wilfully blind in the clearest and most refulgent light. This points out that good which can completely fill all the most extended capacities of the human soul, and which we generally seek for in vain on all sides, catching at it where it is not to be found, but ever neglecting it where alone it is.

But is it then possible at once to be solidly and completely happy? You have not merely the ideas of it, but the thing itself, not only clearly pointed out, but most freely offered, with Divine munificence; so that if you do not obstinately reject the offer, it must be your own; and this happiness consists in returning to the favour and friendship of God, who most mercifully grants us the free pardon of all our sins, if we do with unfeigned repentance, and a heart free of all guile, not only humbly confess and lament them, but entirely forsake, and, with implacable hatred, for ever renounce them. All the names, all the variety of felicities, bliss, and happiness, are accumulated on that man who has known this gift of the right hand of the Most High, on whom this bright day of expiation and pardon has beamed. He easily looks down from on high on all the empty titles and false images of earthly happiness; and when he is bereaved of them all, yea, and beset on every side with what the world calls misfortunes and afflictions, ceases not to be happy. In sorrow he is joyful, in poverty rich, and in chains free; when he seems buried deep, so that not one ray of the sun can reach him, he is surrounded with radiant lustre; when overwhelmed with ignominy, he glories; and in death itself he lives, he conquers, he triumphs. What can be heavy to that man, who is eased of the intolerable burden of sin? How animated was that saying of Luther, "Smite, Lord, smite; for thou hast absolved me from my sins!" Whose anger should he fear who knows that God is propitious to him, that supreme King, whose wrath is indeed the messenger of death, but the light of his countenance is life; who gladdens all by the rays of his favour, and by one smile disperses the darkest clouds, and calms the most turbulent tempest?

But we must now observe the complication of a twofold good, in constituting this felicity; for we have two things here connected, as conspiring to make the person spoken of blessed: The free remission of sin, and the inward purification of the heart. This simplicity and guilelessness are a most excellent part of purity, opposed to all wickedness and arts of deceit; and, in common speech, that which is simple, and has no foreign mixture, is called pure. Pardon presents us as just and innocent before our Judge; and that sanctity is not to be regarded as constituting any part of our justifying righteousness before God, nor as only the condition or sign of our felicity, but truly and properly a part of it. Purity is the accomplishment of our felicity, begun on earth, and to be consummated in heaven: that purity, I say, which is begun here, and shall there be consummated. But if any one think he can divide these two things, which the hand of God has joined by so inseparable a bond, it is a vain dream. Nay, by attempting to separate these two parts of happiness, he will, in fact, only exclude himself from the whole. Jesus, our victorious Saviour, has snatched us from the jaws of eternal death; but to be delivered from the cruel tyranny and bonds of sin, and to be brought into the blessed liberty of the sons of God, was another essential part of our redemption; and if any one does not embrace this with equal alacrity and delight as the other benefit, he is a wretched slave of the most mean and ignoble spirit; and being equally unworthy of both parts of this stupendous deliverance, he will justly forfeit and lose both. And this is the epidemical Antinomianism of the Christian world, because they who labour under it have nothing but the name of Christians; they gladly hear of the pardon of their sins and the salvation of their souls, while they are averse to the doctrine of holiness and repentance. It is a disagreeable message, "a hard saying; and who can bear it?" But oh the incomparable charms of holiness! to be desired not only for the sake of other benefits, which come in its train, but especially for itself: so that he who is not transported with a most ardent love to it, is blind, and deserves to be thrust into the mill, to tread that uncomfortable round, and to grind there—deserves to be a slave for ever, since he knows not how to use liberty when offered to him. Shall the Stoic say, "The servant of philosophy is truly free;" and shall we scruple to assert the same concerning pure religion and evangelical holiness?

Now this freedom from guile, that fair simplicity of which the psalmist speaks, is deservedly reckoned among the chief endowments of a pure soul, and is here named instead of all the rest, as nothing is more like to that God who inspects the very heart; in nothing do we so much resemble him; and therefore it is most agreeable to him, because most like him. He is the most simple of all beings, and is indeed truth itself, and therefore he desires truth in the inward parts, and hates a heart and a heart, as the Hebrew phrase is to express those that are double-hearted. And how much our blessed Redeemer esteems this simplicity, we may learn from the earnestness with which he inculcates it upon his disciples, that they should be simple as doves, Matt. x. 16. We may also learn it from the honourable testimony he bears to this character in Nathanael, when he pronounces him, John i. 47, an Israelite indeed, in whom there is no guile; and especially from his own perfect example, as it is said of him, 1 Pet. ii. 22, He did no sin, neither was guile found in his mouth. Perhaps the psalmist might the more willingly mention this virtue, as he reflected with penitential distress on his crafty and cruel attempt of covering that adultery which he had committed with the veil of murder. But, however that was, it is certain that this guileless sincerity of heart holds the first rank in the graces that attend true repentance. It may be sometimes our duty to open our sins to men, by an ingenuous confession; but it is always our duty to do it to God, who promises to cover them only on this condition, that we do sincerely uncover them ourselves. But if we affect that which is his part, he will, to our unspeakable damage, do that which he had assigned to us. If we hide them, he will bring them into open light, and will discuss and examine each with the greater severity. "He," says Ambrose, "who burdens himself, makes his fault the lighter." "In proportion to the degree," says Tertullian, "in which you are unwilling to spare yourself, God will spare you." But what madness is it to attempt to conceal any action from him, from whom, as Thales wisely declares, "you cannot so much as conceal a thought!" But, not now to insist upon the impossibility of a concealment, a wise man would not wish to cover his wounds and his disease from that physician from whose skilful hand he might otherwise receive healing; and this is what the psalmist presently after, for our instruction, confesses.

VER. 3. *When I kept silence, my bones waxed old through my roaring all the day long.*

WHILE he suppressed the ingenuous voice of confession, the continually increasing weight of his calamity extorted from him a voice of roaring. "While I would not speak as it became a guilty man, I was compelled even to bellow like a beast." Nevertheless, this roaring did not move the Divine compassion, nor atone* his displeasure.

VER. 4. *For day and night thy hand was heavy upon me: my moisture is turned into the drought of summer.*

HITHERTO that voice was wanting, to which the bowels of the father always echo back, the voice of a son full of reverence, and ready to confess his errors; without which, cries and lamentations in misery are no more regarded in the sight of God than the howling of dogs; according to that expression of Hosea vii. 14, They have not cried unto me with their heart, when they howled upon their beds. A dog howls when he is hungry, or when he is lashed: but from a son, when he is chastened, acknowledgments of his fault, and deprecations of his father's displeasure, are expected; and when the son thus acknowledges his offence, and entreats for pardon, it is the part of a compassionate father to for-

* The word atone is here used in its original and etymological meaning—to make at-one.

give, and to spare. Nor do we indeed confess our offences to our Father, as if he were not perfectly acquainted with them; but we fly to him who requires we should repent, that he may not show us by punishment those things which we avoid showing to him by confession. "I confessed unto the Lord," says Augustine, "to whom all the abyss of my sin and misery lay open: so that if I did not confess whatever was hidden in my heart, I should not hide myself from him, but him from me."

Thy hand was heavy upon me. That hand, which when pressing is so heavy, when raising is so sweet and powerful (Ps. xxxvii. 24), and when scattering its blessings so full and so ample, Ps. civ. 28; cxlv. 16. He would not at first be humbled by the confession of his iniquity, and therefore he is humbled by the weight of the hand of God. Oh powerful hand! beyond all comparison more grievous than any other hand to press down, and more powerful to raise up. He who suppresses his sins without confessing them, "Conceals an inward wound, and burns with secret fire." Under the appearance of sparing, he is indeed cruel to himself; and when he has drunk down iniquity, and keeps it within, and it is not covered by the Divine forgiveness, it is like a poison which consumes the marrow in the midst of his bones, and dries up the vital moisture. It may, perhaps, occasion more present pain to draw out the point of the weapon which sticks in the flesh; but to neglect it, will occasion greater danger and more future torment: nor will the dart fall out by his running hither and thither, but, on the contrary, as the poet expresses it with respect to the wounded deer, it fixes deeper and deeper.

But the only healing herb that the sinner can find is true repentance and humble confession, not that which acknowledges sin in a few slight words, when it has hardly looked upon it and known it; but that which proceeds from a previous, true, and vivid compunction of soul, and is inseparably attended with renovation and purity of heart and life, so that, as comprehending this, it is sometimes put for the whole of repentance; 1 John i. 9, If we confess our sins, He is faithful and just to forgive us our sins, and to cleanse us from all unrighteousness. And so in the psalm before us,

VER. 5. *I acknowledged my sin unto thee, and mine iniquity have I not hid. I said, I will confess my transgressions unto the Lord, and thou forgavest the iniquity of my sin.*

TRUE and genuine repentance hath eyes as it were on both sides; it looks back on sins already committed, to lament them; it looks forward, and humbly resolves no more to commit what it has lamented. I entirely agree with him who said, "I had rather feel the inward working of repentance than know the most accurate description and definition of it." Yet how averse sinners are to this free though useful and salutary confession of sin, abundantly appears from this example of so great a man as the psalmist, when taken in this unhappy snare; for he confesses that he lay long senseless and stupid in that quagmire into which he was fallen, and that it was with difficulty that he was as it were racked into a confession, by such exquisite tortures both of body and mind. On the other hand the gracious readiness of the Father of mercies to grant pardon, is so much the more evident, as on the first word of confession that he uttered, or rather the first purpose that he formed in his mind, immediately the pardon, the full and free pardon, came down signed as in the court of heaven—I said, I will confess, and thou forgavest. Oh admirable clemency! It requires nothing but that the offender should plead guilty, and this not that it may more freely punish, but more liberally forgive. He requires that we should condemn ourselves, that so he may absolve us.

VER. 6. *For this shall every one that is godly pray unto thee in a time when thou mayest be found: surely in the floods of great waters they shall not come nigh unto him.*

THIS is the joyful message, this is the great doctrine of the gospel, which opens the first door of hope to sinners; that God is capable of being appeased, yea, that he is actually appeased; that he freely offers peace and favour to those who have deserted him, when they return to his obedience; that he runs forth to meet them, and to receive them with a most affectionate embrace; and having so importunately intreated our return, will not despise those who are treading back with prayers and tears the fatal path which their folly had chosen.

This is what we so frequently read in Scripture, that the Lord is gracious and very merciful, slow to anger and ready to pardon. If he were not such, who could dare to approach him? But seeing he is such a God, who should refuse or delay his return? Surely every rational and pious mind will without delay invoke so gentle and mild a Lord; will pray to him while he is exorable, or, as the Hebrew expresses it, in a time of finding; for he who promises pardon, does not promise to-morrow. There are certain times in which he may be spoken with, and a certain appointed day of pardon and grace, which if a man by perverseness despise, or by sloth neglect, surely he is justly overwhelmed with eternal night and misery, and must necessarily perish by the deluge of Divine wrath; since he has contemned and derided that ark of salvation which was prepared, and in which whoever enters into it shall be safe, while the world is perishing. Though all be one unbounded sea—a sea without shore—yet, as it is here said, the greatest inundation, the floods of deep waters, shall not come nigh unto him. The psalmist exhorts those that have experienced this to teach it, and determines himself to retain it with deep attention, and firm faith in his own mind, as in the following verse.

VER. 7. *Thou art my hiding place; thou shalt preserve me from trouble; thou shalt compass me about with songs of deliverance.*

Thou art my hiding-place; thou hast been, and wilt ever be so. Thou hast surrounded, and thou wilt surround me with songs of deliverance, even me who was so surrounded with clamours of sin. Where he further intimates that songs of praise are perpetually to be offered to God our deliverer. And, that these faithful admonitions and counsels may meet with greater attention and regard, he offers himself to us as a most benevolent teacher and leader.

VER. 8—11. *I will instruct thee and teach thee in the way which thou shalt go, &c.*

SEE to it, only that thou be tractable, and do not with obstinacy repel this friendly and wise counsel, as only capable of being governed by violence, like a mule or unbroken horse, which must be held in by bit and bridle.

But it is added, as the sum of all admonition, and the great axiom most worthy of regard, that many sorrows shall be to the wicked; the Septuagint renders it, many are the scourges of the sinner; but Mercy shall embrace those that hope in the Lord. And the Psalm concludes with this as the burden of it—Rejoice in the Lord, ye righteous; and shout for joy, all ye that are upright in heart. Truly, my dear friends, I have nothing further to wish for myself or you than that we may heartily believe these things, for then it will be impossible that we should not with open arms embrace true religion, and clasp it to our hearts; since nature teaches every one to desire happiness and to fly from misery. So that Epicurus himself would teach us to lay hold on joy and pleasure as the first and proper good. This, therefore, let us lay down as a certain principle, and ever adhere to it, that we may not, like brute beasts, remain in subjection to the flesh—that safety, and joy, and all happiness, is the property of him who is possessed of virtue, and that all virtue is comprehended in true piety; and let us remember what the prophet adds (according to the Greek translators), as the necessary consequence of this principle, that to the wicked there can be no joy.

PSALM CXXX.

VER. 1. *Out of the depths have I cried unto thee, O Lord.*

It is both a useful and pleasant employment, to observe the motions of great and heroic minds in great and arduous affairs; but that mind only is truly great which does in the most placid manner subject itself to God, securely casting all its burdens and cares upon him; in all the uncertain alterations of human affairs, looking at his hand, and fixing its regard upon that alone. Such the royal prophet David declares himself everywhere to have been, and nowhere more evidently than in this Psalm, which seems to have been composed by him. He lifts up his head amidst surrounding waves, and, directing his face and his voice to heaven, he says, Out of the depths, O Lord, do I cry unto thee. For so I would render it, as he does not seem to express a past fact, but, as the Hebrew idiom imports, a prayer which he was now actually presenting.

Out of the depths. Being as it were immersed and overwhelmed in an abyss of misery and calamities. It is indeed the native lot of man to be born to trouble, as the spark to fly upward. Life and grief are congenial; but men who are born again seem, in a redoubled proportion, to be twice born to trouble; with so many and so great evils are they laden, that they may seem sometimes to be oppressed with them. And if any think this is strange, surely, as the apostle expresses it, he cannot see afar off, at best he only looks at the surfaces of things, and cannot penetrate far into those depths. For even the philosophers themselves, untaught by Divine revelation, discovered admirable reasons for such dispensations of providence, and undertook in this respect boldly to plead the cause of God. "God (says the Roman sage) loves his own people truly, but he loves them severely; as the manner in which fathers express their love to their children is generally very different from that of mothers; they order them to be called up early to their studies, and suffer them not to be idle in those days when their usual business is interrupted; but sometimes put them on labouring till the sweat flows down, and sometimes by their discipline excite their tears; while the mother fondles them in her bosom, keeps them in the shade, and knows not how to consent that they should weep, or grieve, or labour. God bears the heart of a father to good men, and there is strength rather than tenderness in his love; they are therefore exercised with labours, sorrows, and losses, that they may grow robust: whereas, were they to be fattened by luxurious fare, and indulged in indolence, they would not only sink under fatigues, but be burdened with their own bulk." Presently after he quotes a remarkable saying of Demetrius the Cynic, to this purpose: "He seems to be the unhappiest of mankind who has never been exercised with adversity, as he cannot have had an opportunity of trying the strength of his own mind." To wish to pass life without it, is to be ignorant of one part of nature; so that I may pronounce thee to be miserable, if thou hast never been miserable. If thou hast passed through life without ever struggling with an enemy, no one, not even thou thyself, can know whether thou art able to make any resistance; whereas, in afflictions, we experience, not so much what our own strength is, as what is the strength of God in us; and what the aid of Divine grace is, which often bears us up under them to a surprising degree, and makes us joyful by a happy exit; so that we shall be able to say, My God, my strength, and my deliverer. Thus the church becomes conspicuous in the midst of the flames, like the burning bush, through the good will of Him that dwelt in it; and when it seems to be overwhelmed with waters, God brings it out of them, cleansed and beautified; he plunges it in the deep, and it rises fairer than before.

We will not here maintain that paradox of the Stoics, That evils which happen to good men, are not to be called evils at all; which, however, is capable of a very good sense, since religion teaches us that the greatest evils are changed, and work together for good. Banishment and poverty are indeed evils in one sense, that is, they have something hard and grievous in them; but when they fall on a good and brave man, they seem to lay aside the malignity of their nature, and the very sharpness of them excites and exercises virtue: by exciting, they increase it, so that the root of faith shoots the stronger, and fixes the deeper, and thereby adds new strength to fortitude and patience; and, as we see in this example before us, affliction does, by a happy kind of necessity, drive the soul to confess its sin, to fly as it were to seek its refuge under the wing of the Divine goodness, and to fix its hope upon God. This is certainly one great advantage which the pious soul gains by adversity, that it calls away the affections from earth and earthly things, or rather tears them away, when obstinately adhering to them. It is necessary that they suffer such hardships as these, as one expresses it, lest they should love this inconvenient stable, in which they are now obliged to lodge, as if it were their own house. It is necessary that they should perceive that they are strangers and foreigners upon earth, that they may more frequently, and with more ardent desire, groan after that better country, and often cry, Home, dear home!

This prayer contains those precious virtues, which, in a grateful temperature, render every prayer acceptable to God—faith, fervour, and humility. Faith, in that he prays out of the deeps; fervour, in that he cries: and again faith, as in the midst of surrounding calamities he does not despair of redress; fervour, as he urges it with repeated importunity. And, to complete all, humility expresses itself in what follows, where he speaks as one that felt himself sinking, as one who was plunged in a sea of iniquities, as well as calamities, and acknowledges he was so overwhelmed with them as to be unable to stand, unless supported by pure mercy and grace. "If thou, Lord, shouldest mark iniquities, who shall stand?" Thus here again, faith manifests itself more clearly, together with its kindred affections of hope and charity, which, like three graces, join their hands, and by an inseparable union support each other. You have faith in the 4th verse, there is forgiveness with thee; hope in the 5th, I wait for the Lord, my soul doth wait, and in thy word do I hope; charity in the 7th and 8th, where he does in a most benevolent manner invite all Israel to a communion of the same faith and hope; and in order to confirm them more abundantly, does in a most animated manner proclaim the riches of the Divine benignity. Such is the composition of this excellent prayer, which, thus compounded, like a pillar of aromatic smoke from myrrh, frankincense, and every other most fragrant perfume, ascends grateful to the throne of God.

Out of the depths. Oh! the immortal power of Divine faith, which lives and breathes in the midst of the waves in which it may be plunged, but cannot be sunk under any of the hugest billows; but raises itself, and the soul in which it resides, and emerges and swims above all. Whatever great things the Stoics may speak of their wise men, and whatever all philosophy may say of fortitude, it is Divine faith that truly and heartily performs all, by which the good man, though stripped of every help and comfort, wraps himself up as it were, not in his own virtue and strength, but in that of God; and hence it is that he cannot be conquered by any tyranny, by any threatenings, by any calamities of life, by any fear of death; for he leans upon Omnipotence.

Nor is this confidence of a pious soul an opinion fluctuating among the waves, or a light conjecture that it shall raise its head above them; but a certain, firm, and infallible assurance. That is a vulgar and weak word of comfort, "To-morrow may be better than today." But the language of Divine faith is stronger and firmer, even when deep calls unto deep, and most certainly determines that it will not be in vain: and, therefore, in the 42nd Psalm, not dubious and trembling, but with a steady voice, he silences all the noisy tumults of an agitated mind, and says, "Amidst all those tempests which rage about me, I am thinking of that hymn of praise which I shall pay to him for my deliverance, and for the happy exit out of all my sorrows." Though at present we have nothing in sight but darkness, and whirlwinds, and rocks, and the raging, foaming sea, let the skill and power of the great Pilot be opposed to all these. And what the psalmist says elsewhere of sailors, may evidently be applied to those that go down into this sea: they gain this by their dangers, that they see the works of this great Pilot in the abyss, and contemplate these wonders in the deep. And he who gives himself up to His care, and fixes his eye and hope wholly on him, though he be, or rather seem to be, shipwrecked, and lose all his goods, yet if he does not make shipwreck of faith, he loses nothing that is properly his own. Nay, when he is swallowed up in the abyss of death, he does not perish, but swims through it, to the further shore of eternity, where he finds a banquet, a palace prepared for him, and a kingdom that cannot be moved, but remains to endless ages.

I cried. Prayer is the natural and genuine voice of the children of God; and as the Latin word *oratio* properly signifies articulate speech, as it distinguishes man from other animals, so in this other signification it expresses that by which the godly are distinguished from the rest of mankind. It is the proper idiom of the citizens of heaven: others may recite some words of prayer, but they do not pray. As parrots and other birds, by the industry of their teacher, may learn to imitate human voices, yet they do not speak; there is something wanting in all their most skilful chattering, which is the very thing that is also wanting in the language of most that are said to pray, and that is mind and meaning, affections correspondent to the words, or rather to which the words may conform, as to their original cause, and of which they may be the true index and sign. The spirit of this world knows not how to pray, nor does a spirit of adoption and liberty know how to forbear praying. Yet affliction often adds vigour to prayers, how lively and assiduous soever they may have been before. Let it be so, that prayer is the natural language of believing souls, by which they daily address their heavenly Father; yet when they are pressed with any uncommon pain or danger, it is no less natural that this voice should be louder than ordinary, and should be raised into a cry; it is, indeed, the breath of faith and heavenly affections; and when they are vehemently pressed by any burden, and almost expiring under it, they breathe quicker than before, and with greater effort. Thus they who have been used to the greatest heights of daily devotion, yet in surrounding calamities pray more fervently and more frequently than ordinary, and this is to be numbered among the chief benefits attending afflictions; and it would surely be well worth our while to experience all the hardest pressures of them, if we may gain this; that the languor and sloth into which our minds are ready to sink, while all is calm and serene, may be happily shaken off by something which the world may call an unhappy event; that some more violent gust of wind may fan the sacred flame, that seems almost extinguished, and blow it up into greater ardour. It will be happy for us, that with the psalmist we should sometimes sink in deep waters, that so we, who in prosperity do but whisper or mutter out our prayers, may from the depths cry aloud unto him. Our vows are cruel to ourselves, if they demand nothing but gentle zephyrs, and flowery fields, and calm repose, as the lot of our life; for these pleasant things often prove the most dangerous enemies to our nobler and dearer life.

Oh! how true is that saying, "that faith is safe when in danger, and in danger when secure; and prayer fervent in straits, but in joyful and prosperous circumstances, if not cold and dead, at least lukewarm." Oh, happy straits, if they hinder the mind from flowing forth upon earthly objects, and mingling itself with the mire; if they favour our correspondence with heaven, and quicken our love to celestial objects, without which, what we call life may more properly deserve the name of death.

VER. 2. *Lord, hear my voice: let thine ears be attentive to the voice of my supplications.*

WE see that he was not only in earnest, which comparatively few that pray are, but that his desires were vehement, and kindled into a flame, which is the case of yet fewer. Nor is it wonderful, as we have elsewhere observed, that those petitions do not ascend which hardly go out, that go not forth from the depth of the breast, and therefore they rise not on high, but are born and die upon the lips. And if he who asks timorously, so much more he that asks with cold indifference, may seem to bespeak a denial.

It is not the much speaking and the vain repetition condemned in the gospel, to redouble the same words again and again, provided it be not from want of care and affection, but proceed from the vehemence and exuberance of it. The great apostle tells us, that he besought the Lord thrice; and the Lord of the apostle, and our Lord, prayed in the garden again and again, speaking the same words. He that pours out his words, inattentive to what he is about, seems to me to pray long if he utters but two sentences. Though his words be ever so few and well chosen, yet is he himself foolish and verbose. For what can be more foolish than the empty noise even of the best words, when they express nothing of the mind? But he who continues long in prayer, and urges the same petitions again and again, bursting out from the fervour of an inflamed breast, he, truly, prays in a vivid and solid manner, and in a manner most acceptable to God.

Hear me. The great Author of nature and of all things does nothing in vain; he instituted not this law, and, if I may so express it, art of praying, as a vain and insignificant thing, but endows it with a wonderful efficacy for producing the greatest and happiest consequences. He would have it to be the key by which all the treasures of heaven should be opened; he has constructed it as a powerful machine, by which we may, with easy and pleasant labour, remove from us the most dire and unhappy machinations of our enemy, and may with equal ease draw to ourselves what is most propitious and advantageous. Heaven and earth, and all the elements, obey and minister to the hands which are often lifted up to heaven in earnest prayer. Yea, all the works, and, which is yet more and greater, all the words of God obey it. Well known in the sacred Scriptures are the examples of Moses and Joshua, and, which James (v. 17) particularly mentions, of Elijah, whom he expressly calls a man subject to like infirmities with ourselves, that he might illustrate the admirable force of prayer, by the common and human weakness of the person by whom it was offered.

It is true, indeed, that our desires and hearts are open to God when our tongues are entirely silent, and that he has a paternal regard to all our concerns; nor do we utter our petitions to him, as if he were ignorant or negligent of our necessities and desires, for we well know that he sees and hears everything. It is also true that his counsels are all fixed and immovable; but it can by no means be inferred from these premises, that the business of prayer is vain and needless; and if any one would represent these things as superseding prayer, surely he deceives himself, and by all his reasonings would make out nothing, unless it were to convict himself of a vast ingratitude to the Divine munificence, and a most shameful unworthiness of so excellent a gift.

Ought not this intercourse of men with God by prayer to be most reverently and gratefully received and cultivated by all, and numbered among the chief favours of the Divine, and dignities of the human nature? And truly this, as much as anything that can be imagined, is a lamentable argument of the stupidity of man, in this fallen state, that such an honour is so little regarded. Opportunities of conversing with nobles or princes of the earth are rare and short; and if a man of inferior station be admitted to such a favour, he glories in it, as if he were raised to heaven; though they are but images made of the same clay with himself, and only set upon a basis a little higher than the rest: but the liberty of daily and free converse with the King of heaven is neglected for every trifle, and indeed is counted as nothing, though his very aspect alone fills so many myriads of blessed spirits above with full and perpetual felicity.

Again, is it not most reasonable to acknowledge, by this spiritual sacrifice of prayer, His infinite power and goodness, and that most providential care by which he governs all human affairs? And when our very being and life depend upon him, and all the comfort and happiness of life, how congruous is it to exhibit this sign and token of his holding us by the hand, and of our being borne up by him! Again, what sweeter lenitive of all those miseries with which life so continually abounds, can be invented, than this, to pour out all our care and trouble into his bosom, as that of a most faithful friend and affectionate Father? Then does the good man lay himself down to sleep with sweet composure, in the midst of waves and storms, when he has lulled al the care and sorrows of his heart to sleep by pouring out his prayer to God. And, once more, how pleasant is it, that these benefits, which are of so great a value both on their own account and that of the Divine benignity from whence they come, should be delivered into our hands, marked as it were with this grateful inscription, That they have been obtained by prayer!

Hear, O Lord. It is certain that the greater part of men, as they babble out vain, languid, and inefficacious prayers, so they seem to set a just estimate upon them, neither hoping for any success from them, nor indeed seeming to be at all solicitous about it, but committing them to the wind, as vain words, which in truth they are. But far be it from a wise and pious man, that he should so foolishly and coldly trifle in so serious an affair; his prayer has a certain tendency and scope, at which he aims with assiduous and repeated desires, and doth not only pray that he may pray, but that he may obtain an answer: and as he firmly believes that it may be obtained, so he firmly, and constantly, and eagerly urges his petition, that he may not flatter himself with an empty hope; for it cannot be that any pious and reasonable desire should be directed toward the throne of God in vain, since he has been pleased to assume it among his titles, that he is a God hearing prayer. And certainly, though the good man does not always obtain the very thing that he asks, yet pure and right petitions never ascend in vain; but he who presents them, either obtains the thing he asks, or receives, instead of what is pleasing, what is truly profitable, and, instead of the things that he wishes for, those that are upon the whole the fittest and best, and that in the fittest and best time.

But oh, how necessary is it that souls worshipping so pure a God, should be purged from all the earthly dregs of impure affections! Most true is that oracle of the psalmist, If I regard iniquity in my heart, the Lord will not hear my prayer. The hands must be washed in innocence before they can be lifted up to him with acceptance. Draw near to God, says the apostle James, and he will draw near to you; but in order to this, he subjoins, Cleanse your hands, ye sinners; and purify your hearts, ye hypocrites, or ye double-minded, who are the impurest of all. These things we only briefly suggest; but I beseech you, my dear charge, that ye embrace this divine study, that you labour to obtain this sacred art. Oh think! it is nothing unpleasant, nothing low and contemptible, to which you are now invited. There is nothing more delightful, nothing more sublime, than to meditate upon heavenly objects, to converse with God, and from thence to imbibe a contempt of this low and transitory world, to be raised above all perishing enjoyments, and to taste the prelibations of that celestial life itself.

But how accurately socver the precepts of this divine oratory may be delivered, none will effectually receive them, unless they are taught the skill by God himself.

We must pray that we may be able to pray, and draw as it were from that superior academy, that faculty of pure and pious speech which flies as with a swift, ready, and natural motion, to heaven from whence it came, and brings down with it the most precious gifts into the bosom of the person that utters it; and, by the way, it is a most certain truth, that the greatest blessings are much more easily obtained from the great God, who is so munificent in his gifts, than others of a meaner nature; so that it were an argument of a low and abject mind, not to ask something noble and excellent: covet earnestly the best gifts, in this sense. If we ask only things of a low and trifling nature, unworthy such a giver, he may answer, as a prince did, "These are not royal gifts;" but if we ask those things that are most precious and valuable—grace and glory, there will be no room to fear denial. If you who are evil know how to give good gifts to your children, how much more your heavenly Father!

VER. 3. *If thou, Lord, shouldest mark iniquities, O Lord, who shall stand?*

AMONG all the virtues which are necessary to offer up our prayers with acceptance, none ascend with greater velocity, and rise higher, than that very humility which causes them, as it were, to descend the deepest of all; nor is there any more indubitable argument of humility, than a conscience which groans under the burden of its own sin and guilt, among all the abyss of calamities, crying especially from this depth. And thus we see the psalmist, while he involves all other evils, how great soever they might be, under one common title, fixed upon this to expatiate upon it at large, If thou, Lord, shouldest mark iniquities, &c. Thus, if any one desire to mount more readily and more favourably from the depth of calamity, let him cry from his depth of profound humility, and plead a penitent sense of sin; for though of all imaginable depths, that of sin be the most remote from the most high and most holy God, yet the depth of the humble soul, depressed under the weight of sin, is nearest of all to the deep bowels of Divine mercy.

One might have been ready perhaps to imagine, from the vehemence with which he begins his address, and from his groanings, as it were, so thick and so short, that he was something of a bold petitioner, that he had some confidence in himself; that he presumed to knock as it were so often and so loud at the door of Divine mercy. But what he here adds plainly shows that this was far from being the case—"Hear me, O Lord, hear me; and I urge the request, because necessity presses urgently upon me. Not that I am, or judge myself to be, one who can merit thine assistance; but that I stand in such need of it, that, if it be not granted me, I must perish. So far am I from being, or appearing to myself, worthy of thy help, that, behold I am overwhelmed with sin more than with sorrows. It is free mercy that I invoke; and I beseech thee, that in order to thy hearing the voice of my prayer, thou wouldest not hearken to the cry of my sins. Wash away the one, that thou mayest graciously smile upon the other: for, If thou, Lord, shouldest mark iniquity, who could stand?" Intimating, that if he were drawn out of the other depths, yet if his sins continued unremitted, he could find no place on which to stand; yea, if it were possible for him in that case to fly away, and hide himself, yet he would rather plunge himself into these depths again, and would rather be, as it were, buried and lost in floods of the greatest calamities, than meet the more dreadful flame of the Divine anger and indignation.

But this humble acknowledgment of his own unworthiness is so far from being inconsistent with the pious confidence of prayer, that it is not only congruous, but even congenial to it, and inseparable, so as to be most agreeable to that great King whom it addresses. Humility and contrition of heart is often thought by men to be the mark of a low and abject mind, but nothing is more honourable in the sight of God. "He," says Augustine, "will bow down his ear, if thou dost not lift up thy neck." There is certainly no more efficacious method of supplicating and obtaining grace than to do it, if I may so speak, *sub formâ pauperis*, confessing and pleading our poverty. He finds the most easy access into the court of heaven, who meets the most frequent repulses on earth. Nay, if I may so express myself, the heavenly court sits and resides in him. The two chief temples and palaces of the great King are that thrice holy place in the third heaven, and the humble and contrite heart upon earth. The best manner of praying, therefore, is that which is made up of faith, fear, and humility. By the equal libration of these wings, the soul mounts on high, while that of fear does not sink too low, nor that of confidence rise too high. By these we are daily and hourly to soar to God; and care must be taken that these wings of the soul be not dragged down by excess, nor scorched by lust, nor clogged and glued together, as it were, by covetousness. But let us now a little more particularly see what this confession of the prophet was.

If thou, Lord, shouldest mark iniquity, O Lord, who shall stand? An uninstructed and incautious reader might perhaps imagine that the psalmist was here seeking for refuge in a crowd, and desirous of sheltering himself under the common lot of human nature. But the design of the sacred writer is far different from this. He confesses, that whatever he, or any other person, may imagine of his innocence, yet when the eye of the mind is directed inward in a serious and fixed manner, then he sees the sum and bulk of his sins to be so immensely great, that he is struck into astonishment by it; so that he finds himself beset on every side with armed troops, which cut off all possibility of escape, otherwise than by flying to Divine mercy. He sees himself overwhelmed with crimes, held at bay, as it were, by his sins on every side, which roar around him like so many savage creatures just ready to devour him. And he that does not see this to be his own case, is either almost blind, or lives abroad, and never descends into his own breast. Gross offences alone strike the eye of our fellow-creatures; but when we seriously consider that we have to do with an all-seeing Judge, who looks at once through every covering, and sees the most secret recesses of our hearts; who considers not only what may be concealed from men, but even from ourselves, so as most clearly to discover every the least stain and speck of our inmost soul, and whose infinite holiness must also abhor it,—is it possible that any one should be so infatuated, as still to retain a false and foolish conceit of his own innocence? They who daily and accurately survey themselves and their own hearts, though they may indeed escape many of those evils which the generality of mankind fall into; yet, in consequence of that very care and study, see so much the more clearly their own impurity, and contract a greater abhorrence of themselves, and a more reverent dread of the Divine judgments. And it is certain that the holier any one is, the viler will he be in his own eyes; and I may also add, the viler he is in his own eyes, the more dear, precious, and honourable will he be in the sight of God. They who bring the whole of their conduct, their deeds and their words, the glances of their eye, and all the inward workings of their affections, and examine them by the pure and strait rule of the Divine law, who feel how wavering and weak their faith is, how lukewarm their piety, how ardent their love of this world, how untamed the flesh, how unguarded the senses, how unbridled the affections, in prayer so light and so wandering,—they, I say, who perceive and reflect on this, with what poignant grief, with what overwhelming shame, must they be seized, and how earnestly and how justly will they cry out, If thou, Lord, shouldest mark iniquity, who shall stand?

There have been great disputes one way and another about the merit of good works; but I truly think, they who have laboriously engaged in them have been very idly, though very eagerly, employed about nothing; since the more sober of the schoolmen themselves acknowledge there can be no such thing as meriting from the blessed God, in the human, or, to speak more accurately, in any created nature whatsoever; nay, so far from any possibility of merit, there can be no room for reward any otherwise than of the sovereign pleasure and gracious kindness of God. But why should I enlarge here, when one single circumstance overthrows all those titles? The most righteous of mankind would not be able to stand, if his works were weighed in the balance of strict justice; how much less then could they deserve that immense glory which is now in question! Nor is this only to be denied concerning the unbeliever and the sinner, but concerning the righteous and pious believer, who is not only free from all the guilt of his former impenitence and rebellion, but endowed with the gift of the Spirit. The interrogation here expresses the most vehement negation, and signifies that no mortal, if called to the strict examination of Divine justice, without daily and repeated forgiveness, could be able to keep his standing, and much less could he arise to that glorious height. "That merit," says Bernard, "on which my hope relies, consists in these three things—the love of adoption, the truth of the promise, and the power of its performance." This is the threefold cord which cannot be broken.

VER. 4. *But there is forgiveness with thee, that thou mayest be feared.*

THIS is the genuine method of Divine grace; it first demands a mind void of all confidence in itself, that so it may be filled with a pure and entire trust in God. Yea, it seems that the riches and magnificence of Divine grace cannot communicate itself, when it is as it were straitened by the receiver; for since it is so great as to be able to fill everything, it requires a free and ample space in which to dilate itself. He who, in the first original of the newborn world, brought all things out of nothing, acts like himself in the regeneration and restoration of mankind to holiness. The Holy Spirit finds nothing but what is without form and void; and whoever of mankind perceives and acknowledges this to be his case, may be assured that the Spirit of God already begins to move upon him, to impregnate the face of the abyss; and then it is said concerning them, Let there be light, and there is light, even that light by which they see themselves unformed and dark, and destitute of everything that is good. It is a great sign of a soul beginning to emerge from its misery, to give up every hope of emerging from it, except that one which arises from free mercy alone; and in this sense it may truly be said, as it is by the poet, "The wretched find no safety but despair;" that is, in themselves, in their own righteousness or innocence, their own industry in fulfilling the law, or any expiation they can make for the breach of it. And what the apostle says of his own danger, may properly enough be applied to a confession of the soul, pressed under the burden of its own guilt: We had received the sentence of death in ourselves, that we might not trust in ourselves, but in God that raises the dead. The poet said with a great deal of justice, "That no sinner is absolved by himself," because he is, as it were, turned informer against himself; yet in another sense the sinner is absolved by that very self-accusation; and, sorrowing for his sins, is freed from the guilt of them; for it is not by any means to be conceived that any one can return into favour with God, unless he return to God; nor that any one can return to God unless he renounce every sin, which if he does, they are all entirely forgiven, and those which he eagerly desires to cast behind his back shall never rise up to condemn him to his face, before the tribunal of the Divine justice. This sentiment runs through all the evangelical discourses of the prophets, by which, as so many heralds, they call a rebellious people to return to the allegiance of God their supreme King: Return, ye backsliding children, and I will heal your backslidings. Yea, the very Fountain of Grace, the Lord of the prophets, who is himself the great Author and Sum of the gospel doctrine, as soon as ever he came forth to publish this grace, said, Repent; for the kingdom of heaven is at hand. Nor can any mind that is not fallen into utter madness and complete distraction, dream of a pardon, how ample and glorious soever, to be imparted to a sinner that will not repent or return: nor indeed can it so much as be wished. For, how unworthy would it be of the Divine Majesty and Wisdom, to throw away such precious graces on those who so obstinately despise them! But there is forgiveness with him. With him there is a treasure of mercy laid up, to be imparted most freely and richly to every humble sinner that applies to him for it. Nor is the dispensing grace in this way at all inconsistent with the riches and freedom of it, since the greatest sins and most aggravated crimes are absolutely forgiven, without any penalty or fine whatsoever imposed upon the offender; yet on this most reasonable and happy condition, that they who are thus received into the Divine favour should express their grateful acknowledgments for it, by love, obedience, and sanctity of life.

Neither is this forgiveness the less free and gracious because Jesus Christ as our Surety and Redeemer has paid the price of it, having been appointed for and destined to this great and arduous work by the Father. For, what does that great Father of mercies herein, but, in order to our complete discharge, by one certain and ever-to-be-admired way, satisfy himself of his own, by fastening his only begotten Son to the cross? The repository of this treasure is opened, the whole price is poured out at once, that great price of redemption, more precious than all the treasures in the world, or even the whole world itself. But they who anxiously debate the point, whether God could simply and absolutely pardon sin without any price, do but trifle; for, whatever may be supposed concerning that, who is there that will deny that this way of the salvation of men which God has chosen, is so full of stupendous mystery, and so illustrious, that nothing can be thought of more worthy the Divine Majesty, nothing sweeter, nothing more munificent with respect to unworthy man? So that it will appear Athanasius speaks very prudently when he says, "We ought not in this matter so much to consider the absolute power of God, as what is most advantageous to man, and what most worthy the Divine Being."

It was fit that our wise Creator should give us a law, and that law was both useful and pleasant to those who would carefully observe it; but when once violated, there would necessarily arise a fatal enmity between the law and transgressors, an enmity which would continually become progressive, and gather new strength in the progress. The law is inviolably safe in its own sanctity, dignity, and immortality; but we, by striving against it, what do we gain but iniquity, disgrace, and death? But that blessed and efficacious Intercessor came from on high; and certainly he was himself a Divine Person who could compose such a controversy, and who, joining by an indissoluble union his infinitely better with our miserable and mortal nature, did so, by a most wonderful method, render to the law all its accuracy of obedience, and to us, though guilty, impunity. And having thus made peace, he animates all that partake of this blessed peace, by his own new, pure, and divine Spirit, that they might not only endeavour diligently to observe the sacred precepts of the law, but might love them, and cordially embrace them; and, on the other hand, he hath tempered the severity of the law towards all those that are received into favour, that their diligent, pious, and affectionate observance of the law, though not entirely complete, should by our indulgent Father be most graciously accepted, even as if it were perfect; and so the honour of the Divine Legislator is secure among men, and his peace descends upon them; and this is what our text observes, There is forgiveness with thee, that thou mayest be feared.

It is well known that the fear of God is commonly used in Scripture to signify, not only the whole of his worship, but all pious affections whatsoever; and, consequently, the whole of true religion. And some translate the expression here, that thou mayest be reverently worshipped: and it is thus used with the greatest propriety. I speak of that fear, which is so far from denoting servile, hostile dread and terror which some might think of, that, on the contrary, it entirely excludes it, being properly a reverence tempered with love. Yet I do not think that we are to exclude all dread of punishment and vindictive justice; nay, I apprehend such a fear to be very necessary, even to those who most ardently love, so long as they live in the flesh, in order to tame and rein in the petulancy of it; yea, love itself places fear as a kind of bit and bridle to the flesh. Psalm cxix. 120, My flesh trembles for fear of thee, and I am afraid of thy judgments. Heb. xii. 28, 29, Let us serve God with reverence and godly fear: for our God is a consuming fire. This is the fear which is called the beginning of wisdom, and marked with other very high titles of honour in the sacred Scripture; without which, we can neither conceive the beginning of divine worship and true piety, nor pursue the improvement of it.

With thee is forgiveness, that thou mayest be feared: that men may not dread thee, and flee thee, as an inexorable judge and enemy; but may reverence, love, and serve thee, as a mild and gracious Lord, as a most merciful and loving Father. And this is that joyful message of the gospel to which sinners run, as soon as they hear and understand it, prostrating themselves with all humility at the feet of so mild a Lord, and so gracious a King. "For no one," as Ambrose says, "will think of repenting, but he who hopes for indulgence." And this is that which the great Messenger and Author of our salvation preached and set forth: Repent, says he; for the kingdom of heaven is at hand. You are not now pursued by wrath and vengeance, threatening utterly to extirpate you and cut you off; but the kingdom of heaven, the dispensation of love, mercy, and grace opens its bosom to embrace you, and freely offers you the full pardon of all your former rebellion. Behold the compassionate father meeting that prodigal son while yet afar off, on his return; and instead of chiding and upbraiding him, burying as it were not only all his sins, but even his very confession, as in a deluge of love, amidst the tenderest embraces, kisses, and tears. Make me to hear, says David, the voice of joy and gladness, that the bones which thou hast broken may rejoice. By that lamentable fall, he had as it were dashed himself against the rock of Divine justice, so that all his bones were broken; but what a voice of joy and gladness is that which should restore full soundness and strength to bones which had as it were been crushed and shattered to pieces! Surely it is no other voice than that so often used by our Saviour in the gospel, Son, be of good cheer; thy sins are forgiven thee. That was the grace, softer than oil, sweeter than roses, which flowed from his lips into the sinner's wounds, and being poured into the contrite heart, not only heals but blesses it, yea, and marks it out for eternal blessedness. But, alas! the greater part of sinners sleep in their misery, and though their distempers are mortal, feel them not. It is therefore no great wonder that his grace, this precious, this invaluable remedy, is despised by them. But oh! how sweet is the voice of pardon to a soul groaning under the burden of sin!

But, as one well expresses it, "He that has never known discomfort, knows not what consolation means.

Men of this world, entangled in the cares of life, and in its crimes, insensible of misery, attend not to mercy." But if any who imagine themselves partakers of this forgiveness do not at the same time feel their hearts struck with a pious fear of the Divine Majesty, let them know that their joys are self-invented dreams, since it is for this very end that there is forgiveness with God, even that he may be feared.

In the remainder of this Psalm the author asserts his confidence in God, and labours to confirm and establish that of all true believers.

VER. 5—8. *I wait for the Lord, my soul doth wait, and in his word do I hope. My soul waiteth for the Lord more than they that watch for the morning: I say, more than they that watch for the morning. Let Israel hope in the Lord: for with the Lord there is mercy, and with him is plenteous redemption. And he shall redeem Israel from all his iniquities.*

I wait for the Lord. With thee is mercy. They who heartily believe this, are drawn by that sweet and amiable force, and desire to be partakers of it. And certainly there is no true faith in the doctrine of salvation, unless it be attended with this magnetic force, by which it draws the soul to God. One would think it would be impossible, where this effect is not produced, that there should be so much as an historical faith; and surely, it is contrary to, and inconsistent with, the rational nature, to see so desirable and excellent a good laid down as it were before us, and freely offered, without running most freely to embrace it, with open arms and an ardent impetuosity of soul.

When a philosopher was asked, why that which is fair attracts our love? he answered, "It is the question of a blind man." Well then might the psalmist, when contemplating the Divine goodness, represent himself as transported with its charms, as though he said, "It is nothing earthly, nothing mortal, that is the object of my wish; my soul hangs on the Lord alone; it thirsts for thee, and till it arrives at the enjoyment of thee, it will still be waiting. Hasten, Lord, to support and comfort me, for I am sick with love; nor is there anything in heaven or earth besides thee, O Lord, which can satiate or delight this soul of mine, pierced through as it were with this sacred passion. And though a heart which loves like mine must find a delay grievous, yet unshaken hope shall alleviate that sickness of the soul. Just as they that watch for the morning, however they may be afflicted with the darkness and coldness of the night, are constantly supported with the assured hope that the dawn will come, and the day arise in all its glory."

Nor does the psalmist envy others their share in those felicities which arise from love and hope; on the contrary, with a cheerful and liberal mind, he invites all to this immense ocean of riches, not shut up, but free to all: Let Israel hope in the Lord. And, lest the confluence of such vast numbers should suggest any fears of straitness and want, he confidently declares that there is wealth enough, and more than enough, to supply all their necessities; for with the Lord, says he, there is mercy, and with him plenteous redemption; grace rich and copious enough to support all sinners, and to forgive all sins; and all that apply to it shall infallibly find that he redeems Israel from all his iniquities. The eye of faith is by no means evil, but bright and sparkling with unbounded charity; it wishes all good to all, and, above all, wishes them a beatific union with the Supreme and Infinite Good. As in that kingdom of glory there is no malignity, no envy, because there can be no straitness, but, according to that emphatical saying of our blessed Saviour, there are many mansions, there is boundless space, and the seats of pious souls are not marked out in any narrow boundaries, but in an ample court; so even in the previous kingdom and banquet of grace, our heavenly Father's house is magnificent, both on account of its amplitude and the rich provision which it contains.

Let me beseech you, therefore, strictly to examine your own souls, inquire what it is that they chiefly wish, hope, and desire; whether they give chace as it were to every painted fly; whether, forsaking the fountain of living waters, they are digging for themselves cisterns of clay, and these leaky too, with great and unprofitable labour. Oh! wretched deceitfulness of every earthly hope, which mocks and deludes us so much the more in proportion to the extravagance of its promises. Blessed are they, and only they, who fix their eyes and their souls above, and say with the psalmist, Lord, I wait on thee, my soul does wait, and in thy word do I trust; and as elsewhere, And now, Lord, what wait I for? my hope is in thee. Happy they who have quitted all those low desires and pursuits, which are unworthy of a generous and immortal spirit, and have fixed their love on one, whose heart and hopes are set upon that one, in whom all things excellent meet and centre. A cheerful joy always shines on their face; nor do their cheeks glow with the shame of repulse and disappointment. While we are wandering hither and thither, in the vicious and perplexed pursuit of flattering objects, what frequent lamentation, what fond complaint of delusive fortune, what crowds of fears and cares divide the mind, and hurry it now one way, and now another! But when we fix our hope and our heart on the only support, on the only true and all-sufficient good, all is safe, and the soul treads firm, as it were, while the whole globe trembles. Let external things be borne this way or that, there is peace within: nor when all methods have been examined, can any other be found for the establishment of the mind, than that it should lay all its stress upon the one immovable and immutable Rock.

EXPOSITORY LECTURES

ON PSALM XXXIX.

LECTURE I.

VER. 1. *I said, I will take heed to my ways, that I sin not with my tongue: I will keep my mouth with a bridle, while the wicked is before me.*

CERTAINLY it is a high dignity that is conferred upon man, that he may, as freely and frequently as he will, converse with Him that made him, the great King of heaven and earth. It is indeed a wonder that God should honour poor creatures so much; but it is indeed no less strange that men having so great privileges, the most part of them do use them so little. Seldom do we come to him in times of ease. And when we are spurred to it by afflictions and pains, commonly we try all other means rather than this, that is the alone true and unfailing comfort. But such as have this way of laying their pained head and heart in his bosom, they are truly happy, though in the world's language they be never so miserable.

The Psalm consists of two parts; his silence to men, and his speech to God; and both of them are set with such sweet notes of music, though they be sad, that they deserve well to be committed, as in the title, To the Chief Musician.

I said, I will take heed to my ways. It was to himself that he said it; and it is impossible for any other to prove a good or a wise man, without much of this kind of speech to himself. It is one of the most excellent and distinguishing faculties of a reasonable creature, much beyond vocal speech, for in that some birds may imitate us; but neither bird nor beast have anything of this kind of language, of reflecting or discoursing with itself. It is a wonderful brutality in the greatest part of men, who are so little conversant in this kind of speech, though framed for it; and which is not only of itself excellent, but of continual use and advantage; but it is a common evil among men, to go abroad, and out of themselves, which is a madness and true distraction. It is true a man hath need of a well-set mind, when he speaks to himself; for otherwise he may be worse company to himself than if he were with others; but he ought to endeavour to have a better with him, to call in God to his heart to dwell with him. If thus we did, we should find how sweet this were to speak to ourselves, by now and then intermixing our speech with discourses unto God. For want of this, the most part not only lose their time in vanity, but do carry in heaps of that vanity to the stock which is in their own hearts, and do converse with that in secret, which is the greatest and the deepest folly in the world.

Other solitary employments, as reading the disputes and controversies that are among men, are things not unuseful, yet all turns to waste if we read not our own heart, and study that; this is the study of every holy man, and between this and the consideration of God, he spends his hours and endeavours. Some have recommended the reading of men more than books: but what is in the one, or both of them, or all the world beside, without this? A man shall find himself out of his proper business, if he acquaint not himself with this, to speak much with God and with himself concerning the ordering of his own ways.

It is true, it is necessary for some men, in some particular charges and stations, to regard the way of others; and besides, something also there may be of a wise observing others, to improve the good and evil we see in them, to our own advantage, and bettering our own ways, looking on them to make the repercussion the stronger on ourselves: but, except it be out of charity and wisdom, it flows either from uncharitable malice or else a curious and vain spirit, to look much and narrowly into the ways of others, to know the manner of living of persons about us, and so to know everything but ourselves; like travellers that are well seen in foreign and remote parts, but strangers in the affairs of their own country at home. The check that Christ gave to Peter is due to such, What is that to thee? follow thou me, John xxi. 22, "Look thou to thine own feet, that they be set in the right way." It is a strange thing that men should lay out their diligence abroad to their loss, when their pains might be bestowed to their advantage nearer at hand, at home within themselves.

This, that the psalmist speaks of here, taking heed to his ways, as it imports his present diligence, so also it hath in it a reflection on his ways past, and these two do mutually assist one another; for he shall never regulate his own ways before him, that has not wisely considered his ways past; for there is wisdom gathered from the observation of what is gone, to the choosing where to walk in time to come, to see where he is weakest, and lies exposed to the greatest hazard, and there to guard. Thus David expresses it in another Psalm, I thought on my ways, and turned my feet unto thy testimonies, Psal. cxix. 59. And this should be done not only in the great change of one's first conversion from sin, but this double observance still continued every day, looking to his rule, and laying that rule to his way, and observing where the baulk and nonconformity to the rule is, and renewing his repentance for that, and amending it the next day, that still the present day may be the better for yesterday's error.

And surely there is much need of this, if we consider how we are encompassed about with hazards and snares, and a variety of temptations, and how little we have, either of strength to overcome, or wisdom to avoid them, especially they being secretly set and unseen (which makes them the more dangerous) everywhere in the way in which we must walk, and even in those ways where we least think. Everywhere does the enemy of our souls lay traps and snares for us; in our table, in our bed, in our company and alone. If the heart be earthly and carnal, there is the snare of riches and gains, or pleasures; and if they delight in spiritual things, that walk is not exempted neither, there are snares of doubtings, presumption, and pride; and in converse of one Christian with another, where spiritual affection hath been stirred, it turns often to carnal passions, as the apostle says of the Galatians, They begin in the Spirit, and end in the flesh, Gal. iii. 3.

This observing and watching, as it is needful, so it is a very delightful thing, though it will be hard and painful to the unexperienced, to have a man's actions and words continually curbed, so that he cannot speak or do what he would: these are fetters and bonds; yet to those that know it, it is a pleasure to gain experience, and to be more skilled in preventing the surprises of our enemies, and upon that to have something added to our own art, and to be more able to resist upon new occasions, and to find ourselves every day outstripping ourselves. That is the sweetest life in the world, the soul to be dressing itself for the espousals of the Great King, putting on more of the ornaments and beauties of holiness; that is our glory, to be made conformable to the image of God and of Jesus Christ. If an image had sense, it would desire nothing so much as to look on the original whence it received its name, and to become more and more like it: so it is the pleasure of renewed souls to be looking on him, and so growing daily more like him, whose living image they are, and to be fitting themselves for that day of glory, wherein they shall be like him in the perfection they are capable of; and this makes death more pleasant than life to the believer. That which seems so bitter to the most of men, is sweetened to them most wonderfully. The continual observance of a man's ways, keeping a watch continually over them, this casts a light upon the dark passage of death, which is at the end of that walk, and conveys him through to the fulness of life: so that man, who observes himself and his ways through his life, hath little to do in examining them when he comes to die. That is a piece of strange folly, that we defer the whole, or a great part, of our day's work to the twilight of the evening, and are so cruel to ourselves, as to keep the great load of our life for a few hours or days, and for a pained sickly body. He who makes it his daily work to observe his ways, is not astonished when that day comes, which long before was familiar to him every day.

That I sin not with my tongue. It is the wise man's advice, Keep thy heart with all diligence, or above all keeping; and he gives the satisfying reason of it, for out of it are the issues of life, Prov. iv. 23. Such as the spring is, so will the streams be; the heart is the spring from whence all the natural life and vital spirits flow through the body, and, in the Scripture sense, it is the spring of all our actions and conversation; for it sends out emissaries through all, through the eye, hand, and all the senses and organs of the body, but through none more constantly and abundantly than the tongue: and therefore Solomon, after these words, immediately adds, Put away from thee a froward mouth, and perverse lips put far from thee. The great current of the heart runs in that channel: for it is the organ of societies, and is commonly employed in all the converse of men; and we can still, when all the other members are useless, use our tongues in regretting their unfitness for their offices. Thus David here, as it seems under some bodily sickness, labours to refrain his tongue; and, lest it should prove too strong for him, he puts a curb upon it. Though it did not free him from inward frettings of his heart, yet he lays a restraint upon his tongue, to stay the progress of sin, that grows in vigour by going out, and produces and begets sin of the same kind in the hearts and mouths of others, when it passes from the heart to the tongue. The apostle James does amply and excellently teach the great importance of ordering the tongue in all a Christian's life; but we are ever learning and never taught. We hear how excellent a guard this is to our lives, to keep a watch over our tongue; but I fear few of us gain the real advantage of this rule.

It is a lamentable thing, that there is nothing, for the most part, in common entertainments and societies of men together, but refuse and trash, as if their tongues were given them for no other end but to be their shame, by discovering their folly and weakness. As is likewise impatient speech in trouble and affliction, which certainly springs from an unmortified spirit, that hath learned nothing of that great lesson of submission to the will of God. But for all the disorders of the tongue, the remedy must begin at the heart: purge the fountain, and then the streams will be clean; keep thy heart, and then it will be easy to keep thy tongue.

It is a great help in the quality of speech, to abate in the quantity; not to speak rashly, but to ponder what we are going to say, Set a watch before the door of thy lips, Psal. cxli. 3. He bids us not build it up like a stone wall, that nothing go in or come out: but he speaks of a door, which may be sometimes open, ofttimes shut, but withal to have a watch standing before it continually. A Christian must labour to have his speech as contracted as can be, in the things of this earth; and even in divine things our words should be few and wary. In speaking of the greatest things, it is a great point of wisdom not to speak much; that is David's resolution, to keep silence, especially before the wicked, who came to visit him, probably, when he was sick: while they were there, he held a watch before his lips, to speak nothing of God's hand on him, lest they should have mistaken him; and a man may have some thoughts of divine things, that were very impertinent to speak out indifferently to all sorts, even of good persons. This is a talkative age, and people contract a faculty to speak much in matters of religion, though their words for the most part be only the productions of their own brain, little of these things in their hearts. Surely these kind of speeches are as bad as any, when holy things are spoken of with a notional freedom, where there is nothing but empty words. They who betake themselves to solitude, choose the best and easiest part, if they have a warrant so to do; for this world is a tempestuous sea, in which there are many rocks, and a great difficulty it is to steer this little helm aright amidst them: however, the apostle James makes it a great character of a Christian's perfection, If any man offend not in word, the same is a perfect man, chap. iii. ver. 2. But where is that man? Seeing we find men generally, and, most of all, ourselves, so far from this, it cannot choose but work this, to stir up ardent desires in us to be removed to that blessed society, where there shall be never a word amiss, nor a word too much.

LECTURE II.

VER. 2—5. *I was dumb with silence, I held my peace, even from good; and my sorrow was stirred. My heart was hot within me, while I was musing the fire burned: then spake I with my tongue, Lord, make me to know mine end, and the measure of my days, what it is; that I may know how frail I am. Behold, thou hast made my days as an handbreadth; and mine age is as nothing before thee: verily every man at his best state is altogether vanity. Selah.*

Among the rest of this holy man's troubles, this was one, that the wicked did reproach him. This is a sharp arrow, that flies thick in the world. It is one of the sharpest stings of poverty, that as it is pinched with wants at home, so it is met with scorn abroad. It is reckoned among the sharp sufferings of holy men, Heb. xi., that they suffered bitter mockings. Now, men commonly return these in the same kind, that is, by the tongue, whereof David is here aware; he refrains himself even from good, not only from his just defence, but even from good and pious discourses. We do so easily exceed in our words, that it is better sometimes to be wholly silent, than to speak even that which is good; for our good borders so near upon evil, and so easy is the transition from the one to the other, that though we begin to speak of God and good things with a good intention, yet quickly run we into another channel; passion and self having stolen in, turn us quite from the first design of our speech; and this chiefly in disputes and debates about religion, wherein, though we begin with zeal for God, yet oft-times in the end we testify nothing but our own passion, and sometimes we do lie one against another in defence of what we call the truth.

It cannot be denied, that to a holy heart it is a great violence to be shut up altogether from the speech of God. It burns within, especially in the time of affliction, as was the case of Jeremiah: Then I said, I will not make mention of him, nor speak any more in his name: but his word was in my heart as a burning fire shut up in my bones; and I was weary with forbearing, and could not stay, Jer. xx. 9; so it is here with David; therefore he breaks out: the fire burns upwards, and he speaks to God.

Let this be our way, when we cannot find ease among men, to seek it in God; he knows the language of his children, and will not mistake it; yea, where there may be somewhat of weakness and distemper, he will bear with it. In all your distresses, in all your moanings, go to him, pour out your tears to him; not only fire, but even water, where it wants a vent, will break upward. These tears drop not in our own lap, but they fall on his, and he hath a bottle to put them in; if ye empty them there, they shall return in wine of strong consolation.

Ver. 4. Now David's request is, *Lord, make me to know mine end, and the measure of my days, what it is; that I may know how frail I am.* In which he does not desire a response from God, about the day of his death, but instruction concerning the frailty and shortness of his life: but did not David know this? Yes, he knew it, and yet he desires to know it. It is very fit we ask of God that he would make us to know the things that we know; I mean, that what we know emptily and barely, we may know spiritually and fruitfully; if there be any measure of this knowledge, that it may increase and grow more. We know that we are sinners but that knowledge commonly produces nothing but cold, dry, and senseless confusion; but the right knowledge of sin would prick our hearts, and cause us to pour them out before the Lord. We know that Jesus is the Saviour of sinners; it were fit to pray that we knew more of him, so much of him as might make us shape and fashion our hearts to his likeness. We know we must die, and that it is no long course to the utmost period of life, yet our hearts are little instructed by this knowledge: how great need have we to pray this prayer with David here, or that with Moses, Teach us to number our days, that we may apply our hearts unto wisdom, Psal. xc. 12. Did we indeed know and consider how quickly we shall pass from hence, it were not possible for us to cleave so fast to the things of this life, and, as foolish children, to wade in ditches, and fill our laps with mire and dirt, to prefer base earth and flesh to immortality and glory.

That I may know how frail I am. Most part of men are foolish, inconsiderate creatures, like unto the very beasts that perish, Psal. xlix. 12, only they are capable of greater vanity and misery: but, in as irrational a way, they toil on and hurry themselves in a multitude of business, by multitudes of desires, fears, and hopes, and know not whither all tends. But one well-advised thought of this thing would temper them in their hottest pursuits, if they would but think how frail they are, how vain and passing things, not only these their particular desires and projects are, but they themselves, and their whole life. David prays that he may know his end; and his prayer is answered, Behold, thou hast made my days as an handbreath, ver. 5. If we were more in requests of this kind, we should receive more speedy and certain answers. If this be our request, to know ourselves, our frailties and vanity, we should know that our days are few and evil, both the brevity and vanity of them.

Ver. 5. *Thou hast measured out my days as an handbreadth.* That is one of the shortest measures; we need not long lines to measure our lives by, each one carries a measure about with him, his own hand, that is the longest and fullest measure. It is not so much as a span: that might possibly have been the measure of old age in the infancy of the world, but now it is contracted to an handbreadth, and that is the longest; but how many fall short of that! Many attain not to a fingerbreadth; multitudes pass from the womb to the grave; and how many end their course within the compass of childhood!

Whether we take this handbreadth for the fourscore years, that is ordinarily the utmost extent of man's life in our days, or for the four times of our age, in which we use to distinguish it, childhood, youth, manhood, and old age; there are great numbers we see take up their lodging ere they come near the last of any of these, and few attain to the utmost border of them. All of us are but a handbreadth from death, and not so much; for many of us have passed a great part of that handbreadth already, and we know not how little of it is behind. We use commonly to divide our lives by years, months, weeks, and days, but it is all but one day; there is the morning, noon, afternoon, and evening: Man is as the grass that springs in the morning, Psal. xc. 5. As for all the days that are past of our life, death hath them rather than we, and they are already in its possession: when we look back on them, they appear but as a shadow or dream; and if they be so to us, how much more short are they in the sight of God! So says David here, when I look on thee and thy eternity, mine age is as nothing before thee; what is our life, being compared to God, before whom a thousand years are but as one day, and less, like yesterday when it is past, and that is but a thought! The whole duration of the world is but a point in respect of eternity, and how small a point is the life of man, even in comparison with that!

The brevity of our life is a very useful consideration; from it we may learn patience under all our crosses and troubles; they may be shorter than life, but they can be no longer. There are few that an affliction hath lain on all the days of their life; but though that were the case, yet a little time, and how quickly is it done! While thou art asleep, there is a cessation of thy trouble; and when awake, bemoaning and weeping for it, and for the sin that is the cause of it, in the mean time it is sliding away. In all the bitter blasts that blow on thy face, thou, who art a Christian indeed, mayest comfort thyself in the thought of the good lodging that is before thee. To others it were the greatest comfort, if their afflictions in this life were lengthened out to eternity.

Likewise, this may teach us temperance in those things that are called the good things of this world. Though a man had a lease of all those fine things the world can afford for his whole life (which yet never any man that I know of had), what is it? a feigned dream of an hour long. None of these things, that now he takes so much delight in, will accompany the cold lump of clay to the grave. Within a little while, those that are married and rejoice shall be as if they rejoiced not, 1 Cor. xii. 29, nor ever had done it; and if they shall be so quickly, a wise man makes little difference, in these things, betwixt their presence and absence.

This thought should also teach us diligence in our business. We have a short day, and much to do: it were fit to be up early, to remember our Creator in the days of our youth; and ye that are come to riper years, be advised to lay hold on what remains, ye know not how little it is.

The more you fill yourselves with the things of this life, the less desires you will have after those rivers of pleasures that are at God's right hand; those shall never run dry, but all these other things shall be dried up within a little space; at the furthest, when old age and death come, if not sooner. And on the other side, the more we deny ourselves the sensual enjoyments of a present world, we grow the liker to that divine estate, and are made the surer of it; and I am sure all will grant that this is a very gainful exchange.

Verily every man at his best state is altogether vanity. It is no wonder that the generality of men are strangers to God, for they are strangers to themselves. The cure of both these evils is from the same hand. He alone can teach us what He is, and what we are ourselves. All know and see that their life is short, and themselves vanity. But this holy man thought it needful to ask the true notion of it from above, and he receives the measure of his life, even an handbreadth. There is a common imposture among people, to read their fortunes by their hands; but this is true palmistry indeed, to read the shortness of our life upon the palms of our hands.

Our days are not only few, but we ourselves are vanity. Every man, even a godly man, as he is a partaker of this life, is not exempted from vanity, nay, he knows it better than any other: but this thought comforts him, that he hath begun that life that is above, and beyond all vanity. The words are weighty and full. It is not a problem, or a doubtful thing, but *surely* every man is vanity. I may call it a definition, and so it is proven, Psal. cxliv. 2, 3, What is man? He is like to vanity, and his days are as a shadow that passes away. His days do not only soon decline and pass away as a shadow, but also they are like vanity. While he appears to be something, he is nothing but the figure and picture of vanity.

This is a very profitable truth to think on, though some kind of hearers, even of the better sort, would judge it more profitable to hear of cases of conscience; but this is a great case of conscience, to consider it well, and carry the impression of it home with you on your hearts. The extreme vanity of ourselves, that we are nothing but vanity; and the note that is added here, *Selah*, if it import anything to the sense and confirmation of what it is added to, it agrees well to this: but if it be only a musical note, to direct, as some think, the elevation, or, according to others, the falling of the voice, it fits the sense very well. For you have man here lifted up and cast down again; lifted up, "man at his best state," and from that thrown down to nothing, even in that state "he is altogether vanity." What is that? It is, as the word signifies, an earthly vapour, and it is generally used to signify things of the least and meanest use, the most empty airy things. So idols are oft called by that name; they are nothing, in respect of what is attributed to them by the children of men; and such a thing is man, he seems to be something, and is indeed nothing, as it is, Psal. lxii. 9, Men of low degree are vanity. Possibly that may be granted for a truth, and they pass for such; but he adds, Men of high degree are a lie; they promise something, and look bigger, but they are nothing more, except this, a lie; and the greater they are, the louder lie.

This it is, then, that we should acquaint ourselves with, that man, in this present life, in all the high advantages of it, is an empty, feeble, fading thing. If we look to the frame of man's body, what is he but a muddy wall, an house of clay, whose foundation is in the dust? If we look within, there is nothing there but a sink, a heap of filth. The body of man is not only subject to fevers, hectics, &c., that make the wall to moulder down; but, take him in his health and strength, what is he but a bag of rottenness? And why should he take delight in his beauty, which is but the appearance of a thing, which a fit of sickness will so easily deface, or the running of a few years spoil the fashion of? A great heat or a cold puts that frame into disorder; a few days' sickness lays him in the dust; or much blood gathered within gathers fevers and pleurisies, and so destroys that life it should maintain; or a fly or a crumb of bread may stop his breath, and so end his days.

If we consider men in societies, in cities and towns, often hath the overflowing scourge of famine and pestilence laid them waste. If we could see all the parts and persons in a great city at once, how many woes and miseries should we behold there! how many either want bread, or scarcely have it by hard labour! Then, to hear the groans of dying persons, and the sighs and weepings of those about them; how many of these things are within the walls of great cities at all times! Great palaces cannot hold out death, but it breaks through and enters there; and thither oft-times the most painful and shameful diseases that are incident to the sons of men resort. Death, by vermin, hath seized on some of the greatest kings that have ever been in the world. If we look on generals, who have commanded the greatest armies, they carry about with them poor frail bodies, as well as others; they may be killed with one small wound, as well as the meanest soldier; and a few days' intemperance hath taken some of the most gallant and courageous of them away in the midst of their success. And, sure I am, he who believes and considers the life to come, and looks on this, and sees what it is, makes little account of those things that have so big a sound in the world, the revolutions of states, crowns, kingdoms, cities, towns; how poor inconsiderable things are they, being compared with eternity! And he that looks not on them as such is a fool.

LECTURE III.

VER. 6. *Surely every man walketh in a vain show: surely they are disquieted in vain: he heapeth up riches, and knoweth not who shall gather them.*

THERE is a part of our handbreadth past since we last left this place, and, as we are saying this, we are wearing out some portion of the rest of it; it were well if we considered this so as to make a better improvement of what remains, than of what is past. Let us see if we can gain the space of an hour, that we may be excited to a better management of the latter part of our time than we have made of the former.

We are all, I think, convinced of the vanity of man, as to his outside, that he is a feeble, weak, poor creature; but we may have hope of somewhat better, in that which is the man indeed, his mind and intellectual part. It is true, that that was originally excellent, and that there is somewhat of a radical excellency still in the soul of man; yet it is so desperately degenerate, that, naturally, man, even in that consideration, is altogether vanity, in all the pieces of him; his mind is but a heap of vanity, nothing there but ignorance, folly, and disorder; and if we think not so, we are the more foolish and ignorant. That which passes with great pomp, under the title of learning and science, it is commonly nothing else but a rhapsody of words and empty terms, which have nothing in them to make known the internal nature of things.

But even those who have the improvement of learning and education, who understand the model and government of affairs, that see their defects, and entertain themselves with various shapes of amending and reforming them, even in those we shall find nothing but a sadder and more serious vanity. It is a tormenting and vexing thing for men to promise to themselves great reformations and bettering of things; that thought usually deludes the wisest of men; they must at length come to that of Solomon, after much labour to little purpose, that crooked things cannot be made straight, Eccles. i. 15, yea, many things grow worse by labouring to rectify them; therefore he adds, but he that increaseth knowledge increaseth sorrow.

As for knowledge in religion, we see the greatest part of the world lying in gross darkness; and even amongst Christians, how much ignorance of these things: which appears in this, that there are such swarms and productions of debates and contentions, that they are grown past number, and each party is confident that truth is on his side, and ordinarily, the most ignorant and erroneous are the most confident and most imperious in their determinations. Surely it were a great part of our wisdom to free our spirits from these empty, fruitless janglings, that abound in the Christian world.

It were an endless toil to go through all degrees, professions, and employments of men in the world; we may go through nations, countries, crafts, schools, colleges, courts, camps, councils of state, and parliaments, and find nothing in all these, but still more of this trouble and vexation in a more fine dress and fashion, altogether vanity.

Every man walks in a vain show. His walk is nothing but a going on in continual vanity, adding a new stock of vanity, of his own coining, to what he has already within, and vexation of spirit woven all along in with it. He was in an image, as the word is, conversing with things of no reality, and which have no solidity in them, and he himself as little. He himself is a walking image, in the midst of these images. Every man's fancy is to himself a gallery of pictures, and there he walks up and down, and considers not how vain these are, and how vain a thing he himself is.

My brethren, they are happy persons (but few are they in number) that are truly weaned from all those images and fancies the world doats so much upon. If many of the children of men would turn their own thoughts backwards in the evening but of one day, what would they find for the most part, but that they have been walking among these pictures, and passing from one vanity to another, and back again to and fro—to as little purpose as the running up and down of children at their play! He who runs after honour, pleasure, popular esteem, what do you think? does not that man walk in an image, pursuing after that, that hath no other being but what the opinion and fancy of men give to it, especially the last, which is a thing so fluctuating, uncertain, and inconstant, that while he hath it he hath nothing? The other image, that man follows and worships, is that in the text, that wretched madness of heaping up riches: this is the great foolishness and disease, especially of old age, that the less way a man has to go, he makes the greater provision for it; when the hands are stiff, and fit for no other labour, they are fitted and composed for scraping together. But for what end dost thou take all this pains? If for thyself, a little sober care will do thy turn, if thy desires be sober; and if not so, thy diligence were better bestowed in imparing and diminishing of these, and that is the easier way a great deal. And if it be for others, why dost thou take a certain unease to thyself for the uncertain ease of others? And who these are thou dost not know; may be, such as thou never intended them for. It were good we used more easy and undistracting diligence for increasing of these treasures, which, we cannot deny, are far better; and whosoever hath them, may abound therein with increase; he knows well for whom he gathers them; he himself shall possess them through all eternity.

If there were not a hope beyond this life, there were reasons for that passionate word in Psal. lxxxix. 47, Why hast thou made all men in vain? To what purpose were it for poor wretched man to have been all his days tossed upon the waves of vanity, and then to lie down in the grave and be no more heard of? But it is not so: he is made capable of a noble and blessed life beyond this; and our forgetfulness of this is the cause of all our misery and vanity here.

It is a great folly to complain of the shortness of our life, and yet to lavish it out so prodigally on trifles and shadows: if it were well managed, it would be sufficient for all we have to do. The only way to live, indeed, is to be doing service to God, and good to men: this is to live much in a little time. But when we play the fool in mispending our time, it may be indeed a sad thought to us, when we find it gone, and we are benighted in the dark so far from our home. But those that have their souls untied from this world and knit to God, they need not complain of the shortness of it, having laid hold on eternal life; for this life is flying away, there is no laying hold on it; it is no matter how soon it goes away, the sooner the better, for to such persons it seems rather to go too slow.

LECTURE IV.

VER. 7. *And now, Lord, what wait I for? my hope is in thee.*

To entertain the minds of men with thoughts of their own vanity, and discourses of their own misery, seems to be sad and unpleasant; but certainly it is not unprofitable, unless it be our own choice to make it so; and that were the greatest vanity and misery of all. Indeed, if there were no help for this sore evil, then the common shift were not to be blamed, yea, it were to be chosen as the only help in such a desperate case, not to think on it, to forget our misery, and to divert our thoughts from it, by all possible means, rather than to increase it, and torment ourselves, by insisting and pondering on it; and in that case, shallow minds would have the advantage, that they could not converse with these sad thoughts: for to increase this knowledge were but to increase sorrow. But far be it from us thus to determine; there is a hope which is a help to this evil, and this is it that this holy man fixes on, And now, Lord, &c., otherwise it were strange that the most excellent piece of the visible creation should be made subject to the most incurable unhappiness, to feel misery which he cannot shun, and to be tormented with desires that cannot be satisfied. But there is some better expectation for the souls of men, and it is no other but Himself who made them.

The wisest natural men have discoursed of man's vanity, and passionately bemoaned it, but in this they have fallen short, how to remedy it. They have aimed at it and come near it, but were not able to work it; they still laboured to be satisfied in themselves; they speak somewhat of reason, but that will not do it; for man being fallen under the curse of God, there is nothing but darkness and folly in himself. The only way to blessedness is by going out of ourselves unto God. All our discourses of our own vanity will but further disquiet us, if they do not terminate here, if they do not fix on His eternal happiness, goodness, and verity.

I am persuaded, if many would ask this question of themselves, What wait I for? they would puzzle themselves and not find an answer: there are a great many things that men desire and are gaping after, but few after one thing chiefly and stayedly: they float up and down, and are carried about without any certain motion, but by fancy and by guess; and no wind can be fair for such persons that aim at no certain haven.

If we put this question to ourselves, What would I have? it were easy for many to answer, I would have an easy, quiet, peaceable life in this world; so would an ox or a horse: and is that all? May be you would have a greater height of pleasure and honour; but think on this one thing, that there is this one crack and vanity that spoils all these things, that they will not bear you up when you lean on them in times of distress; and besides, when you have them, they may be pulled from you; and if not, you must be plucked away from them within a little while: there is much seeming content in the pursuit of these things, but they are lost with greater discontent. It is God's goodness to men, to blast all things in the world to them, and to break their fairest hopes, that they may be constrained to look above to himself: he beats them from all shores, that he may bring them to the Rock that is higher than they, Ps. lxi. 2.

Oh that God would once touch some of your hearts that are under the chains of darkness, that ye might once bethink where to rest your heads in the midst of all our confusions; and here is the resting-place—Hope in God: Now, Lord, what wait I for? my hope is in thee. Blessed soul that can say, "Lord, thou seest I desire nothing but thyself (as Peter said, Lord, thou knowest I love thee), all the corners of my heart stand open in thy sight; thou seest if there be any other desire or expectation but to please thee; and if there be any such thing in me (for I see it not), I pray thee discover it to me, and through thy grace it shall lodge no longer. My heart is thine alone, it is consecrated to thee; and if anything would profane thy temple, if it will not go forth by fair warning, let it be scourged out by thy rod, yea, any rod whatsoever it pleaseth thee to choose."

My hope is in thee. This holy man, seeing the vanity of all other expectations and pursuits of men, at length runs to this; And now, Lord, what wait I for? my hope is in thee: he finds nothing but moving sand everywhere else; but he finds this eternal Rock to be a strong foundation, as the Hebrew word, by which he is styled, doth signify. It is true, the union of the heart with God is made up by faith and love; but yet both these, in this our present condition of our absence and distance from God, do act themselves much by the third grace, which is joined with them, and that is hope. For faith is conversant about things that are not seen, and in a great part that are not yet, but are to come; and the spirit of faith, choosing things that are to come, is called hope. It is true that they are not so wholly deferred as that they possess nothing; but yet the utmost they possess is but a pledge and earnest-penny, a small thing in respect of that eternal inheritance they look for. What they have here is of the same kind with what they expect; but it is but a little portion of it, the smiles and glances of their Father's face, foretastes of heaven, which their souls are refreshed with.

Hope is the great stock of believers, it is that which upholds them under all the faintings and sorrows of this life, and in their going through the valley and shadow of death. It is the helmet of their salvation, which, while they are looking over to eternity, beyond this present time, covers and keeps their head safe amidst all the darts that fly round about them. In the present discomfort and darkness of mind, and the saddest hours they meet with in this life, hope is that which keeps up the soul, and is that which David cheered up his soul with, Ps. xlii. 5, Why art thou cast down, O my soul? and why art thou disquieted in me? Hope thou in God; for I shall yet praise him for the help of his countenance. And even in this point the children of the world have no great advantage of the children of God, as to the things of this life; for much of their satisfaction, such as it is, does hang, for the most part, on their hope; the happiest and richest of them do still piece it out with some further expectation, something they look for beyond what they have; and the expectation of that pleases them more than all their present possessions. But this great disadvantage they have, all their hopes are but heaps of delusions and lies; and either they die and obtain them not, or if they obtain them, yet they obtain them not, they are so far short of what they fancied and imagined of them beforehand. But the hope of the children of God, as it is sure, so it is inconceivably full and satisfying, far beyond what the largest apprehension of any man is able to reach. Hope in God! what is wanting there?

This hope lodges only in the pure heart; it is a

precious liquor that can only be kept in a clean vessel, and that which is not so cannot receive it: but what it seems to receive, it corrupts and destroys. It is a confidence arising from peace, agreement, and friendship, which cannot be betwixt the God of purity and those who allow unholiness in themselves. It is a strange impudence for men to talk of their trust and hope in God, who are in perfect hostility against him. Bold fellows go through dangers here, but it will not be so hereafter, Jer. ii. 27, They turn to me the back and not the face; yet in their trouble they say, Arise and save us: they do it as confidently as if they never had despised God; but they mistake the matter, it is not so. Go and cry, says he, to the gods whom ye have chosen, Judges x. 14. When men come to die, then they catch hold of the mercy of God; but from that their filthy hands are beat off, there is no help for them there, and so they fall down to the pit. A holy fear of God and a happy hope in him are commonly linked together: Behold, the eye of the Lord is upon them that fear him, upon them that hope in his mercy, Ps. xxxiii. 18.

And even in those who are more purified from sin, yet too large draughts of lawful pleasures do clog the spirits, and make this hope grow exceeding weak; surely the more we fill ourselves with these things, we leave the less appetite for the consolations of this blessed hope. They cannot know the excellency of this hope, who labour not to keep it unmixed: it is best alone, as the richest wines and oils, which are the worst of mixtures.

Be sober and hope, 1 Pet. i. 13; keep your mind sober, and your hope shall be pure. Any thing or person that leans on two supporters, whereof the one is whole and sound, and the other broken or crooked, that which is unsound breaks, though the other remains whole, and they fall; whereas the one that was whole had been sufficient. Thus it is when we divide our hopes betwixt God and this present world, or any other good; those that place their whole hopes on God, they gather in all their desires to him; the streams of their affections are not scattered and left in the muddy ditches of the world, they do not fall into sinking pools, but being gathered into one main torrent, they run on in that channel to the sea of his eternal goodness.

My hope is in thee. We cannot choose but all of us think that God is immensely good in himself; but that which is nearer, whereon our hearts most rise, is a relative goodness, that he is good to us, and that he is so perfectly and completely good, that having made choice of him, and obtained union with him, we need no more. Were once the hearts of the children of men persuaded of this, all their deliberations were at an end; they would not only choose no other, but defer no longer to fix on him. And what can trouble the soul that is thus established? No change or overturning of outward things: though the frame of the world itself were shaken to pieces, yet still the bottom of this hope is Him that changeth not: and whatever thy pressures be, poverty, sickness, or disquiet of mind, thou mayest draw abundant consolation from him in whom thou hast placed thy hope. There is only one thing that cruelly assaults it by the way, and that is the guilt of sin. All afflictions and troubles we meet with are not able to mar this hope or quench it; for where it is strong, it either breaks through them or flies above them; they cannot overcome it, for there is no affliction inconsistent with the love of God, yea, the sharpest affliction may sometimes have the clearest characters of his love upon it; but it is sin that presents him as angry to the view of the soul. When he looks through that cloud, he seems to be an enemy; and when we apprehend him in that aspect, we are affrighted, and presently apprehend a storm; but even in this case, this hope apprehends his mercy. And thus David here.

LECTURE V.

VER. 8, 10—12. *Deliver me from all my transgressions: make me not the reproach of the foolish. Remove thy stroke away from me: I am consumed by the blow of thine hand. When thou with rebukes dost correct man for iniquity, thou makest his beauty to consume away like a moth: surely every man is vanity. Selah. Hear my prayer, O Lord, and give ear unto my cry: hold not thy peace at my tears: for I am a stranger with thee, and a sojourner, as all my fathers were.*

THIS is indeed the basis and foundation of all our other hopes—the free pardon of our sins; but none must entertain these sins, if they desire to be pardoned. Repentance and remission of sins are still linked together in the Scriptures; and he that would have sin pardoned, and yet live in it, or retain the love of it, would have God and sin reconciled together, and that can never be. David finds his sins pressing him down; he sees them as an army of men set in battle array about him: and whither flies he for a deliverance? even to Him whom he had offended.

Remove thy stroke away from me: I am consumed by the blow of thine hand. We are naturally very partial judges of ourselves; and, as if we were not sufficiently able by nature, we study and devise by art to deceive ourselves. We are ready to reckon any good that is in us to the full, nay, to multiply it beyond what it is; and to help this, we commonly look on those who have less goodness in them, who are weaker and worse than ourselves; and so we magnify the sense of our own worth and goodness by that comparison. And as in the goodness we have, or imagine we have, so likewise in the evils we suffer, we use to extol them very much in conceit. We account our lightest afflictions very great; and to heighten our thoughts of them, we take a view of those who are more at ease and less afflicted than ourselves. By these devices we nourish in ourselves pride, by the overweening conceit of our goodness, and impatience, by the overfeeling sense of our evils. But if we would help ourselves by comparison, we should do well to view those persons who have been eminent for holiness, and by this means we should lessen the great opinion we have of our own worth; and so likewise should we consider the many instances of great calamities and sorrows, which would tend to quiet our minds, and enable us to possess our souls in patience under the little burden of trials that lies upon us: and we shall find those instances to fall in together, that as persons have been very eminent in holiness, they have also been eminent in suffering very sore strokes from the hand of God. If we would think on their consuming blows and broken bones, their bones burnt as an hearth, and their flesh withered as grass, certainly we should entertain our thoughts sometimes with wonder of God's indulgence to us, that we are so little afflicted, when so many of the children of men and so many of the children of God suffer so many and so hard things; and this would very much add to the stock of our praises. We should not think that we are more innocent in not deserving these things that are inflicted on others, but rather, that He who thus measures out to them and to us, knows our size, and sees how weak we are in comparison of them; and that therefore he is indulgent to us, not because we are better, but because we are weaker, and are not able to bear so much as he lays on the stronger shoulders. Even in the sharpest of these rods there is mercy. It is a privilege to the sheep that is ready to wander, to be beaten into a right way. Certainly he that finds any cure of the evils of his spirit by the hardest sufferings of his flesh, gets a very gainful bargain. If thou account sin thy greatest unhappiness and mischief, thou wilt be glad to have it removed on any terms. But there is one great benefit of affliction, which follows in the text, that it gives him the true measure of himself.

When with rebukes thou dost correct man, thou makest his beauty to consume away like a moth: surely every man is vanity. Selah. Man at his best state is altogether vanity: but at his lowest state it appears best unto him how much vanity he is, and how much vanity he was at his best state, seeing he was then capable of such a change, to fall so low from such a height. As that great man, who was seeking new conquests, when he fell upon the sand, and saw the print of his own body, "Why," says he, "so small a parcel of earth will serve me, who am seeking after new kingdoms." Thus it is when a man is brought down, then he hath the right measure of himself, when he sees how vain a thing he is.

Thus the psalmist represents it here, both as an argument to move God to compassion, and to instruct himself and other men. So Job xiii. 25, Wilt thou break a leaf driven to and fro with the wind? and wilt thou pursue dry stubble? Ps. ciii. 14, For he knoweth our frame; he remembereth that we are dust. And his beauty, which seemed to be his perfection, yet, when the hand of God is on him, it is blasted as a moth-eaten garment; this should teach us humility, and to beware of sin, which provokes God to pour out his heavy judgments upon us. If any be proud of honour, let him remember Nebuchadnezzar and Herod; or of riches, or of wit and endowments of mind, let him think how soon God can make all these to wither and melt away. Surely every man is vanity.

Hear my prayer, O Lord, and give ear unto my cry; hold not thy peace at my tears: for I am a stranger with thee, and a sojourner, as all my fathers were. What is this life we cleave so fast to, and are so uneasy to hear of parting with; what is it but a trance, and a succession of sorrows, a weary tossing upon the waves of vanity and misery? No estate or course of life is exempted from the causes of this complaint; the poorer sort are troubled with wants, and the richer with the care of what they have, and sometimes with the loss of it; and the middle sort betwixt the two partake of the vexations of both, for their life is spent in care for keeping what they have, and in turmoil for purchasing more. Neither does godliness exempt the best of men from the sufferings of this life. David, who was both a great man and a good man, did share deeply in these; so that his conclusion still holds true, no instance can be found to infringe it; Surely every man is altogether vanity.

It remains only to inquire what manner of men they are who are furnished with the best helps, and with the most comfortable mitigations of their trouble, and with the strongest additions of support and strength to bear them up under it? And it will certainly be found that godliness alone hath this advantage. And among the many consolations godly men have under their trouble, this is one, and the chief one, their recourse unto prayer. So here, and Ps. cxlii. 4, 5. Isa. xxxviii. 2, Hezekiah turned his face towards the wall; he turns his back on all worldly councils and vain helps, and betakes himself to prayer; and prayer brings ease and support, and seasonable deliverance to the godly man: but their sorrows shall be multiplied that hasten after other gods, Ps. xvi. 4. And this all ungodly men do when they are afflicted: they run to other imaginary helps of their own, and they prove but the multipliers of sorrows, and add to their torment: they are miserable or troublesome comforters; like unskilful physicians, that add to the patient's pain by nauseous, ill chosen, and, it may be, pernicious drugs.

Now, in this prayer of David we find three things, which are the chief qualifications of all acceptable prayers.

The first is *humility*. He humbly confesses his sins, and his own weakness and worthlessness. We are not to put on a stoical, flinty kind of spirit under our afflictions, that so we may seem to shun womanish repinings and complaints, lest we run into the other evil of despising the hand of God; but we are to humble our proud hearts, and break our unruly passions. There is something of this in the nature of affliction itself; as in the daytime men are abroad, but the night draws them home, so in the day of prosperity men run out after vanities and pleasures, and when the dark night of affliction comes, then men should come home, and wisely lay the matter to heart. It is meet we humble ourselves under the mighty hand of God. It is meet to say unto him, as Job xxxiv. 31, I have been chastised, or have borne chastisement, and I will not offend any more: that is a kind of language that makes the rod fall out of his hand. That prayer ascends highest that comes from the lowest depth of a humbled heart. But God resists the proud; he proclaims himself an enemy to pride and stiffness of spirit, but his grace seeks the humble heart, as water does the low ground.

If a holy heart be the temple of God, and therefore a house of prayer, certainly when it is framed and builded for such, the foundation of that temple is laid in deep humility; otherwise no prayers that are offered up in it have the smell of pleasing incense to him.

The second qualification of this prayer is *fervency* and *importunity*, which appears in the elegant gradation of the words, Hear my prayer, my words; if not that, yet give ear to my cry, which is louder; and if that prevail not yet, hold not thy peace at my tears, which is the loudest of all: so David, elsewhere, calls it the voice of his weeping. Though this gift of tears doth often flow from the natural temper, yet where that temper becomes spiritual and religious, it proves a singular instrument of repentance and prayer. But yet there may be a very great height of piety and godly affections where tears are wanting; yea, this defect may proceed from a singular sublimity of religion in their souls, being acted more in the upper region of the intellectual mind, and so not communicating much with the lower affections, or these expressions of them. We are not to judge of our spiritual proficiency by the gift of prayer, for the heart may be very spiritually affected where there is no readiness or volubility of words: the sure measure of our growth is to be had from our holiness, which stands in this, to see how our hearts are crucified to the world, and how we are possessed with the love of God, and with ardent longings after union with him, and dwelling in his presence hereafter, and in being conformed to his will here.

It is the greatest folly imaginable in some to shed tears for their sins, and within a little while to return to them again; they think there is some kind of absolution in this way of easy venting themselves by tears in prayer, and when a new temptation returns they easily yield to it. This is lightness and foolishness, like the inconstancy of a woman, who entertains new lovers in her mourning apparel, having expressed much sorrow and grief for her former husband.

Now, fervency in prayer hath in it, 1st, Attentiveness of mind. If the mind be not present, it is impossible that much of the heart and affections can be there. How shall we think that God shall hear these prayers which we do not hear ourselves? And shall we think them worthy of his acceptance that are not worthy of our thoughts? Yet we should not leave off prayer because of the wanderings of our hearts in it, for that is the very design of the devil; but still we must continue in it, and amend this fault as much as we can. 2ndly, Fervency of prayer hath in it an intense bent of the affections, to have our desires as ardent as can be for the pardon of sin, the mortifying our lusts and passions, the delivering us from the love of ourselves and this present world; and for such spiritual things to pray often, and with importunity, that is, to pray fervently, and never to rest till an answer come.

The third qualification is *faith.* Heb. xi. 6, He who comes to God must believe that he is, and that he is a rewarder of all that diligently seek him. And certainly, as he that comes to God must believe this, so he that believes this cannot but come to God; and if he be not presently answered, he that believes makes no haste, he resolves patiently to wait for the Lord, and to go to no other.

Surely there is much to be had in prayer: all good may be obtained, and all evil averted by it; yea, it is a reward to itself. It is the greatest dignity of the creature to be admitted to converse with God; and certainly the soul that is much in prayer grows in purity, and is raised by prayer to the despising of all those things that the world admires, and is in love with, and by a wonderful way is conformed to the likeness of God.

For I am a stranger with thee, and a sojourner, as all my fathers were. In the law, God recommended strangers to the care and compassion of his people; now David returns the argument to him,—for I am a stranger with thee, that is, before thee, "in this world wherein thou hast appointed me to sojourn a few days, and I betake myself to thy protection in this strange country; I seek shelter under the shadow of thy wings, therefore have compassion upon me." He that looks on himself as a stranger, and is sensible of the darkness both round about him in this wilderness, and also with him, he will often put up that request with David, Ps. cxix. 19, I am a stranger on this earth; hide not thy commandments from me: do not let me lose my way. And as we should use this argument to persuade God to look down upon us, so likewise to persuade ourselves to send up our hearts and desires to him. What is the joy of our life, but the thoughts of that other life, our home before us? And certainly he that lives much in these thoughts, set him where you will here, he is not much pleased nor displeased: but if his Father call him home, that word gives him his heart's desire.

LECTURE VI.

VER. 13. *Oh spare me, that I may recover strength, before I go hence, and be no more.*

WHY is it that we do not extremely hate that which we so desperately love, sin? For the deformity of it is unspeakable; and besides, it is the cause of all our woes; sin hath opened the sluices, and lets in all the deluges of sorrows, which make the life of poor man nothing else but vanity and misery; so that the meanest orator in the world may be eloquent enough on that subject. What is our life but a continual succession of many deaths? Poor creatures are ofttimes tossed betwixt two, the fear of death and the tediousness of life; and under these fears they cannot tell which to choose. Holy men are not exempted from some apprehensions of God's displeasure because of their sins; and that may make them cry out with David, Oh spare me, that I may recover strength before I go hence, and be no more. Or perhaps this may be a desire, not so much simply for the prolonging of life as for the intermitting of his pain: if it be the desire of a recovery, and the spinning out of the thread of his life a little longer, surely he intended to employ it for God and his service; but long life was suitable to the promises of that time; so Hezekiah, Isa. xxxviii. There is no doubt these holy men, under the law, knew somewhat of the state of immortality, Heb. xi.; they calling themselves strangers on earth, argued that they were no strangers to these thoughts; but it cannot be denied that that doctrine was but darkly laid out in these times; it is Christ Jesus that hath brought life and immortality to light, who did illuminate life and immortality, that before stood in the dark.

Surely the desire of life is, for the most part, sensual and base, when men desire that they may still enjoy their animal pleasures, and are loath to be parted from them. They are pleased to term it, a desire to live and repent; and yet few do it when they are spared: like evil debtors, who desire forbearance from one term to another, but with no design at all to pay. But there is a natural desire of life, something of abhorrence of nature against the dissolution of these tabernacles. We are loath to go forth, like children who are afraid to walk in the dark, not knowing what may be there. In some, such a desire of life may be very reasonable; being surprised by sickness, and apprehensions of death, and sin unpardoned, they may desire a little time before they enter into eternity; for that change is not a thing to be hazarded upon a few days' or hours' preparation. I will not say that death-bed repentance is altogether desperate, but certainly it is very dangerous, and to be suspected; and therefore, the desire of a little time longer, in such a case, may be very allowable.

I will not deny but it is possible, even for a believer, to be taken in such a posture, that it may be very uncomfortable to him to be carried off so, through the affrightments of death, and his darkness as to his after-state. On the other hand, it is an argument of a good measure of spirituality and height of the love of God, to desire to depart, and be dissolved, in the midst of health and the affluence of worldly comforts. But for men to desire and wish to be dead, when they are troubled and vexed with anything, is but a childish folly, flowing from a discontented mind, which being over, they desire nothing less than to die.

But there is a spiritual desire of death, which is very becoming a Christian; for Jesus Christ hath not only opened very clearly the doctrine of eternal life, but he himself hath passed through death, and lain down in the grave; he hath perfumed that passage, and warmed that bed for us; so that it is sweet and amiable for a Christian to pass through and follow him, and to be where he is. It is a strange thing, that the souls of Christians have not a continual desire to go to that company which is above (finding so much discord and disagreement among the best of men that are here), to go to the spirits of just men made perfect, where there is light and love, and nothing else; to go to the company of angels, a higher rank of blessed spirits; but most of all, to go to God, and to Jesus the Mediator of the New Covenant. And, to say nothing positively of that glory (for the truth is, we can say nothing of it), the very evils that death delivers the true Christian from, may make him long for it; for such an one may say, "I shall die, and go to a more excellent country, where I shall be happy for ever, that is, I shall die no more, I shall sorrow no more, I shall be sick no more; and, which is yet more considerable, I shall doubt no more, and shall be tempted no more; and, which is the chiefest of all, I shall sin no more."

EXHORTATIONS

TO THE

CANDIDATES FOR THE DEGREE OF MASTER OF ARTS IN THE UNIVERSITY OF EDINBURGH.

EXHORTATION I.

Were I allowed to speak freely what I sincerely think of most of the affairs of human life, even those that are accounted of the highest importance, and transacted with the greatest eagerness and bustle, I should be apt to say, "that a great noise is made about the merest trifles:" but if you should take this amiss, as a little unseasonable upon the present occasion, and an insult upon your solemnity, I hope you will the more easily forgive me, that I place in the same rank with this philosophical convention of yours, the most famous councils and general assemblies of princes and great men; and say of their golden crowns, as well as your crowns of laurel, "that they are things of no value, and not worth the purchasing." Even the triumphal, inaugural, or nuptial processions of the greatest kings and generals of armies, with whatever pomp and magnificence, as well as art, they may be set off, are, after all, so far true representations of their false, painted, and tinsel happiness, that, while we look at them, they fly away; and, in a very short time, they are followed by their funeral processions, which are the triumphs of death over those who have themselves triumphed during their lives. The scenes are shifted, the actors also disappear; and, in the same manner, the greatest shows of this vain world likewise pass away. Let us, that we may lop off the luxuriant branches of our vines, take a nearer view of this object, and remember, that what we now call a laurel crown, will soon be followed by cypress wreaths. It will be also proper to consider how many, who, in their time, were employed as we are now, have long ago acted their parts, and are now consigned to a long oblivion; as also, what vast numbers of the rising generation are following us at the heels, and, as it were, pushing us forward to the same land of forgetfulness; who, while they are hurrying us away, are at the same time hastening thither themselves. All that we see, all that we do, and all that we are, are but mere dreams; and if we are not sensible of this truth, it is because we are still asleep: none but minds that are awake can discern it; they, and they only, can perceive and despise these illusions of the night. What is it, pray, to which, with the most ardent wishes, you have been aspiring throughout the whole course of these four last years? Here you have a cap and a title, and nothing at all more.

But, perhaps, taking this amiss, you secretly blame me in your hearts, and wish me to congratulate you upon the honour you have obtained. I cheerfully comply with your desire, and am willing to explain myself. These small presents are not the principal reward of your labours, nor the chief end of your studies; but honorary marks and badges of that erudition and knowledge wherewith your minds have been stored by the uninterrupted labours of four whole years. But whatever attainments in learning you have reached, I would have you seriously to reflect, how inconsiderable they are, and how little they differ from nothing; nay, if what we know is compared with what we know not, it will be found even vastly less than nothing: at least, it is an argument of little knowledge, and the sign of a vain and weak mind, to be puffed up with an overbearing opinion of our own knowledge: while on the contrary, it is an evidence of great proficiency in knowledge, to be sensible of our ignorance and inability. "He is the wisest man," says Plato, "who knows himself to be very ill qualified for the attainment of wisdom."

You, young gentlemen, I imagine, entertain good hopes with regard to your future fortune; nor would I discourage those hopes, yet I would gladly moderate them a little by this wholesome advice: lean not upon a broken reed, neither let any one who values his peace, his real dignity, and his satisfaction, give himself up to hopes that are uncertain, frail, and deceitful. The human race are, perhaps, the only creatures that by this means become a torment to themselves; for, as we always grasp at futurity, we vainly promise ourselves many and great things, in which, as commonly happens, being for the most part disappointed, we must, of necessity, pay for our foolish pleasure with a proportionate degree of pain. Thus, the greatest part of mankind find the whole of this wretched life chequered with delusive joys and real torments, ill-grounded hopes, and fears equally imaginary: amidst these, we live in continual suspense, and die so too.

But a few—alas! a few only, having set their hearts upon heavenly enjoyments, take pleasure in despising, with a proper greatness of mind, and trampling upon, the fading enjoyments of this world. These make it their only study, and exert their utmost efforts, that, having the more divine part of their composition weaned from the world and the flesh, they may be brought to a resemblance and union with the holy and supreme God, the Father of spirits, by purity, piety, and an habitual contemplation of divine objects: and this, to be sure, is the principal thing, with a noble ambition whereof I would have your minds inflamed; and whatever profession or manner of life you devote yourselves to, it is my earnest exhortation and request, that you would make this your constant and principal study. Fly, if you have any regard to my advice, fly far from that controversial, contentious school-divinity, which, in fact, consists in fruitless disputes about words, and rather deserves the name of vain and foolish talking.

Almost all mankind are constantly catching at something more than they possess, and torment themselves in vain; nor is our rest to be found among these enjoyments of the world, where all things are covered with a deluge of vanity, as with a flood of fluctuating, restless waters; and the soul, flying about, looking in vain for a place on which it may set its foot, most unhappily loses its time, its labour, and itself at last, like the birds in the days of the flood, which having long sought for land, till their strength was quite exhausted, fell down at last, and perished in the waters.

Oh! how greatly preferable to these bushes, and briars, and thorns, are the delightful fields of the gospel, wherein pleasure and profit are agreeably mixed together, whence you may learn the way to everlasting peace; that poverty of spirit, which is the only true riches; that purity of heart, which is our greatest beauty; and that inexpressible satisfaction, which attends the exercise of charity, humility, and meekness! When your minds are stored and adorned with these graces, they will enjoy the most pleasing tranquillity, even amidst the noise and tumults of this present life; and you will be, to use the words of Tertullian, candidates for eternity—a title infinitely more glorious and sublime than what has been this day conferred upon you. And that great and last day, which is so much dreaded by the slaves of this present world, will be the most happy and auspicious to you; as it will deliver you from a dark, dismal prison, and place you in the regions of the most full and marvellous light.

Let us pray.

MOST exalted God, who hast alone created, and dost govern this whole frame, and all the inhabitants thereof, visible and invisible, whose name is alone Wonderful, and to be celebrated with the highest praise, as it is indeed above all praise and admiration! Let the heavens, the earth, and all the elements, praise thee; let darkness, light, and all the returns of days and years, and all the varieties and vicissitudes of things, praise thee; let the angels praise thee, the archangels, and all the blessed court of heaven, whose very happiness it is, that they are constantly employed in celebrating thy praises. We confess, O Lord, that we are of all creatures the most unworthy to praise thee; yet, of all others, we are under the greatest obligations to do it; nay, the more unworthy we are, our obligation is so much the greater. From this duty, however unqualified we may be, we can by no means abstain, nor indeed ought we. Let our souls bless thee, and all that is within us praise thy holy name, who forgivest all our sins, and healest all our diseases, who deliverest our souls from destruction, and crownest them with bounty and tender mercies. Thou searchest the heart, O Lord, and perfectly knowest the most intimate recesses of it:

reject not those prayers which thou perceivest to be the voice and the wishes of the heart. Now it is the great request of our hearts, unless they always deceive us, that they may be weaned from all earthly and perishing enjoyments; and if there is anything to which they cleave with more than ordinary force, may they be pulled away from it by thy Almighty hand, that they may be joined to thee for ever in an inseparable marriage covenant; and, in our behalf, we have nothing more to ask. We only add, in behalf of thy church, that it may be protected under the shadow of thy wings, and everywhere, throughout the world, be watered by thy heavenly dew, that the spirit and heat of worldly hatred against it may be cooled, and its intestine divisions, whereby it is much more grievously scorched, extinguished. Bless this nation, this city, and this university, in which we beg thou wouldest be pleased to reside, as in a garden dedicated to thy name, through Jesus Christ our Lord. Amen.

EXHORTATION II.

Would you have me to speak the truth with freedom and brevity? The whole world is a kind of stage, and its inhabitants mere actors. As to this little play of yours, it is now very near a conclusion, and you are upon the point of applying to the spectators for their applause. Should any superciliously decline paying this small tribute, you surely may, with great ease, retort their contempt upon themselves, merely by saying, "Let your severity fall heavy on those who admire their own performances; as to this affair of ours, we know it is nothing at all:" for I will not allow myself to doubt but you are very sensible, that there is indeed nothing in it.

It would, to be sure, be very improper, especially as the evening approaches, to detain you and my other hearers with a long and tedious discourse, when you are already more than enough fatigued, and almost quite tired out, with hearing. I shall therefore only put you in mind of one thing, and that in a few words. Let not this solemn toy, however agreeable to youthful minds, so far impose upon you, as to set you a dreaming of great advantages and pleasures to be met with in this new period of life you are entering upon. Look round you, if you please, and take a near and exact survey of all the different stations of life that are set before you. If you enter upon any of the stations of active life, what is this but jumping into a bush of thorns, where you can have no hope of enjoying quiet, and yet cannot easily get out again? But if you rather choose to enter upon some new branch of science, alas! what a small measure of knowledge is to be thus obtained, with what vast labour is even that little to be purchased, and how often, after immense toil and difficulty, will it be found, that truth is still at a distance, and not yet drawn out of the well! We indeed believe that the soul breathed into man when he was first made, was pure, full of light, and every way worthy of its divine original: but ah! Father of mankind, how soon, and how much was he changed from what he was at first! He foolishly gave ear to the fatal seducer, and that very moment was seized upon by death, whereby he at once lost his purity, his light and truth, and, together with himself, ruined us also.

As for you, young gentlemen, especially those of you that intend to devote yourselves to theological studies, it is my earnest advice and request to you, that you fly far from that infectious curiosity which would lead you into the depths of that controversial, contentious theology, which, if any doctrine at all deserves the name, may be truly termed, "science falsely so called." And that you may not, in this respect, be imposed upon by the common reputation of acuteness and learning, I confidently affirm, that, to understand and be master of those trifling disputes that prevail in the schools, is an evidence of a very mean understanding; while, on the contrary, it is an argument of a genius truly great, to slight and despise them, and to walk in the light of pure and peaceable truth, which is far above the dark and cloudy region of controversial disputes. But, you will say, it is necessary, in order to the defence of truth, to oppose errors, and blunt the weapons of sophists. Be it so; but our disputes ought to be managed with few words, for naked truth is most effectual for its own defence; and when it is once well understood, its natural light dispels all the darkness of error: "for all things that are reproved are made manifest by the light," saith the apostle.

There is but one useful controversy and dispute, one sort of war, most noble in its nature, or most worthy of a Christian, and this not to be carried on against enemies at a great distance, but such as are bred within our own breasts; against those it is most reasonable to wage an endless war, and them it is our duty to persecute to death. Let us all, children, young men and old, exert ourselves vigorously in this warfare; let our vices die before us, that death may not find us indolent, defiled, and wallowing in the mire; for then it will be most truly, and to our great misery, death to us: whereas, to those sanctified souls who are conformed to Christ, and conquerors by his means, it rather is to be called life, as it delivers them from their wanderings and vices, from all kinds of evils, and from that death which is final and eternal.

Let us pray.

Eternal God, who art constantly adored by thrones and powers, by seraphim and cherubim, we confess that thou art most worthy to be praised; but we of all others are the most unworthy to be employed in showing forth thy praise. How can polluted bodies and impure souls, which, taken together, are nothing but mere sinks of sin, praise thee, the pure and holy Majesty of heaven? Yet, how can these bodies which thou hast wonderfully formed, and those souls which thou hast inspired, which owe entirely to thine unmerited favour all that they are, all that they possess, and all that they hope for, forbear praising thee, their wise and bountiful Creator and Father? Let our souls, therefore, and all that is within us, bless thy holy name; yea, let all our bones say, O Lord, who is like thee; who is like unto thee? Far be it, most gracious Father, from our hearts, to harbour anything that is displeasing to thee: let them be, as it were, temples dedicated to thy service, thoroughly purged from every idol and image, from every object of impure love and earthly affection. Let our most gracious King and Redeemer dwell and reign within us; may he take full possession of us by his Spirit, and govern all our actions. May he extend his peaceable and saving kingdom throughout the whole habitable world, from the rising of the sun to the going down thereof.

Let the nations acknowledge their King, and the isles be glad in him, and particularly that which we inhabit, with those in its neighbourhood; and, that they may be truly blessed in him, may they daily submit, more perfectly and dutifully, to his golden sceptre, and the holy laws of his gospel. Bless this nation and city, and this our university; may it be continually watered with the dew of thy Spirit, and plentifully produce fruit acceptable in thy sight, through Jesus Christ our Lord. Amen.

EXHORTATION III.

This day, which has been the object of your earnest wishes throughout the course of four whole years, is now almost over, and hastening to a close. What has it produced for your advantage? Can he that has reaped most successfully of you all, say he has filled his arms with sheaves? Though possibly you would permit me to express myself with great freedom on this occasion, yet I will not take the liberty to depreciate too much your past studies, the specimens you have given to-day of your abilities, and the degree that has been conferred upon you. This at least, I imagine, I may say without offence, the most of those things we greedily catch at, and labour most earnestly to obtain, and consequently even your philosophy, is a real and demonstrative truth of that great paradox, that there is a vacuity in the nature of things. And, in truth, how great is this vacuity, seeing even the human race is no inconsiderable part of it! Though this day is marked with more than ordinary solemnity, it is, after all, but the conclusion and period of a number of days that have been idly spent, and is itself elapsing to little or no purpose, as well as the rest. But oh! how glorious must that blessed day be, which all purified souls, and such as are dear to God, earnestly long for throughout the whole of this perishing life, and constantly wait, with a kind of impatience, until it dawn, and the shadows fly away!

I am, indeed, of opinion, that those of you who think most justly, will readily own your attainments, hitherto, are of no great moment. But, possibly, henceforth you intend to begin life, as it were, anew; you aspire to greater matters, and entertain views worthy of human nature; you already begin to live, and to be wise; you form desires, and conceive hopes of rising to arts, riches, and honours: all this is very well. Yet there is one consideration I would have you to admit among these ingenious projects and designs. What if death should come upon you, and, looking with an envious eye upon this towering prospect, put a stop to a project that extends itself so far into futurity, and, like a spider's web, entirely destroy it with a gentle breath of wind? Nor would this be any prodigy, or indeed an extraordinary event, but the common fate of almost all mankind. "We are always resolving to live, and yet never set about life in good earnest." "At the age of fifty," says one, "I will retire and take my ease; or, the sixtieth year of my life shall entirely disengage me from public offices and business." Fool! art thou not ashamed to reserve to thyself the last remains and dregs of life? Who will stand surety that thou shalt live so long? And what immense folly is it, so far to forget mortality, as to think of beginning to live at that period of years to which a few only attain!

As for you, young gentlemen, I heartily wish you may think more justly: let your souls, as it were, retire into themselves, and dwell at home; and having shaken off the trifles that make a bustle and noise around you, consider seriously, that the remaining part of your life is long only in one respect, (and in this indeed its length may be justly complained of), that it is fraught with every sort of misery and affliction, and has nothing agreeable in it, but the study of heavenly wisdom alone; for everything else is "vanity." Look about you and see, whether there is anything worthy of your affection, and whether everything you see does not rather excite your indignation and aversion. At home are contentions and disputes; abroad, in the fields, robbers; clamour and noise at the bar; wickedness in the camp; hypocrisy in the church; and vexation or lamentable mistakes everywhere. Among the rich and great there are false and inconstant friendships, bitter enmities, envy, fraud, and falsehood; and cares in great numbers flutter round the most stately and sumptuous palaces.

What a considerable part of mankind are struggling with open and sharp afflictions! To whatever side you turn yourself, what do you commonly hear but lamentation and mourning? How many complaints of the poor, that are distressed for want of daily bread, or drag a most wretched life under the grievous oppression of powerful tyrants! How frequent are the groans of the sick and languishing! How great the multitude of those that lament their friends and relations carried off by death, and will themselves, in a short time, and for the same reason, be lamented by others! And, to conclude, how innumerable are the miseries and afflictions of various kinds, that seem alternately to re-echo to one another!

But you are now philosophers, and, amidst these dismal calamities, you comfort yourselves with the inward and hidden riches of wisdom, and the sciences you have acquired. The sciences! Tell us in what part of the earth they are to be found. Let us know, pray, where they dwell, that we may flock thither in great numbers. I know, indeed, where there is abundance of noise, with vain and idle words, and a jarring of opinions, between contending disputants; I know where ignorance, under the disguise of a gown and a beard, has obtained the title of science: but where true knowledge is to be found, I know not. We grope in the dark; and though it is truth only we are in quest of, we fall into innumerable errors. But, whatever may be our case with respect to the knowledge of nature, as to that of heavenly and divine things, let us cheerfully embrace that rich present which Infinite Goodness has made us, and be thankful that the dayspring from on high hath visited us. "Because there was no wisdom on this earth," says Lactantius, "he sent a teacher from heaven." Him let us follow as our guide; for he that follows his directions shall not walk in darkness.

Let us pray.

INFINITE, eternal Creator, and King of heaven and earth, bodies and spirits; who, being unmoved thyself movest all things, and changest them at thy pleasure, while thou remainest thyself altogether unchangeable; who supportest all things by thy powerful hand, and governest them by thy nod, the greatest as well as the least; so that the greatest are no burden to thee, nor dost thou contemn the least. Behold, the nations before thee are as the drop of the bucket, and like the small dust of the balance; and these isles of ours, with all the rest in the world, are, in thy sight, but a very little thing. Yet thou deignest to be present in our assemblies, and take notice of our affairs, which are very inconsiderable. Let our souls adore thee, and fall down, with the greatest humility, at the footstool of thy throne, continually entreating thy grace, and constantly offering thee glory. Our praises add nothing to thee; but they exalt ourselves, enhance our happiness, and unite us with the society of angels; yet thou receivest them with a gracious hand, as most acceptable sacrifices, and incense of a sweet-smelling savour. Let us celebrate thee, O Lord, who art great, and greatly to be praised. Let all nations praise thee, from the rising of the sun to the going down thereof. Set our hearts on fire with the flames of thy Divine love, that they may wholly ascend to thee as burnt-offerings, and nothing of ours may remain with us. Oh! blessed transmigration, where the blind confidence of the flesh is transformed into a lively and pure faith, that has no dependence but upon thee alone; where self-love, and the love of the world, is exchanged for the love of thy infinite beauty; when our will shall centre in thine, and be altogether absorbed by it. Let this change, O bountiful Father, be brought about, for it is a change only to be effected by the power of thy hand; and as soon as our souls are made sensible of it, thy praise shall be for ever sounded within us, as in temples devoted to thy service.

Let thy whole church, O Lord, flourish and rejoice in the light of thy favour. Be favourable to this our university, city, and nation. Dispel, we pray thee, the thick clouds, and quiet the winds and storms; for when they rage most, and make the greatest noise, they know thy voice and obey it. Thou art the only God of peace, who createst it with a word, and makest righteousness and peace mutually to kiss one another. We depend upon thee only; and to thee alone we render praise and glory, as far as we can, through Jesus Christ. Amen.

EXHORTATION IV.

Besides those common divisions of human life into the four stages of childhood, youth, manhood, and old age, which suppose the yet smaller divisions of years and months, men have many various ways of distributing the periods of their life, according to the different occupations and studies they have been engaged in. And I doubt not but you, young gentlemen, look upon this present instant of time as the beginning of a new period of your life. You have my leave to do so, provided you seriously consider, at the same time, that the whole life we live in this world is of a frail and fleeting nature, and, in some respect, nothing at all.

A great part of mankind no sooner look upon themselves to be capable of worldly affairs, and think on entering upon some profession suitable to a state of manhood, but they are cut off, in the very beginning of their course, by an unforeseen and untimely death. Yet, by their desires and designs, they launch out a great way into futurity, and form a series of projects for many years to come; while, in the mean time, they rarely, or at least very superficially, consider, how foolish and precarious it is to depend upon to-morrow, and how soon this present form of ours may disappear; how soon we may return to our original dust. It is not the common sort of mankind only that impose upon themselves in this respect, but the generality of those who desire to be accounted not only men of learning, but also adepts in wisdom, and actually pass for such. Not that I would prohibit your making an early and prudent choice, under the Divine direction, of the employment and profession of life you intend to pursue; nay, I would use every argument to persuade you to make use of such a choice, and when you have made it, to prosecute the intention of it with the greatest diligence and activity. I only put you upon your guard, not to entertain many and towering hopes in this world, nor form a long series of connected projects; because you will find them all more vain and fleeting than illusions of the night. Some necessary means will fail, some favourable opportunity be missed; after all your industry, the expected even may not happen, or the thread of your life may be cut, and thereby all your projects rendered abortive. And, though your life should be drawn out to ever so great a length, and success constantly answer your expectations, yet you know, and I wish you would remember it, the fatal day will come at last, perhaps when it is least expected; that fatal and final day, I say, will at last come, when we must leave all our enjoyments, and all our schemes, those we are now carrying on, and those we have brought to perfection, as well as those that are only begun, and those that subsist only in hopes and ideas.

And these very arguments, that have been used to confine your minds from indulging themselves in too remote prospects, will also serve to persuade you, in another sense, to look much further; not with regard to worldly enjoyments, for such prospects, strictly speaking, cannot be called long, but to look far beyond all earthly and perishing things, to those that are heavenly and eternal: and those that will not raise their eyes to such objects, as the apostle Peter expresses it, "are blind, and cannot see afar off."

But of you, my dear youths, I expect better things. I need not, I imagine, use many words to persuade you to industry, and a continual progress in human studies, and philosophical learning. You are not ignorant, that our schools are only intended for laying the foundations of those studies, upon which years and indefatigable industry are to raise the superstructure of more complete erudition; which, by the accession of the Divine Spirit, may be consecrated into a temple for God. And this is what I would recommend to your esteem, and your earnest desires, beyond any other study whatever, "That you may be holy, because our God is holy;" that, when you leave this university, those with whom you converse may not find you puffed up with pride, on account of a little superficial learning, nor bigoted, talkative, or fond of entering into unseasonable disputes; but consider you all as patterns and examples of piety, purity, temperance, modesty, and all Christian virtues; particularly that humility that shone so brightly in Christ himself, and which he earnestly exhorts all his disciples to learn from him. I earnestly exhort and beseech you, my dear young men, to make it, above all other things, your principal study, to have your hearts purged from all impure and ignoble love of the world and the flesh, that, in this earth, you may live to God only; and then, to be sure, when you remove out of it, you will live with him for ever in heaven.

May the honorary title you have this day received be happy and auspicious; but I earnestly pray the Father of lights, that he would deign to bestow upon you a title more solid and exalted than is in the power of man to give, that you may be called the sons of God, and that your conversation may be suitable to so great a name, and so glorious a Father.

Let us pray.

ETERNAL King, thy throne is established and immovable from everlasting, and will continue so throughout all the ages of eternity. Before the mountains were brought forth, before thou hadst formed the earth and the world, even from everlasting to everlasting thou art God. All things that exist, whether visible or invisible, derive from thee their being, and all that they possess; and they all, from the least to the greatest, are subservient to thy purposes, who art their supreme King and Father. Many of them, indeed, act without knowledge or design, yet serve thee with a constant and unerring obedience; others pay their homage from principles of reason and inclination; and all the rest are forced to promote thy intentions, though by constraint, and against their wills. Thou art great, O Lord, thou art great, and greatly to be praised, and of thy greatness there is no end. The heavens are far raised above the earth, but thy majesty is much farther exalted above all our thoughts and conceptions. Impress, we pray thee, on our hearts, most bountiful Father, a profound sense of our meanness and insignificancy; and make us acceptable to thee, through thy grace, in thy beloved Son, blotting out all our sins by the blood of his cross, and purifying our hearts by the effusion of thy Spirit from on high. Illuminate, most gracious God, this assembly of ours by the light of thy Divine favour, and let thy effectual blessing, we pray thee, attend the work we are now employed about (by thy approbation, and the gracious disposition of thy providence), and may the result of all be to the glory of thy name, through Jesus Christ our Lord. Amen.

EXHORTATION V.

THE complaint, with regard to the vanity of all perishing and transitory enjoyments, which has been long general among mankind, is indeed just and well-founded; but it is no less true, that the vanity which resides in the heart of man himself exceeds everything of that kind we observe in the other parts of the visible creation. For, among all the creatures that we see around us, we can find nothing so fleeting and inconstant; it flutters hither and thither, and, forsaking that only perfect good which is truly suited to its nature and circumstances, grasps at phantoms and shadows of happiness, which it pursues with a folly more than childish.

For how few are there that seriously and frequently consider with themselves, whence they came, whither they are going, and what is the purpose of their life; who are daily reviewing the state of their own minds, and often descend into themselves, that they may as frequently ascend, by their thoughts and meditations, to their exalted Father, and their heavenly country; who take their station upon temporal things, and view those that are eternal! Yet these are the only men that can be truly said to live, and they only can be accounted wise.

And to this it is, my dear youths, that I would willingly engage your souls; nay, I heartily wish they were carried thither by the fiery chariots of celestial wisdom. Let the common sort of mankind admire mean things; let them place their hopes on riches, honours, and arts, and spend their lives in the pursuit of them; but let your souls be inflamed with a far higher ambition. Yet I would not altogether prohibit you these pursuits; I only desire you to be moderate in them. These enjoyments are neither great in themselves, nor permanent; but it is surprising how much vanity is inflated by them. What a conceited, vain nothing is the creature we call man! For, because few are capable of discerning true blessings, which are solid and intrinsically beautiful, therefore the superficial ones, and such as are of no value at all, are catched at; and those who, in any measure, attain to the possession of them, are puffed up and elated thereby.

If we consider things as they are, it is an evidence of a very wrong turn of mind to boast of titles and fame, as they are no part of ourselves, nor can we depend upon them. But he that is elevated with a fond conceit of his own knowledge, is a stranger to the nature of things, and particularly to himself; since he knows not that the highest pitch of human knowledge ought, in reality, rather to be called ignorance. How small and inconsiderable is the extent of our knowledge! Even the most contemptible things in nature are sufficient to expose the greatness of our ignorance. And with respect to divine things, who dares to deny, "that the knowledge mankind have of them is next to nothing"? Because the weak eyes of our understanding, confined as they are within such narrow houses of clay, cannot bear the piercing light of divine things; therefore the Fountain of all wisdom hath thought proper to communicate such imperfect discoveries of himself, as are barely sufficient to direct our steps to the superior regions of perfect light. And whoever believes this truth, will, doubtless, make it his chief care and principal study constantly to follow this lamp of divine light, that shines in darkness, and not to deviate from it either to the right hand or to the left. It is, indeed, my opinion, that no man of ingenuity ought to despise the study of philosophy, or the knowledge of languages; but what I would recommend with the greatest earnestness is, that you would inseparably unite with such measures of learning and improvements of your minds as you can attain, purity of religion, divine love, moderation of soul, and an agreeable, inoffensive behaviour. For you are not ignorant, what a low and empty figure the highest attainments in human sciences must make, if they be compared with the dignity and duration of the soul of man; for however considerable they may be in themselves, yet, with regard to their use and their whole design, they are confined within the short space of this perishing life. But the soul, which reasons, which is employed in learning and teaching, in a few days will for ever bid farewell to all these things, and remove to another country. Oh how inconsiderable are all arts and sciences, all eloquence and philosophy, when compared with a cautious concern that our last exit out of this world may be happy and auspicious, and that we may depart out of this life candidates of immortality, at which we can never arrive but by the beautiful way of holiness.

Let us pray.

INFINITE and eternal God, who inhabitest thick darkness, and light inaccessible, whom no mortal hath seen, nor can see; yet all thy works evidently declare and proclaim thy wisdom, thy power, and thy infinite goodness. And, when we contemplate these thy perfections, what is it our souls can desire, but that they may love thee, worship thee, serve thee, for ever proclaim thy praises, and celebrate thy exalted name, which is above all praise, and all admiration? Thy throne is constantly surrounded with thousands and ten thousands of glorified spirits, who continually adore thee, and cry out, without ceasing, Holy, holy, holy, Lord God Almighty, who was, who is, and who is to come. Let others seek what they will, and find and embrace what they can; may we have always this one fixed and settled purpose, that it is good for us to draw near to God. Let the sea roar, the earth be shaken, and all things go to ruin and confusion; yet the soul that adheres to God will remain safe and quiet, and shall not be moved for ever. O blessed soul! that has thee for its rest, and all its salvation; it shall be like a tree planted by the rivers of water; it shall not fear when heat cometh, nor shall it be uneasy in a year of drought. It is our earnest petition and prayer, O Father, that thy hands may loosen all our chains, and effectually deliver our souls from all the snares and allurements of the world and the flesh, and that, by that same bountiful and most powerful hand of thine, they may be for ever united to thee, through thy only begotten Son, who is our union and our peace. Be favourably present, most gracious God, with this assembly of ours, that whatever we undertake, in obedience to thy will, may be carried to perfection by the aid of thy grace, and tend to the glory of thy name, through Jesus Christ our Lord. Amen.

EXHORTATION VI.

I AM not ignorant, that it is one of the common arts of life, to set off our own things with all the pomp we can; and if there is any worth in them, by no means to depreciate it, but rather to endeavour, with all our might, to enhance their value as much as possible; nay, those of them which are quite vain and worthless, we use to magnify with pompous expressions, and daub with false colours; and to do otherwise is reckoned a kind of rustic simplicity. But you, young gentlemen, who are acquainted with my manner, will, I imagine, easily forgive this indifference of mine; and therefore I say, if there are any that despise these performances of ours, we leave them at full liberty, for we ourselves held them in contempt before; but, to speak freely, together with them we undervalue all worldly things: they are all made of the same mean materials. O life, short with regard to duration, long in consideration of thy miseries, involved in darkness, beset with snares, still fluctuating between false joys and real torments, groundless hopes and fears equally imaginary, yet foolishly, and even to distraction, loved by most. We will not die, and yet we know not how to live. Our present possessions are loathsome as food to a man in a fever, and we greedily catch at future enjoyments, which, when they come to be present, will be received with the same indifference: for, among the advantages of this fleeting life, nothing is equally agreeable to those who have it in possession, and those who have it only in desire and hope.

We are all in general of such a nature, that we are weary of ourselves, and what we lately preferred to everything else, upon experience we reject. This inconstancy is undoubtedly a sign of a mind distempered, forcibly drawn away from its centre, and separated from its only durable rest. Nor need you go far, young gentlemen, to look for an instance of this distemper.

Let any of you descend into himself (which very few do, and even they but rarely), he will find it within him: upon a very slight inquiry, he will surely be sensible of it; for, passing other considerations, with what fervent wishes have you, in your hearts, longed for this day! Yet I forewarn you, that all your pleasure will either die with the day itself, or but for a very short time survive it. And, as commonly happens, it will be succeeded by the anxious cares of beginning life, as it were, anew, or, which is much more grievous, by those temptations and allurements of vice which tend to debauch and ruin you; for these allurements, after the manner of some robbers, attack the unwary and unexperienced with blandishments and caresses, that thereby they may have an opportunity to undo them. If therefore, as soon as ye enter upon a life of freedom, those deceitful and deadly pleasures of sense tempt you with their delusive smiles, I would put you in mind, how unworthy it is of a free and generous mind, especially that of a Christian, to become an abject slave, and submit to the most shameful bondage; how disgraceful and wretched a choice it is, to become the slave of a mad, distracted master; and how much more generous and exalted is the pleasure of despising them all, and trampling them under foot, when they come in competition with the pure and permanent delights of Divine love!

As to exalted degrees of honour, and heaps of riches, the idols of all ranks of mankind, they have nothing divine in them; and they are entirely void of real goodness. All the beauty and brightness of these idols resemble the decorations of a stage, that dazzle the eyes of the vulgar; and the enjoyment of them is in reality but a splendid kind of slavery, and gilded misery. It is a pathetic expression of St Bernard, "O ambition, the torture of the ambitious, how happens it, that though thou tormentest all, thou yet makest thyself agreeable to all?" Oh how easily does even the least glimpse of eternal and infinite beauty rase out of the mind all the impressions made upon it by the objects we daily converse with on this earth, and turn its admiration of them into contempt and disdain!

But if any one, having thoroughly examined and despised these shadows, resolves solely to pursue a more complete knowledge of things and follow the streams of learning, we cannot deny that he judges more justly; yet, after all, he must know, if he is wise, or at least he ought to know, that he may be wise, what vanity and superfluity is to be met with even here: for often, when one has applied himself to his books and studies with the greatest assiduity, and almost spent his life upon them, all his pains evaporate into smoke, and the labour of years is entirely lost. And, what is most of all to be lamented, this is sometimes the case with respect to theology, which is the chief of all arts and sciences, as so large a portion of that vineyard is still possessed with briars and thorns. How many are the disputes and controversies, how many the trifling arguments and cavils, which possibly may have something of the sharpness of thorns, but undoubtedly a great deal of their barrenness and their hurtful quality! A philosopher of old severely reproves the sophisters of his time in these words: "What was formerly the love of wisdom, is now become the love of words." We, to be sure, may substitute, in place of this, a complaint still more bitter, that what was theology before, is now become foolish talking; and that many of our divines, though they serve one God, and *that* the God of peace, "yet split into parties upon the slightest occasions, and with great impiety divide the whole world into factions." And I am much afraid this evil, in a great measure, derives its original from the education of youth in schools and colleges. For the most part of men manage this business, as if disputing was the end of learning, as fighting is the design of going to war: hence the youth, when they enter the school, begin disputing, which never ends but with their life. Death imposes silence; and so, at last, "these fierce passions of their minds, and these inveterate contentions, are composed to rest by the weight of a little dust thrown upon them."

As for you, young gentlemen, if my earnest wishes and sincere advice can have any weight with you, you will early extricate yourselves out of these flames of contention, that your minds, being lighted up by the pure and celestial fire of the Divine Spirit, may shine forth in holiness, and burn with the most fervent charity.

Let us pray.

HONOUR and praise are due to thee, O infinite God! This is the universal voice of all the blessed spirits on high, and all the saints on earth: Worthy art thou, O Lord, to receive glory, and honour, and power, because thou hast created all things, and for thy pleasure they are. We, here before thee, with united hearts and affections, offer thee, as we can, the sacrifice of gratitude, love, and praise. How much are we indebted to thee for ourselves, and for all that we possess! for in thee we live, move, and have our being. Thou hast redeemed us from our sins, having given the Son of thy love, as a sacrifice and ransom for our souls; the chastisement of our peace fell upon him, and by his stripes we are healed. On this consideration, we acknowledge, we are no longer at our own disposal, since we are bought with a price, and so very great a price, that we may glorify thee, O Father, and thy Son, in our souls and our bodies, which are so justly thine. May we devote ourselves to thee through the whole remaining part of our life, and disdain the impure and ignoble slavery of sin, the world, and the flesh, that, in all things, we may demean ourselves as becomes the sons of God, and the heirs of thy celestial kingdom, and make, daily, greater progress in our journey towards the happy possession thereof.

Bless thy church, and our nation, and this our university: may it be thine, we pray thee. We entreat thou wouldest become our Father, our Protector, and our supreme Teacher, who hast thy throne in heaven, and teachest the hearts of men on this earth. May the youth flourish under thy instruction, that they may be not only learned, but especially upright, pious, and true Christians, entirely devoted to the honour of thy name, through our Lord Jesus Christ. Amen.

EXHORTATION VII.

These academical exercises of ours are, to be sure, no great matter, nor do we make any high account of them; yet, after all, we set no higher, perhaps even a less value, upon the bustling affairs of mankind, which make a much greater noise, and the farces that are acted upon the more exalted theatres of the world, which are for the most part outwardly more pompous than these of ours, but inwardly equally vain. Or if you choose to be more severe upon the fruitless labours of mankind, you may, with a great man, that knew all these things by experience, compare them to the "fluttering of frightened flies, the toilsome hurry of the ants, and the motions of puppets." But he that, amidst all the confusions and commotions which happen in human affairs here below, has recourse to divine contemplation, and the hopes of eternity, as the lofty, impregnable tower of true wisdom, "is the only person that enjoys uninterrupted ease and tranquillity, like the heavenly bodies, which constantly move on in their orbits, and are never, by any violence, diverted from their course."

And, indeed, what wonder is it, that he can easily view all the dreadful appearances of this wretched life with a resolute and steady countenance, who, by frequent interviews and daily conversation with death itself, has rendered it familiar to him, and thereby not only divested it of its terrors, but also placed it in a beautiful, pleasant, and quite amiable light. By this means, he dies daily, and, doubtless, before he suffers a natural death, he dies in a more exalted sense of the word, by withdrawing, as far as possible, his mind from the incumbrance of earthly things, and, even while it lodges in the body, weaning it from all the worldly objects that are placed about him.

And, indeed, young gentlemen, I am of opinion, that a view and meditation of death will not be unsuitable, or improper, even for you, though you are in the prime of life, and your minds in their full vigour; nay, I would gladly hope you yourselves will not imagine it would, nor be at all offended at me, as if, by mentioning that inauspicious word unseasonably, I disturbed your present joy, drew a kind of black cloud over this bright day of festivity, or seemed to mix among your laurels a branch of the hated cypress. For a wise man would not willingly owe his joy to madness, nor think it a pleasure foolishly to forget the situation of his affairs.

The wise man alone feels true joy, and real wisdom is the attainment of a Christian only, who bears with life, but hopes for death; and passes through all the storms and tempests of the former with an undaunted mind, but with the most fervent wishes looks for the latter, as the secure port, and the "fair havens" in the highest sense of the expression; whose mind is humble, and, at the same time, exalted, neither depending upon foreign, that is, external advantages, nor puffed up with his own; and neither elevated nor depressed by any turns or vicissitudes of fortune.

He is the wise man who relishes things as they really are; who is not, with the common sort of mankind, that are always children, terrified by bugbears, nor pleased with painted rattles; who has a greatness of soul, vastly superior to all fading and perishing things. The only thing he desires, is the favour and countenance of the Supreme King; the only thing he fears, is his displeasure; and, without doubt, a mind of this cast must, of necessity, be the habitation of constant serenity, exalted joy, and gladness springing from on high. And this is the man that is truly possessed of that tranquillity and happy disposition of mind, which the philosophers boast of, the divines recommend, but few attain. And though he will neither willingly suffer himself to be called a philosopher, nor a philologer, yet he is, in reality, well versed in the things of God, and, by a kind of divine influence and instruction, has attained to the light of pure and peaceable truth; where he passes his days in the greatest quietness and serenity, far above the cloudy and stormy regions of controversy and disputation.

If any of you has been thus instructed, he has certainly attained the highest of all arts, and has entered upon the most glorious liberty, even before he hath received any university degree. But the rest, though they are presently to have the title of Master of Arts, still continue a silly, servile set of men, under a heavy yoke of bondage, whereby even their minds will be cramped with oppressive laws, far more intolerable than any discipline however severe. It is my earnest prayer, that you will retire from the seminary with your minds excited to a keen and wholesome thirst after true learning, rather than blown up with the wildfire of science, falsely so called: and, what of all other attainments is of greatest consequence, that you will leave us, deeply affected with the most ardent love of heavenly wisdom. Whatever may be your fate with respect to other things, it is my earnest request, that it may be your highest ambition and your principal study to be true Christians; that is, to be humble, meek, pure, holy, and followers of your most auspicious Captain, the Lamb, wherever he goeth; for he that followeth him shall not walk in darkness, but be conducted, through the morning light of Divine grace, to the meridian and never-ending brightness of glory.

Let us pray.

Eternal Father of mercies and of lights, the only rest of the immortal souls which thou hast created, and their never-failing consolation: into what bypaths of error do our souls divert, and to what dangers are they exposed on every hand, when they stray away from thee! But while they keep within thy hiding place, O Most High, they are safe under the shadow of thy wings. Oh how happy are they, and how well do they live, who pass their whole lives in that secret abode, where they may continually refresh themselves with the delicious fruits of thy love, and show forth thy praise; where they may taste and see that thou art good, O Lord, and be thoroughly persuaded of the immense riches of thy bounty, which all our miseries cannot exceed, nor our poverty exhaust; nay, which the constant effusion of them upon the whole universe, and all its parts, cannot in the least diminish! As for us, who are before thee, the most unworthy of all thy creatures, yet at the same time the most excessively loaded with all the instances of thy goodness, can we avoid crying out with the united voices of our hearts, Let praise be ascribed to the Lord, because he is good, and his mercy endureth for ever? Who shall declare the great and wonderful works of God? Who shall show forth his praise, who ruleth by his power for ever, and his eyes observe the nations, that the rebellious may not exalt themselves; who restores our souls to life, and suffers not our feet to be moved? But, on the other hand, alas! how justly may our songs be interrupted with bitter lamentations, that, under such strong and constant rays of his bounty, our hearts are so cold towards him! Oh how faint and languid is our love to him! How very little, or near to nothing, is the whole of that flame which we feel within us; and, as that love fails within us, we misplace our affections upon the things around us; and as we follow vanity, we become vain and miserable at the same time. But may thy Spirit, O Lord, whom we humbly and earnestly beg of thee, descending into our hearts, inspire us thoroughly with life, vigour, and celestial purity.

Bless this city, and this celebrated university. Grant, most gracious Father, that the numbers of youth we send out from it this day, and every year, may be, by thy effectual grace, consecrated and devoted to thy service. Let this fountain of learning be continually enriched with thy heavenly influences, that it may constantly supply pure and limpid streams, for the welfare and improvement of thy church and people, to the glory of thy exalted name, through our Lord Jesus Christ; to whom, with thee, and the Holy Spirit, be honour, praise, and glory, world without end. Amen.

EXHORTATION VIII.

Amidst these amusements, we are unhappily losing a day. Yet some part of the weight of this complaint is removed, when we consider, that while the greatest part of mankind are bustling in crowds, and places of traffic, we are trifling our time more innocently than they. But what should hinder us from closing this last scene in a serious manner, that is, from turning our eyes to more divine objects, whereby, though we are fatigued with other matters, we may terminate the work of this day, and the day itself, agreeably; as the beams of the sun use to give more than ordinary delight when he is near his setting?

You are now initiated into the philosophy, such as it is, that prevails in the schools, and, I imagine, intend, with all possible despatch, to apply to higher studies. But oh! how pitiful and scanty are all those things which beset us before, behind, and on every side! The bustling we observe, is nothing but the hurrying of ants eagerly engaged in their little labours. The mind must surely have degenerated, and forgotten its original, as effectually as if it had drunk of the river Lethe, if, rising above this visible world, it does not return to its Father's bosom, where it may contemplate his eternal beauty, where contemplation will inflame love, and love be crowned with the possession of the beloved object. But, in the contemplation of this glorious object, how great caution and moderation of mind is necessary, lest by prying presumptuously into his secret councils, or his nature, and rashly breaking into the sanctuary of light, we be involved in darkness! And, with regard to what the infinite, independent, and necessarily existent Being has thought proper to communicate to us concerning himself, and we are concerned to know, even that is by no means to be obscured by curious, impertinent questions, nor perplexed with the arrogance of disputation; because by such means, instead of enlarging our knowledge, we are in the fair way to know nothing at all; but readily to be received by humble faith, and entertained with meek and pious affections. And if in these notices of him, that are communicated to us, we meet with anything obscure, and hard to be understood, such difficulties will be happily got over, not by perplexed controversies, but by constant and fervent prayer. "He will come to understand," says, admirably well, the famous bishop of Hippo, "who knocks by prayer, not he who, by quarrelling, makes a noise at the gate of truth." But what can we, who are mortal creatures, understand with regard to the inexpressible Being we now speak of, especially while we sojourn in these dark prisons of clay, but only this, that we can by no means comprehend him? For though, in thinking of him, we remove from our idea all sort of imperfection, and collect together every perceivable perfection, and adore the whole with the highest titles, we must, after all, acknowledge, that we have said nothing, and that our conceptions are nothing to the purpose. Let us, therefore, in general acknowledge him to be the immovable Being, that moveth everything; the immutable God, that changeth all things at his pleasure; the infinite and eternal fountain of all good, and of all existence, and the Lord and sole Ruler of the world.

If you, then, my dear youths, aspire to genuine Christianity, that is, the knowledge of God and divine things, I would have you consider, that the mind must first be recalled, and engaged to turn in upon itself, before it can be raised up towards God, according to that expression of St Bernard, "May I return from external things to those that are within myself, and from these again rise to those that are of a more exalted nature." But the greatest part of men live abroad, and are, truly, strangers at home; you may sooner find them anywhere than with themselves. Now, is not this real madness, and the highest degree of insensibility? Yet, after all, they seem to have some reason in their madness, when they thus stray away from themselves, since they can see nothing within them that, by its promising aspect, can give them pleasure or delight. Everything there is ugly, frightful, and full of nastiness, which they would rather be ignorant of than be at the pains to purge away; and therefore prefer a slothful forgetfulness of their misery, to the trouble and labour of regaining happiness. But how preposterous is the most diligent study and the highest knowledge, when we neglect that of ourselves! The Roman philosopher, ridiculing the grammarians of his time, observes, "that they inquired narrowly into the misfortunes of Ulysses, but were quite ignorant of their own." The sentiments of a wise and pious man are quite different, and I wish you may adopt them. It is his principal care to be thoroughly acquainted with himself, he watches over his own ways, he improves and cultivates his heart as a garden, nay, a garden consecrated to the King of kings, who takes particular delight in it; he carefully nurses the heavenly plants and flowers, and roots up all the wild and noxious weeds, that he may be able to say, with the greater confidence, "Let my Beloved come into his own garden, and be pleased to eat of his fruits." And when, upon this invitation, the great King, in the fulness of his goodness, descends into the mind, the soul may then easily ascend with him, as it were, in a chariot of fire, and look down upon the earth, and all earthly things, with contempt and disdain: "Then rising above the rainy regions, it sees the storms falling beneath its feet, and tramples upon the hidden thunder."

Let us pray.

WHATEVER satisfaction we look for without thee, O heavenly Father, is mere delusion and vanity; yet, though we have so often experienced this, we have not, this day, learned to renounce this vain and fruitless labour, that we may depend upon Thee, who alone canst give full and complete satisfaction to the souls of men. We pray, therefore, that by thy almighty hand, thou wouldest so effectually join and unite our hearts to thee, that they may never be separated any more. How unhappy are they who forsake thee, and whose hearts depart from thy ways! They shall be like shrubs in the desert, they shall not see when good cometh, but dwell in a parched and barren land. Blessed, on the contrary, is he who hath placed his confidence in thee; he shall be like a tree planted by the rivers of water; he shall not be afraid when heat cometh, nor be uneasy in the time of drought. Take from us, O Lord, whatever earthly enjoyments thou shalt think proper; there is one thing will abundantly make up all our losses, let Christ dwell in our hearts by faith, and the rays of thy favour continually refresh us in the face of thine Anointed; in this event, we have nothing more to ask, but, with grateful minds, shall for ever celebrate thy bounty, and all our bones shall say, Who is like unto thee, O Lord; who is like unto thee?

Let thy church be glad in thee, and all in this nation, and everywhere throughout the world, that regard and love thy name; by the power and efficacy of the gospel, may their number be daily augmented, and let the gifts of thy grace be also increased in them all. Bless this university; let it be like a garden watered by thy heavenly hand, that thy tender shoots may grow, and in due time produce abundant fruit, to the eternal honour of thy most glorious name, through our Lord Jesus Christ. Amen.

VALEDICTORY ORATION.

Though this, I imagine, is the last address I shall ever have occasion to make to you, I will not detain you long from your studies, nor encroach on the time allowed you for recreation. This is, to be sure, the first time that some of you have heard me; but I have a great many others to bear witness of the constant design of all my dissertations in this place. They will testify, that the intention of all my discourses was, "that the form of sound words," that is, the Christian doctrine, and consequently the fear and love of God, might not only be impressed, but also engraven upon your hearts in lasting and indelible characters; and that you might not only admit as a truth, but also pay the highest regard to this indisputable maxim, that piety and religion are the only real good among men. Moreover, that your minds might be the less encumbered in their application to this grand study of religion, and the more expeditious in their progress therein, I constantly endeavoured, with all possible warmth, to divert you from those barren and thorny questions and disputes, that have infected the whole of theology: and this at a time, when the greatest part of divines and professors, and those of no small reputation, engaging furiously in such controversies, have split into parties, and unhappily divided the whole world. It was my constant practice to establish those great and uncontroverted articles of our holy religion, which are but few and clear; some part whereof are confirmed by the common consent of nations, and of all the human race; and all the rest by the unanimous voice of the whole Christian world. Of the first sort are those we have often advanced in treating of the being and perfections of the one supreme and eternal Principle, and the production of all things by him; the continual preservation and government of the world by his providence; the law of God given to mankind, and the rewards and punishments annexed to it. The other class of the grand articles of religion are indeed peculiar to Christian philosophy, but believed in common by all the professors of that religion. These are the great foundations of our faith, and of all our hope and joy, with regard to the incarnation of the Son of God, his death and resurrection for the destruction of sin, and consequently of death; his ascension into the highest heavens, with that same flesh of ours in which he died, and his exaltation there above all ranks of angels, dominions, and thrones, whence we expect he will return in great glory, in that day when he will be glorious in all his saints, and admired in those that believe. As many, therefore, as desire to receive him in this his last manifestation, with joy and exultation, must of necessity be holy, and, in conformity to their most perfect and glorious Head, sober, pious, upright, and live in full contempt of this perishing transitory world, their own mortal flesh, and the sordid pleasures of both: in a word, all the enjoyments which the mean and servile admire, they must trample under foot and despise. For whoever will strive for this victory, and strive so as at last to obtain it, the Lord will own him for his servant, and the great Master will acknowledge him for his disciple. He will attain a likeness to God in this earth, and, after a short conflict, will triumph in the Divine presence for ever. These are the doctrines which it is our interest to know, and in the observation of which our happiness will be secured. To these you will turn your thoughts, young gentlemen, if you are wise; nay, to these you ought to give due attention, that you may be wise. The phantoms we catch at, fly away; this shadow of a life we now live, is likewise on the wing. Those things that are without the verge of sense, and above its reach, are the only solid and lasting enjoyments. "Why are ye fond of these earthly things," says St Bernard, "which are neither true riches, nor are they yours? If they are yours, take them with you." And Lactantius admirably well observes, that, "whoever prefers the life of the soul, must, of necessity, despise that of the body; nor can he aspire to the highest good, unless he despise advantages of an inferior kind. For the all-wise God did not choose that we should attain to immortality in a soft, indolent way, but that we should gain that inexpressible reward of eternal life with the highest difficulty and severest labour." And, that you may not be discouraged, remember the great Redeemer of souls, your exalted Captain, hath gone before you, and we have to do with an enemy already conquered. Let us only follow him with courage and activity, and we have no ground to doubt of victory. And indeed it is a victory truly worthy of a Christian, to subdue the barbarous train of our appetites, and subject them to the empire of reason and religion; while, on the other hand, it is the most shameful bondage to have the more divine part of our composition meanly subjected to an ignoble, earthly body. Now, this victory can only be secured by steadfast believing, vigorous opposition to our spiritual enemies, unwearied watching, and incessant prayer. Let prayer be not only the key that opens the day, and the lock that shuts out the night; but let it be also, from morning to night, our staff and stay in all our labours, enabling us to go cheerfully up into the mount of God. Prayer brings consolation to the languishing soul, drives away the devil, and is the great medium whereby all grace and peace is communicated to us. With regard to your reading, let it be your particular care to be familiarly acquainted with the sacred Scriptures above all other books whatever; for from thence you will truly derive light for your direction, and sacred provisions for your support on your journey.

May our dear Redeemer Jesus impress upon your minds a lively representation of his own meek and immaculate heart, that, in that great and last day, he may, by this mark, know you to be his, and, together with all the rest of his sealed and redeemed ones, admit you into the mansions of eternal bliss. Amen.

Let us pray.

ETERNAL Creator, and supreme Governor of the world, songs of praise are due to thee in Zion; nay, as thou art infinitely superior to all our songs and hymns, even silence in Zion redounds to thy praise. Let the

CPSIA information can be obtained
at www.ICGtesting.com
Printed in the USA
LVHW100521120522
718524LV00004B/180

9 783375 002985